NUMBER SEVENTEEN

NUMBER SEVENTEEN

A Tale of Intrigue and Murder in London

By Louis Tracy

Skyhorse Publishing

Copyright © 2014 by Skyhorse Publishing, Inc.

All Rights Reserved. No part of this book may be reproduced in any manner without the express written consent of the publisher, except in the case of brief excerpts in critical reviews or articles. All inquiries should be addressed to Skyhorse Publishing, 307 West 36th Street, 11th Floor, New York, NY 10018.

Skyhorse Publishing books may be purchased in bulk at special discounts for sales promotion, corporate gifts, fund-raising, or educational purposes. Special editions can also be created to specifications. For details, contact the Special Sales Department, Skyhorse Publishing, 307 West 36th Street, 11th Floor, New York, NY 10018 or info@skyhorsepublishing.com.

Skyhorse® and Skyhorse Publishing® are registered trademarks of Skyhorse Publishing, Inc.®, a Delaware corporation.

Visit our website at www.skyhorsepublishing.com.

10 9 8 7 6 5 4 3 2 1

Library of Congress Cataloging-in-Publication Data is available on file.

ISBN: 978-1-62873-764-0

Printed in the United States of America

CHAPTER I

"TAXI, sir? Yes, sir. No. 4 will be yours."

A red-faced, loud-breathing commissionaire, engaged in the lucrative task of pocketing sixpences as quickly as he could summon cabs, vanished in a swirl of mackintoshes and umbrellas.

People who had arrived at the theater in fine weather were emerging into a drizzle of rain. "All London," as the phrase goes, was flocking to see the latest musical comedy at Daly's, but all London, regarded thus collectively, is far from owning motor cars, or even affording taxicabs, so the majority of the playgoers were hurrying on foot towards tube railways and omnibus routes.

Still, a popular light opera could hardly fail to draw many patrons from the upper ranks of society, and, in the crush at the main exit, Francis Berrold Theydon, hesitating whether to walk or wait the hazard of a cab, deemed himself fortunate when a panting commissionaire promised to secure a taxi "in half a minute."

Automobiles of every known variety were snorting up to the curb and bustling off again as promptly as their users could enter and bestow themselves in dim interiors. Being a considerate person—wishful also to light a cigarette—Theydon moved out of the way. In so doing, he was cannoned against by an impetuous footman, whose cry, "Your car, sir," led him to follow the man's alert eyes.

He saw a tall, elderly gentleman, with clean-shaven, shrewd, and highly intelligent features, of the type which finance, or the law, or a combination of both, seems to evolve only in big cities, escorting a young lady from the vestibule. Then Theydon remembered that he had noticed this self-same girl's remarkable beauty as she was silhouetted in white against the dark background of a first-tier box. He had even speculated idly as to her identity, and had come to the conclusion, on catching her face in profile, that she must be the daughter of the man seated by her side but half-hidden behind a heavy curtain.

The likeness was momentarily lost now while the two neared him, yet discovered anew when they halted for a second at his elbow. Oddly enough, the man was carrying an umbrella, which he proceeded to open, and his daughter's astonished question put their relationship beyond doubt.

"Dad," she said, with a charming smile in

which there was just a hint of a pout, "aren't you coming home with me?"

"No. I must look in at the Constitutional Club. It's only a step. I'll take no harm. This sleet looks worse than it is when every drop shines in the glare of so many lamps. Now, in with you, Evelyn! Tell Downs to come back, and don't forget which club. Anyhow, I'll tell him myself."

"Shall I wait up for you?"

"Well—er—I shan't be late. I'll be free by the time Downs returns."

"No. 4 taxi!" came a voice, and Theydon saw his commissionaire perched on the step of a cab swinging in deftly behind the waiting car. The girl, gazing at her father, happened to look for an instant at Theydon, who, fearful lest his candidly admiring glance might have been a trifle too sustained, pretended a hurried interest in an unlighted cigarette. That was all. The three crossed the pavement almost simultaneously.

The next moment the unknown goddess was gone, though Theydon snatched a final glimpse of her, faintly visible, yet no less radiantly lovely, as she leaned forward from the depths of the limousine, and waved a white-gloved hand to her father through a window jeweled with raindrops.

There was nothing in the incident to provoke a second thought. Assuredly, Frank Theydon

—as his friends called him—was not the only man in the vestibule of Daly's Theater who had found the girl well worth looking at, and it was the mere accident of propinquity which enabled him to overhear the quite commonplace remarks of father and daughter.

A score of similar occurrences had probably taken place in the like circumstances that night in London, and the maddest dreamer of fantastic dreams would not have heard the fluttering wings of the spirit of romance in connection with any one of them. It was by no means marvelous, therefore, but rather in obedience to the accepted law of things as they are when contrasted with things as they might be, if Theydon both failed to attach any importance to that chance meeting and proceeded forthwith to think of something else.

He did not forget it, of course. His artist's eyes had been far too interested in a certain rare quality of delicate femininity in the girl's face and figure, and his ear too quick to appreciate the music of her cultured voice, that he should not be able to recall such pleasant memories later. Indeed, during those fleeting moments on the threshold of the theater, he had garnered quite a number of minor impressions, not only of the girl, but of her father.

In some respects they were singularly alike. Thus, each had the same proud, self-reliant carriage, the same large, brilliant eyes, serene

4

brow and firm mouth, the same repose of manner, the same clear, incisive enunciation. Neither could move in any company, however eclectic, without evoking comment.

They held in common that air of refinement and good breeding which is, or should be, the best-marked attribute of an aristocracy. It was impossible to imagine either in rags, but, given such a transformation, each would be notable because of the amazing difference that would exist between garb and mien.

It must not be imagined that Theydon indulged in this close analysis of the physical characteristics of two complete strangers while his cab was wheeling into the scurry of traffic in Cranbourn Street. Rather did he essay a third time to light the cigarette which he still held between his lips. And yet a third time was his intent balked.

A policeman stopped the east-bound stream of vehicles somewhat suddenly at the corner of Charing Cross road; owing to the mud, the taxi skidded a few feet beyond the line; a lamp was torn off by a heavy wagon coming south; and a fierce argument between taxi driver and policeman resulted in "numbers" being demanded for future vengeance. Then Theydon took a hand in the dispute, poured oil on the troubled waters by tipping the policeman half a crown and the driver half a sovereign—these sums being his private estimate of damages to dignity and lamp—and the journey was resumed, with a net loss, to the person who had absolutely nothing to do with the affair, of twelve and sixpence in money and nearly ten minutes in time.

Theydon was not rich, as shall be seen in due course, but he was generous and impulsive. He hated the notion of any one suffering for having done him a service, and the taxi man might reasonably be deemed a real benefactor on that sloppy night.

So far as he was concerned, the delay of ten minutes was of no consequence. It only meant a slightly deferred snuggling down into an easy chair in his flat with a book and a pipe. That is how he would have expressed himself if questioned on the point. In reality it influenced and controlled his future in the most vital way, because, once the cab had crossed Oxford Street and turned into the quiet thoroughfare on which the first block of Innesmore Mansions abutted, he passed into a new phase of existence.

The cigarette, lighted at last after the altercation, had filled the cab with smoke to such an extent that Theydon lowered a window. At that moment the driver was slowing down to take the corner of the even more secluded road which contained Innesmore Mansions and the gardens appertaining thereto, and nothing else. Necessarily, Theydon was looking out, and he was very greatly surprised at seeing the unknown gentleman of the theater walking rapidly round the same corner.

He could not be mistaken. The stranger tilted back his umbrella and raised his eyes to ascertain the name of the street, as though he was not quite sure of his whereabouts, and the glare of a lamp fell directly on his clean-cut, almost classical face.

Being thus occupied, he did not glance at the passing cab, or recognition might possibly have been mutual—possibly, though not probably, because, during that brief pause on the steps of the theater, he stood beside Theydon; hence, he was half-turned toward his daughter while they were discussing the night's immediate program.

, In itself the fact that he had gone in the direction of Innesmore Mansions rather than toward the Constitutional Club was in nowise remarkable. Nevertheless, he had deceived his daughter—deceived her intentionally, and the knowledge came as a shock to his unsuspected critic in Theydon.

He did not look the sort of man who would stoop to petty evasion of the truth. It was as though a statue of Praxiteles, miraculously gifted with life, should express its emotions, not in Attic Greek, but in the up-to-date slang of the Strand.

"Well, I'm dashed!" said Theydon, or

words to that effect, and his cab sped on to the third doorway. Innesmore Mansions arranged its roomy flats in blocks of six, and he occupied No. 18.

He held a florin in readiness; the rain, now falling heavily, did not encourage any loitering on the pavement. For all that, he saw out of the tail of his eye that the other man was approaching, though he had paused to examine the numbers blazoned on a lamp over the first doorway.

"Good night, sir, and thank you!" said the taxi driver.

The cab made off as Theydon ran up a short flight of steps. Innesmore Mansions did not boast elevators. The flats were comfortable, but not absurdly expensive, and their inmates climbed stairs cheerfully; at most, they had only to mount to a second storey. Each block owned a uniformed porter, who, on a night like this, even in May, needed rousing from his lair by a bell if in demand.

Theydon took the stairs two at a stride, opened the door of No. 18, which, with No. 17, occupied the top landing. He was valeted and cooked for by an ex-sergeant of the Army Service Corps and his wife, an admirable couple named Bates, and the male of the species appeared before Theydon had removed coat and opera hat in the tiny hall.

"Bring my tray in fifteen minutes, Bates,

and that will be all for tonight," said Theydon.

"Yes, sir," said Bates. "Remarkable change in the weather, sir."

"Rotten. Who would have expected this downpour after such a fine day?"

Bates took the coat and hat, and Theydon entered his sitting room, a spacious, square apartment which faced the gardens. He had purposely prevented Bates from coming immediately with his nightly fare, which consisted of a glass of milk and a plate of bread and butter.

Truth to tell, the artistic temperament contains a spice of curiosity, which is, in some sense, an exercise of the perceptive faculties. Theydon wanted to raise a window and look out, an unusual action, and one which, therefore, would induce Bates to wonder as to its cause.

For once in his life a man who bothered his head very little about other people's business was puzzled, and meant to ascertain whether or not the unknown was really calling on some resident in Innesmore Mansions. It was a harmless bit of espionage. Theydon scarcely knew the names of the other dwellers in his own block, and his acquaintance did not even go that far with any of the remaining tenants of 48 flats, all told.

Still, to a writer, the vagaries of the tall stranger were decidedly interesting, so he did open a window, and did thrust his head out, and was just in time to see the owner of the limousine which would call at the Constitutional Club in a quarter of an hour mount the steps leading to Nos. 13-18. Somehow, the discovery gave Theydon a veritable thrill.

Could that pretty girl's father, by any chance, be coming to visit him? A wildly improbable development had been whittled down to a five-to-one chance. He closed the window and waited, yes, actually waited, for the bell to ring!

The sitting room door was open, and it faced the hall door. Footsteps sounded sharply on the slate steps of the stairway; when Theydon heard some one climbing to the topmost landing he was almost convinced that, as usual, the unexpected was about to happen. It did happen, but took its own peculiar path. The unknown rang the bell of No. 17, and, after a slight delay, was admitted.

Theydon smiled at the anticlimax. A trivial mystery had developed along strictly orthodox lines. A rather good-looking and distinctly well-dressed lady, a Mrs. Lester, occupied No. 17. She lived alone, too, he believed. At any rate, he had never seen any other person, except an elderly servant, enter or leave the opposite flat, and he had encountered the tenant herself so seldom that he was not quite certain of recognizing her apart from the environment of the staircase which provided their occasional meeting place.

Then he sighed. Romance evidently denied her magic presence to one who wooed her assiduously by his pen. He was yet to learn that the alluring sprite had not only favored him with her attentions during the past twenty minutes, but meant to stick to him like his own shadow for many a day. And he frowned, too.

He did not approve of that pretty girl's father visiting the attractive Mrs. Lester in conditions which savored of something underhanded and clandestine. The man had deliberately misled his daughter. He left her with a lie on his lips; yet never were appearances more deceptive, for the stranger had the outward aspect of one whose word was his bond.

"Oh, dash it all, what business is it of mine, anyhow?" growled Theydon, and he laughed sourly as he sat down to write a letter which Bates could take to the post, thus himself practicing a slight deceit intended solely to account for the deferred bringing of the tray.

It was apparently an unimportant missive which could well have been postponed till the morning, being merely an announcement to a firm of publishers that he would pay a business call later in the week. In less than five minutes it, and another, making an appointment for Wednesday, this being the night of Monday, were written, sealed, directed and stamped.

He rang. Bates came, with laden hands, thinking the tray was in demand.

"Kindly post those for me," said Theydon, glancing at the letters. "Better take an umbrella. It's raining cats and dogs."

The man had found the door open, and left it so when he entered. Before he could answer, the door of No. 17 was opened and closed, with the jingle inseparable from the presence of many small panes of glass in leaden casing, and footsteps sounded on the stairs. For some reason—probably because of the unusual fact that any one should be leaving Mrs. Lester's flat at so late an hour, both men listened.

Then Bates recollected himself.

"Yes, sir," he said.

Oddy enough, the man's marked pause suggested a question to his employer.

"Mrs. Lester's visitor didn't stop long," was the comment. "He came up almost on my heels."

"I thought it must ha' bin a gentleman," said Bates.

"Why a 'gentleman'?" laughed Theydon.

"I mean, sir, that the step didn't sound like a lady's."

"Ah, I see."

Vaguely aware that he had committed himself to a definite knowledge as to the sex of Mrs. Lester's visitor, Theydon added:

"I didn't actually see any one on the stairs, but I heard an arrival, and jumped to the same conclusion as you, Bates."

Tacitly, master and man shared the same opinion—it was satisfactory to know that Mrs. Lester's male visitors who called at the unconventional hour of 11:30 p. m. were shown out so speedily. Innesmore Mansions were intensely respectable.

No lady could live there alone whose credentials had not satisfied a sharp-eyed secretary. Further, Theydon was aware of a momentary disloyalty of thought toward the distinguished-looking father of that remarkably handsome girl, and it pleased him to find that he had erred.

Bates went out, closing the door behind him: he donned an overcoat, secured an umbrella and presently descended to the street. Yielding again to impulse, Theydon reopened the window and peered down. The stranger was walking away rapidly. A policeman, glistening in cape and overalls, stood at the corner, near a pillar box.

The tall man, who topped the burly constable by some inches, halted for a moment to post a letter. Whether by accident or design he held his umbrella so that the other could not see his face. Then he disappeared. Bates came into view. He dropped Theydon's letters into the box, but he and the policeman exchanged a few words, which, his employer guessed, must surely have dealt with the vagaries of the weather.

For an author of repute Theydon's surmises had been wide of the mark several times that night. The policeman had seen the unknown coming out from the doorway of Nos. 13-18, and had noted his stature and appearance.

"Who's the toff who just left your lot?" he said, when Bates arrived.

"Dunno," said Bates. "Some one callin' on Mrs. Lester, I fancy. Why?"

"O, nothing. On'y, if I was togged up regardless on a night like this I'd blue a cab fare."

"I didn't see him meself," commented Bates. "My boss 'eard him come, an' both of us 'eard him go. He didn't stay more'n five minnits."

"Wish I was in his shoes. I've got to stick round here till six in the morning," grinned the policeman.

"Well, cheer-o, mate."

"Cheer-o."

Bates looked in on his master before retiring for the night.

"What time shall I call you, sir?" he said.

Theydon was in the pipe and book stage, having exchanged his dress coat for a smoking jacket. He was reading a treatise on aeronautics, and, like every novice, had already formulated a flying scheme which would supersede all known inventions.

"Not later than 8," he said. "I must be out by 9. And, by the way, I may as well tell you now. After lunch tomorrow I am going to Brooklands. I return to Waterloo at 6:40. As I have to dine in the West End at 7:30, and my train may be a few minutes behind time, I want you to meet me with a suitcase at the hairdresser's place on the main platform. I'll dress there and go straight to my friend's house. It would be cutting things rather fine if I attempted to come here."

"I'll have everything ready, sir."

Bates was eminently reliable in such matters. He could be depended on to the last stud.

The storm which had raged overnight must have cleared the skies for the following day, because Theydon never enjoyed an outing more than his trip to the famous motor track. His business there, however, lay with aviation. A popular magazine had commissioned him to write an article summing up the progress and practical aims of the airmen and he was devoting afternoon and evening to the quest of information. A couple of experts and a photographer had given him plenty of raw material in the open, but he looked forward with special zest to an undisturbed chat that night with Mr. James Creighton Forbes, millionaire and philanthropist, whose peculiar yet forcible theories as to the peaceful conquest of the air were for the hour engaging the attention of the world's press.

He had never met Mr. Forbes. When on the point of writing for an appointment he had luckily remembered that the great man was a lifelong friend of the professor of physics at his (Theydon's) university, and a delightfully cordial introductory note was forthcoming in the course of a couple of posts. This brought the invitation to dinner. "On Tuesday evening I am dining *en famille*," wrote Mr. Forbes, "so, if you are free, join us at 7:30, and we can talk uninterruptedly afterward."

The train was not late. Bates, erect and soldierly, was standing at the rendezvous. With him were two men whom Theydon had never before seen. One, a bulky, stalwart, florid-faced man of forty, had something of the military aspect; the other supplied his direct antithesis, being small, wizened and sallow.

The big man had a round, bullet head, prominent bright blue eyes, and the cheek bones, chin and physical development of a heavy-weight pugilist. His companion, whose dark and recessed eyes were noticeably bright, too, could not be more than half his weight, and Theydon would not have been surprised if told that this diminutive person was a dancing master. Naturally he classed both as acquaintances of his valet, encountered by chance on the platform at Waterloo.

He was slightly astonished, therefore, when the two faced him, together with Bates. A dramatic explanation of their presence was soon supplied.

"These gentlemen, sir, are Chief Inspector Winter and Detective Inspector Furneaux of Scotland Yard," said the ex-sergeant, in the awed tone which some people cannot help using when speaking of members of the Criminal Investigation Department.

Though daylight had not yet failed it was rather dark in that corner of the station, and Theydon saw now what he had not perceived earlier, that the usually sedate Bates was pale and harassed looking.

"Why, what's up?" he inquired, gazing blankly from one to the other of the ominous pair.

"Haven't you seen the evening papers, Mr. Theydon?" said Winter, the giant of the two.

"No, I've been at Brooklands since two o'clock. But what is it?"

"You don't know, then, that a murder was committed in the Innesmore Mansions last night or early this morning?"

"Good Lord, no! Who was killed?"

"A Mrs. Lester, the lady—"

"Mrs. Lester, who lives in No. 17?"

"Yes."

"What a horrible thing! Why, only the day before yesterday I met her on the stairs."

It was a banal statement, and Theydon knew it, but he blurted out the first crazy words that would serve to cloak the monstrous thought which leaped into his brain. And a picture danced before his mind's eye, a picture, not of the fair and gracious woman who had been done to death, but of a sweet-voiced girl in a white satin dress who was saying to a fine-looking man standing by her side: "Dad, aren't you coming home with me?"

His blurred senses were conscious of the strange medley produced by the familiar noises of a railway station blending with the quietly authoritative voice of the chief inspector.

"Mr. Furneaux and I have the inquiry in hand, Mr. Theydon," the detective was saying. "We called at your flat, and Bates told us of the sounds you both heard about 11:30 last night. I'm afraid we have rather upset you by coming here, but Bates was unable to say what time you would return home, so I thought you would not mind if we accompanied him in order to find out the hour at which it would be convenient for you to meet us at your flat—this evening, of course."

"You have certainly given me the shock of my life," Theydon gasped. "That poor woman dead, murdered! It's too awful! How was she killed?"

"She was strangled."

"O, this is dreadful! Shall I wire an apology to the man I'm dining with?"

"No need for that, Mr. Theydon," said Winter, sympathetically. "I'm sorry now we blurted out our unpleasant news. But you had to be told, and it was essential that we should get your story some time tonight. Can you be home by eleven?"

"Yes, yes. I'll be there without fail." --

"Thank you. We have a good many inquiries to make in the meantime. Goodby, for the present."

The two made off. Winter had done all the talking, but Theydon was far too disturbed to pay heed to the trivial fact that Furneaux, after one swift glance, seemed to regard him as a negligible quantity. It was borne in on him that the detective evidently believed he had something of importance to say, and meant to render it almost impossible that he should escape questioning while his memory was still active with reference to events of the previous night.

And he had so little, yet so much, to tell. On his testimony alone it would be a comparatively easy matter to establish beyond doubt the identity of Mrs. Lester's last known visitor. And what would be the outcome? He dared hardly trust his own too lively imagination. Whether or not his testimony gave a clew to the police, the one irrevocable issue was that somewhere in London there was a girl named Evelyn who would regard a certain young man, Francis Berrold Theydon to wit, as a loathsome and despicable Paul Pry.

Bates, somewhat relieved by the departure of the emissaries of Scotland Yard, recalled his master's scattered wits to the affairs of the moment.

" It's getting on for seven, sir," he said. "I've engaged a dressing room."

"Tell you what, Bates," said Theydon abstractedly, "it is my fixed belief that you and I could do with a brandy and soda apiece."

"That would be a good idea, sir."

The good idea was duly acted on. While Theydon was dressing Bates told him what little he knew of the tragedy, which was discovered by Mrs. Lester's maid when she brought a cup of tea to her mistress' bedroom at ten o'clock that morning.

Bates himself was the first person appealed to by the distracted woman, and he had the good sense to leave the body and its surroundings untouched until a doctor and the police had been summoned by telephone. Thenceforth the day had passed in a whirl of excitement, active in respect to police inquiries and passive in its resistance to newspaper interviewers. He saw no valid reason why his employer's plans should be disturbed, so made no effort to communicate with him at Brooklands.

"Them 'tecs were very pressin', sir," said Bates, rather indignantly, "very pressin', especially the little one. He almost wanted to know what we had for breakfast."

At that Theydon laughed dolefully, and, as it happened, Bates's grim humor prevented him from ascertaining the exact nature of Furneaux's pertinacity. Moreover, the time was passing. At 7:15 Theydon called a taxi and was carried swiftly to Mr. Forbes's house in Belgravia, while Bates disposed himself and the dressing case on top of a northbound omnibus.

The mere change of clothing, aided by the stimulant, had cleared Theydon's faculties. Though he would gladly have foregone the dinner, he realized that it was not a bad thing

21

that he should be forced, as it were, to wrench his thoughts from the nightmare of a crime with which such a man as "Evelyn's" father might be associated, even innocently.

At any rate, he was given some hours to marshal his forces for the discussion with the representatives of Scotland Yard. He knew well that he must then face the dilemma boldly. Two courses were open. He could either share Bates's scanty knowledge, no more and no less, or avow his ampler observations. And why should he adopt the first of these alternatives? Was he not bringing himself practically within the law?

Why should any man be shielded, no matter what his social position or how beautiful his daughter, who might possibly have caused the death of the pleasant-mannered and ladylike woman fated now to remain for ever a tragic ghost in the memory of one who had dwelt under the same roof with her for five months?

It was a thorny problem, yet it permitted of only one solution. Duty must be done though the heavens fell.

This conviction grew on Theydon as his cab scurried across the Thames and along Birdcage Walk. A pretty conceit could not be allowed to sweep aside the first principles of citizenship. Indeed, so reassuring was this reasoned judgment that he felt a sense of relief as he paid off the cab and rang the bell of the Forbes mansion.

He gave his name to a footman, who disposed of his overcoat and hat, and led him to an upstairs drawing room. Even the most fleeting glances at hall and staircase revealed evidences of a highly trained artistic taste gratified by great wealth. The furniture, the china, the pictures, were each and all rare and well chosen.

"Mr. Theydon," announced the man, throwing wide the door.

A lady, bent over some prints spread on a distant table, turned at the words, and hastened to greet the guest.

"My father is expecting you, Mr. Theydon," she said. "He was detained rather late in the city, but will be here now at any moment."

Theydon was no neurotic boy, whose surcharged nerves were liable to crack in a crisis demanding some unusual measure of self-control. Yet the room and its contents—and, not least, the graceful girl advancing with outstretched hand—swam before his eyes.

Because this was "Evelyn," and it was certain as the succession of night to day that Mrs. Lester's mysterious visitor must have been "Evelyn's" father, James Creighton Forbes.

CHAPTER II

THE COMPACT

So petrified was Theydon by coming face to face with the last person breathing whom he expected to meet in that room, that he stumbled over a small chair which lay directly between him and his hostess. At any other time the gaucherie would have annoyed him exceedingly; in the existing circumstances, no more fortunate incident could have happened, since it brought Evelyn Forbes herself unwittingly to the rescue.

"I have spoken twenty times about chairs being left in that absurd position," she cried, as their hands met, "but you know how wooden-headed servants are. They will not learn to discriminate. People often sit in that very place of an afternoon, because any one seated just there sees the Canaletto on the opposite wall in the best light. When the lamps are on, the reason for the chair simply ceases to exist, and it becomes a trap for the unwary. You are by no means the first who has been caught in it."

Theydon realized, with a species of irritation, that the girl was discoursing volubly about the offending chair merely in order to extricate an apparently shy and tongue-tied young man from a morass of his own creation.

That an author of some note should not only behave like a country bumpkin, but actually seem to need encouragement so that he should "feel at home" in a London drawing room, was a fact so ridiculous that it spurred his bemused wits into something approaching their normal activity.

"I have not the excuse of the Canaletto," he said, compelling a pleasant smile, "but may I plead an even more distracting vision? I came here expecting to meet an elderly gentleman of the class which flippant Americans describe as 'high-brow,' and I am suddenly brought face to face with a Romney 'portrait of a lady' in real life. Is it likely that such an insignificant object as a chair, and a small one at that, would succeed in catching my eye?"

Evelyn Forbes laughed, with a joyous mingling of surprise and relief. Most certainly, Mr. Theydon's manner of speech differed vastly from the disconcerting expression of positive bewilderment, if not actual fright, which marred his entrance.

"Do I really resemble a Romney? Which one?" she cried.

"An admitted masterpiece."

"Ah, but people who pay compliments deserve to be put on the rack. I insist on a definition."

"Lady Hamilton as Joan of Arc."

He drew the bow at random, and was gratified to see that his hearer was puzzled.

"I don't know that particular picture," she said, "but I cannot imagine any model less adapted to the subject."

"Romney immortalized the best qualities of both," he answered promptly. "Please, may I look at the Canaletto which indirectly waylaid me?"

She turned to cross the room, but stopped and faced him again with a suddenness that argued an impulsive temperament.

"Now, I remember," she said. "Dad told me you had written novels and some essays. Have you ever really seen Romney's portrait of Lady Hamilton as Joan of Arc?"

Those fine eyes of hers pierced him with a glance of such candid inquiry that he cast pretence to the winds.

"No," he said.

"Then you just invented the comparison as an excuse for colliding with the chair?"

"Yes. At the same time I throw myself on the mercy of the court."

"It was rather clever of you."

He laughed, and their eyes met, at very close range.

"May I share the joke?" said a voice, and Theydon knew, before he turned, that the man he had last seen disappearing around the corner of Innesmore Mansions in a heavy rainstorm was in the room.

"Why did you tell me that Mr. Theydon was a serious scientific person?" cried the girl. "He is anything but that. He can talk nonsense quite admirably."

"So can a great many serious scientific persons, Evelyn. Glad to see you, Mr. Theydon. Professor Scarth's letter paved the way for something more than a formal meeting, so I thought you wouldn't mind giving us an evening. My wife is not in town. She is a martyr to hay fever, and has to fly from London to the sea early in May to escape. If caught here in June nothing can save her. Tonight, as it happens, you're our only guest, but my daughter is going to a musicale at Lady de Winton's after dinner, so you and I will be free to soar into the empyrean through a blaze of tobacco smoke."

Standing there, in that delightful drawing room, made welcome by a man like Forbes, and admitted to a degree of charming intimacy by a girl like Forbes's daughter, Theydon tried to believe that his meeting with those ill-omened detectives at Waterloo Station was, in some sort, a figment of the imagination.

But he was instantly and effectually brought back to a dour sense of reality by Evelyn Forbes's next words. She, by chance, looked at Theydon just as she had looked at him the previous night.

"Were you at Daly's Theater last night?" she inquired suddenly.

"Yes," he said. Then, finding there was no help for it, he went on:—

"You and I have hit on the same discovery, Miss Forbes. We three stood together at the exit. I was waiting for a taxi, and saw you get into your car. Now you know just why I fell over the chair."

Forbes glanced up quickly.

"Don't tell me Tomlinson forgot to move that infernal chair again!" he cried. "Really, I must get rid either of our butler or the Canaletto, yet I prize both."

"Don't blame Tomlinson, Dad," laughed the girl. "If Mr. Theydon hadn't made an unconventional entry we would have talked about the weather, or something equally stupid."

At that moment Tomlinson himself, imperturbable and portly, announced that dinner was served. The three descended the stairs, chatting lightly about the musical comedy witnessed overnight. It was no new revelation to Theydon that truth should prove stranger than fiction, but the trite phrase was fast assuming a fresh and sinister personal significance. He believed, and not without good reason, that no man living had ever undergone an experience comparable with his present adventure.

When he left that house he was going straight to two officers of the law whose bounden duty it would become to call upon Mr. Forbes for a full and true explanation of his visit to Mrs. Lester—provided, that is, he (Theydon) told them what he knew. Talk about a death's-head grinning at a feast! At that bright dinner-table he was a prey to keener emotion than ever shook a Borgia entertaining one whom he meant to poison.

In sheer self-defense he talked with an animation he seldom displayed. Evelyn was evidently much taken by him, and, fired by her manifest interest, he indulged in fantastic paradox and wild flights of fancy. Seemingly his exuberance stimulated Forbes, himself a well-informed and epigrammatic talker.

An hour sped all too soon. The girl rose with a sigh.

"It's too bad that I should have to go," she said. "I shall be bored stiff at Lady de Winton's. But I can't get out of it except by telling a positive fib over the telephone. Dad, next time you ask Mr. Theydon to dinner, please let me know in good time, and neither of you will be rid of me so easily."

She shook hands with Theydon. While she was giving her father a parting kiss the guest moved to the door and held it open. As she passed out she smiled and her eyes said plainly:

"I like you. Come again soon."

Then she was gone and the pleasant room lost some of its glow and color.

"Don't sit down again, Theydon," said Forbes, rising. "We'll have coffee brought to my den. What is your favorite liqueur— or shall we tell Tomlinson to send along that decanter of port? It's a first-rate wine. Another glass won't hurt you, or me, for that matter."

Theydon had hardly dared to touch the champagne supplied during the meal. Abstemious at all times, because he found that wine or spirits interfered with his capacity for work, he felt that a clear head and steady nerves were called for that night more than any other night in his life. Following the lead given by his host, therefore, he elected for the port.

"You are right, too," said Forbes. "You remember Dr. Johnson's dictum: 'Claret is the liquor for boys; port for men; but he who aspires to be a hero must drink brandy'?

Tonight, not aspiring to the heroic, we'll stick to port.''

"It is a curious fact that on my return from Brooklands today I took a glass of brandy,'' confessed Theydon. "I seldom, if ever, drink any intoxicant before dining, but I needed a stimulant of a sort, and some unknown tissue in me cried aloud for brandy.''

He hoped vaguely that the comment would lead to something more explicit, and thus bring him, without undue emphasis, so to speak, to the one topic on which he was now resolved to obtain a decisive statement from the man chiefly concerned before he faced the representatives of Scotland Yard.

But Forbes, motioning to an easy chair in a well-appointed library, and flinging himself into another, gave heed only to the one word —Brooklands.

"Did you fly?'' he asked.

"No. I was soaking in theory, not practice.''

"Ah, theory. It would, indeed, seem to be true that folded away in some convolution of our brain are the faculties of the fish and the bird. Those latent powers are expanding daily. The submarine has already gone far beyond the practical achievement of aerial craft. But why, in the name of humanity, should every such development of man's al-

most immeasurable resources be dedicated to
warlike purposes? I am sick at heart when I
hear the first question put in these days to each
inventor: 'Can you enable us to kill more of our
fellowmen than we can kill with existing appli-
ances?' Is it a new engine, a new amalgam
of metals, a new explosive, a new field of
electrical energy, one hears the same vulture's
cry—'How many, how far, how safely can we
slay?' I regard this lust for destruction as
contemptible. It is a strange and ignomini-
ous feature of modern life. Forgive me,
Mr. Theydon, if I speak strongly on this matter. The men who spread the bounds of
science today are, nominally, at any rate,
Christians. They tell of peace and goodwill
to all, yet prepare unceasingly for some awful
Armageddon.* We teach Christ's gospel in
pulpit and schoolhouse, strive to express it in
our laws, obey it in our lives and social relations, yet we are armed to the teeth and ever
arming, adding strength to the plates of our
warships and distance to the range of our
guns, constantly riveting and welding and forg-
ing monsters which shall shatter men and cities
and States.''

It was not the younger man now who talked
brilliantly and forcibly. Theydon, frankly
abandoning the effort to twist the conversation to that enigma which, the more he saw

* This story was written before the outbreak of war in 1914.

and heard of Forbes the more incredible it became, listened enthralled to one who spoke with the conviction and earnestness of a prophet.

"Don't imagine that I am framing an indictment against Christianity," went on Forbes passionately. "The Sermon on the Mount inspires all that is great and noble in our everyday existence, all that is eternally beautiful in our dreams of the future. But why this din of war, this smoke of arsenals, this marching and drilling of the world's youth? Nature's law appears to have two simple clauses. It enforces a principle in the struggle for existence, a test in the survival of the fittest. Great heavens, are not these enough, without having our ears deafened by powder and drumming? That is why I am devoting a good deal of time and no small amount of money to an international crusade against the warlike idea, and I see no reason why a beginning should not be made with the airship and the airplane. We are too late with the submarine, but, before the golden hour passes, let us stop the navigation of the air from forming part of the equipment of murder. Surely it can be done. England and the United States, Italy, France and the rest of Europe—the founts of civilization—can write the edict, with all the blazonry of their glorious histories to illuminate the page—'There shall be no war in the air!' "

Theydon was carried away in spite of himself.

"You believe that the airship might develop along the unemotional lines of the parcel post?" he inquired.

Forbes laughed.

"Exactly," he said. "I like your simile. No one suggests that we Britons should endeavor to destroy our hated rivals by sending bombs through the mails. Why, then, in the name of common sense, should the first—I might almost say the only use of which the airship is commonly supposed capable—be that of destruction? Don't you see the instant result of a war-limiting ordinance of the kind I advocate? Suppose the peoples and the rulers declared in their wisdom that soldiers and war material should be contraband of the air—and suppose that airships do become vehicles of practical utility—what a farce would soon be all the grim fortresses, the guns, the giant steel structures now designed as floating hells! Humanity has yet time to declare that the flying machine shall be as harmless and serviceable as the penny post. I believe it can be done. Come now, Mr. Theydon, I think you've caught on to my scheme—will you help?"

Help! Here was a man expounding a new

evangel, which might, indeed, be visionary and impracticable, but was none the less essentially noble and Christian in spirit, yet Theydon was debating whether or not he should give testimony which would bring to that very room a couple of detectives whose first questions would make clear to Forbes that he was suspected of blood-guiltiness!

The notion was so utterly repellent that Theydon sighed deeply; his host not unnaturally looked surprised.

"Of course, such a revolutionary idea strikes you as outside the pale of common sense," he began, but the younger man stayed him with a gesture. Here was an opportunity that must not be allowed to pass. No matter what the cost—if he never saw Evelyn Forbes or her father again—he must dispel the waking nightmare which held him in such an abnormal condition of uncertainty and foreboding.

"Now that your daughter is gone I may venture to speak plainly," he said. "I told you that I felt the need of a brandy and soda at Waterloo. As a matter of fact, I did not leave the Brooklands track until six o'clock, and, as Innesmore Mansions, where I live, lie north, and I was due here at 7:30, I had my man meet me at the station with a suitcase, meaning to change my clothes in the dressing room there, and come straight

here. Guess my astonishment when I found
Bates—Bates is the name of my factotum—
in the company of two strangers, whom he
introduced as representing the Criminal Investigation Department.''

He paused. He had brought in his own
address skilfully enough, and kept his voice
sufficiently under control that no tremor betrayed a knowledge of Forbes's vital interest
in any mention of that one block of flats
among the multitude.

Now, for the first time, Innesmore Mansions figured as his abode, the correspondence
which led to the dinner having centered in
his club. But not a flicker of eyelid nor
twitch of mobile lips showed the slightest
concern on Forbes's part. Rather did he display at once a well-bred astonishment on
hearing Theydon's concluding words.

''Do you mean detectives from Scotland
Yard?'' he cried.

''Yes.''

Forbes smiled, and commenced filling a
pipe.

''Evidently they did not want you as a principal,'' he said.

His tone was genial, but slightly guarded.
Theydon realized that this man of great
wealth and high social position had reminded
himself that his guest, though armed with
the best of credentials, was quite unknown to

him otherwise, and that, perhaps, he had acted unwisely in inviting a stranger to his house without making some preliminary inquiry. This reversal of their rôles was a conceit so ludicrous that Theydon smiled too.

At any rate, he meant now to pursue an unpleasing task, and have done with it.

"No," he said slowly. "It seems that I am the worst sort of witness in a murder case. I may have heard, I may even have seen, the person suspected of committing the crime, or, if that is going too far, the person whom the police have good reason to regard as the last who saw the poor victim alive and in ordinary conditions. But my testimony, such as it is, is so slight and inconclusive that, of itself, no one could hang a cat on it."

"Good gracious! That sounds interesting, though you have my sympathy. It must be rather distressing to be mixed up in such an affair, even indirectly."

Forbes struck precisely the right note of friendly inquiry. He wished to hear more, and was at the same time relieved to find that Professor Scarth had not introduced a notorious malefactor in the guise of a young writer seeking material for an article on airships!

Theydon could have laughed aloud at this

comedy of errors, but the fact that at any moment it might develop into a tragedy exercises a wholesome restraint.

"I happen to live at No. 18 Innesmore Mansions," he said. "Opposite—on the same floor, I mean—lives, or did live, a Mrs. Lester. I do not—"

"Are you telling me that a Mrs. Lester of No. 17 Innesmore Mansions is dead—has been murdered?"

Forbes's voice rang out vibrant, incisive. His ordinarily pale face had blanched, and his deep-set eyes blazed with the fire of some fierce emotion, but, beyond the slight elevation of tone and the change of expression, he revealed to Theydon's quietly watchful scrutiny no sign of the terror or distress which an evil-doer might be expected to show on learning that the law's vengeance was already shadowing him, even in so remote a way as was indicated by the presence under his roof of a witness regarded by the police as an important one.

"Yes!" stammered Theydon, quite taken aback by his companion's vehemence. "Do you—know the lady? If so—I am sorry—I spoke so unguardedly—"

"Good heavens, man, don't apologize for that! I am not a child or weakling, that I should flinch in horror from one of life's dramatic surprises! But, are you sure of what you are saying? Mrs. Lester murdered! When?"

"About midnight last night, the doctor believes. That is what Bates told me. I was so shaken on hearing his news, which was confirmed by the two detectives, that I really gave little heed to details. . . . She was strangled—a peculiarly atrocious thing where an attractive and ladylike woman is concerned. I have never spoken to her, but have met her at odd times on the stairs. I was immeasurably shocked, I assure you. In fact, I was on the point of telegraphing an excuse to you for this evening, but the Chief Inspector —Winter, I think his name is—said it would suffice for his purpose if I met him at my flat about eleven o'clock, as he was engaged on other inquiries which would occupy the intervening hours."

"But if the news of this dastardly crime only reached you tonight at Waterloo Station, and you have no personal acquaintance with Mrs. Lester, what evidence can you give that will assist the police?"

"Mrs. Lester received a visitor last night, an incident so unusual that I, who heard him arrive, and Bates, who was in my sitting room when we both heard him depart, commented on the strangeness of it. That, I suppose, is the reason why I am in request by Scotland Yard."

"You say 'him.' How did you know it was a man? Did you see him?"

"Er—that was impossible. We were in my flat, behind its closed door. Bates and I deduced his sex from the sound of his footsteps."

Again Theydon nearly stammered. Events had certainly turned in the most amazing way. Instead of carrying himself almost in the manner of a judge, he was figuring rather as an unwilling witness in the hands of a skilled and merciless cross-examining counsel.

"Did the police officers supply any theory of motive for the crime? Was this poor woman killed for the sake of her few trinkets?"

By this time Theydon was stung into a species of revolt. It was he, not Forbes, who should be snapping out searching questions.

"I regret to say that my nerves were not sufficiently under control at Waterloo that I should listen carefully to each word," he said, almost stiffly. "Bates had picked up such information as was available; but he, though an ex-sergeant in the Army, was so upset as to be hardly coherent. When I meet the detectives in the course of another hour I shall probably gather something definite and reliable in the way of details."

Forbes laid the pipe which he had filled but not lighted on the table. He poured out a glass of port and drank it.

"Try that," he said, pushing the decanter toward Theydon. "They cannot trouble you greatly. You have so little to tell."

"No, thanks. Nothing more for me tonight until the Scotland Yard men have cleared out."

Forbes rose as he spoke and strode the length of the room and back with the air of a man debating some weighty and difficult point.

"Mr. Theydon," he said, at last, halting in front of the younger man and gazing down at him with a direct intensity that was highly embarrassing to one who had good cause to connect him with the actual crime. "I want you to do me a favor—a great favor. It was in my mind at first to ask you to permit me to go with you to Innesmore Mansions, and to be present during the interview with the detectives. But a man in my position must be circumspect. It would, perhaps, be unwise to appear too openly interested. I don't mind telling you in confidence that I have known Mrs. Lester many years. The shock of her death, severe as it must have been to you, is slight as compared with my own sorrow and dismay. More than that I dare not say until better informed. I remember now hearing the newsboys shouting their ghoulish news, and I saw contents bills making large type display of 'Murder of a lady,' but little did I imagine

41

that the victim was one whom—one whose loss
I shall deplore. . . . Are you on the telephone?"

"Yes," said Theydon, thoroughly mystified
anew by the announcement that Forbes had
even contemplated, or so much as hinted at,
the astounding imprudence of visiting Innesmore Mansions that night.

"Ring me up when the detectives have gone.
I shall esteem your assistance during this
crisis as a real service."

For the life of him, Theydon could not
frame the protest which ought to have been
made without delay and without hesitation.

"Yes," he said. "I'll do that. You can
trust me absolutely."

Thus was he committed to secrecy. That
promise sealed his lips.

CHAPTER III

THEYDON, though blessed, or cursed, with an active imagination—which must surely be the prime equipment of a novelist—was shrewd and level-headed in dealing with everyday affairs.

It was no small achievement that the son of a country rector, aided only by a stout heart, a university education and an excellent physique—good recommendations, each and all, but forming the stock-in-trade of many a man on whose subsequent career "failure" is writ large—should have forced himself to the front rank of the most overcrowded among the professions before attaining his twenty-sixth year.

It may be taken for granted, therefore, that he was not lacking in the qualities of close observation and critical analysis. He would, for instance, be readier than the majority of his fellows to note the small beginnings of events destined to become important.

Often, of course, his deductions would prove erroneous, but the mere fact that he habitually exercised his wits in such a way

43

rendered it equally certain that his judgment would be accurate sometimes. One such occasion presented itself a few seconds after he had left the Forbes mansion.

A taxi, summoned by a footman, was in waiting, and Theydon was crossing the pavement when he noticed a gray landaulet car at rest beneath the trees at some distance. Mr. Forbes's house stood in a square, and the gray car had been drawn up on the quiet side of the roadway, being stationed there, apparently, to await its owner's behest. Gray cars are common enough in London, but they are usually of the touring class.

Not often does one see a gray-painted landaulet; hence, the odd though hardly remarkable fact occurred to Theydon that a precisely similar gray automobile had occupied the center of the station yard at Waterloo when he took a taxi from the rank.

Admittedly he was in a nervous and excited state. It could hardly be otherwise after the strain of that astounding conversation with Forbes, and there was no prospect of the tension being relaxed until the close of the interview with the detectives, which he now regarded as the worse ordeal of the two.

But this subconscious neurasthenia in no wise affected the reflex action of his ordinary faculties. When, on leaving the square, and while his cab was rattling along an aris-

tocratic thoroughfare leading to Knights-
bridge, he peered through a tiny observation
window in the back of the vehicle, and ascertained that the gray car was stealing along
quietly about a hundred yards in the rear,
he began to believe that its presence both at
Waterloo and outside Mr. Forbes's residence
could not be wholly accidental. When he had
watched its persistent treading on his heels
along Piccadilly its intent became almost un-
mistakable.

The route to Innesmore Mansions traversed
some of London's main arteries, but, despite
the rush of traffic due to the first flight of
homewardbound playgoers, the gray car kept
steadily on his track. Amused at first, be became angry because of a notion which grew
out of the wonderment of finding himself the
object of this persistent espionage.

To make sure, and at the same time discover the sort of person who was spying on
him, he adopted a ruse. Leaning out, when
about to cross Oxford Street into Totten-
ham Court Road, he said to his driver: "Turn
sharp to the right in Store Street, and pull
up. I'll tell you when to go on again."

The man obeyed. Theydon posted himself
at the outer window, and in a space of time
so short that the excellence of the gray car's
accelerator was amply demonstrated, the pur-
suer swung into sight. A stolid-faced chauf-

feur at the wheel did not appear discomfited at coming on his quarry thus unexpectedly. He whirled past, seemingly quite oblivious of Theydon's fixed stare. Though the weather was mild he wore an overcoat with upturned collar, so that between its protecting flaps and a low-peaked cap his face was well hidden. Still, Theydon received an impression of a curiously wooden physiognomy.

The man might have been an automaton for all the heed he gave to the taxi or its inquisitive occupant. But his aspect was almost forgotten in the far stranger discovery that the car was empty. Both windows were open, and the bright lights of a corner shop flashed into the interior, yet not a soul was visible. Moreover, the car sped on unhesitatingly, stopping some two hundred yards ahead.

So far as Theydon could tell, no one alighted. He jotted down the number—XY 1314—on his shirt cuff.

"Did you happen to see that car waiting near the house I came from?" he said to the taxi man, who, of course, provided an interested audience of one.

"Yes, sir," was the ready answer. "It's not a London car. I've never seen them letters afore."

"In other words, it may be a faked number."

"Likely enough, sir, but rather risky. The police are quick at spotting that sort of thing."

"Can you take a hand in the game? I want to know where that car goes to."

The man grinned.

"I wouldn't like to humbug you, sir. That there machine can lose me quicker'n a Derby winner could pass a keb horse. Didn't you hear the hum of the engine as it went by?"

"Thanks. Now go ahead to Innesmore Mansions."

He was paying the driver when the gray car stole quietly past the end of the street, and that was the last he saw of it.

"There it goes again, sir," said the man. "Tell you wot, gimme your name an' address. I'll make a few inquiries, an' keep me eyes open as well. Then, if I hear anythink, I'll let you know."

Theydon scribbled the number of his flat on a card.

"There you are," he said. "Even if I happen to be out, I'll leave instructions that you are to be paid half a crown for your trouble if you call. By the way, what is your name?"

"Evans, sir."

There was really little doubt in Theydon's mind as to the reason why he had been followed. He was fuming about it when Bates met him in the hall of No. 18 with the whisper:

"Them two are waiting here now, sir."

Theydon glanced at his watch. The hour was ten minutes past eleven.

"Sorry I'm late, gentlemen," he said, on entering the sitting room and finding the detectives seated at his table, seemingly comparing notes, because the Chief Inspector was talking, while Furneaux, the diminutive, was glancing at a notebook.

"We have no reason to complain of being kept waiting a few minutes in such comfortable quarters," said Winter pleasantly.

"O, I fancy I was detained by some zealous assistant of yours," said Theydon, determined to carry the war into the enemy's territory.

At that Furneaux looked up quickly.

"Will you kindly tell me just what you mean, Mr. Theydon?" said Winter.

"Why? Is it news to you that a gray limousine car stalked me from Waterloo to— to my friend's house, waited there three hours or more, and has carefully escorted me home? I dislike that sort of thing. Moreover, it strikes me as stupid. I didn't kill Mrs. Lester. It will save you and me a good deal of time and worry if you accept that plain statement as a fact."

"Won't you sit down?" said Winter

quietly. "And—may I smoke? I didn't like to ask Bates for permission to light up in your absence."

Theydon was not to be outdone in coolness. He opened a corner cupboard and produced various boxes.

"The cigars are genuine Havanas," he said. "A birthday present from a maiden aunt, who is wise enough to judge the quality of tobacco by the price. Here, too, are Virginian, Turkish and Egyptian cigarettes."

Winter inspected the cigars gravely.

"By Jove!" he cried, his big eyes bulging in joyous surprise. "Last year's crop from the Don Juan y Guerrero plantation. Treasure that aunt of yours, Mr. Theydon. None but herself can be her equal."

Theydon saw that the little man did not follow his chief's example.

"Don't you smoke?" he said.

"No, but if you'll not be horrified, I would like to smell one of those Turks."

"Smell it?"

"Yes. That is the only way to enjoy the aroma and avoid nicotine poisoning. My worthy chief dulls a sound intellect by the cigar habit. What is worse, he excites a nervous system which is normally somewhat bovine. You, also, I take it, are a confirmed smoker, so both of you are at cross-purposes already."

Furneaux's voice was pitched in the curious piping note usually associated with comic relief in a melodrama, but his wizened face was solemn as a red Indian's. It was Theydon who smiled. His preconceived ideas as to the appearance and demeanor of the London detective were shattered. Really, there was no need to take these two seriously.

Winter, while lighting the cigar, grinned amiably at his colleague. Furneaux passed a cigarette to and fro under his nostrils and sniffed. Theydon reached for a pipe and tobacco jar and drew up a chair.

"Well," he said, "it is not my business to criticise your methods. I have very little to tell you. I suppose Bates—"

"The really important thing is this car which followed you tonight," broke in Winter. "The details are fresh in your memory. What type of car was it? Did you see the driver and occupants? What's its number?"

Theydon had not expected these questions. He looked his astonishment.

"Ha!" cackled Furneaux. "What did I tell you?"

"O, shut up!" growled Winter. "I am asking just what you yourself are itching to know."

"May I take it that the car has not been dogging me by your instructions?" said Theydon. He was inclined to be skeptical, yet the Chief Inspector seemed to have spoken quite candidly.

"Yes," said Winter, meeting the other's glance squarely. "We have no reason on earth to doubt the truth of anything you have said, or may say, with regard to this inquiry. The car is not ours. This is the first we have heard of it. We accepted your word, Mr. Theydon, that you were dining with a friend. Perhaps you will tell us now what his name is and where he lives."

Theydon hesitated the fraction of a second. That, he knew instantly, was a blunder, so he proceeded to rectify it.

"I was dining with Mr. James Creighton Forbes, of No. 11, Fortescue Square," he said. "Probably you are acquainted with his name, so you will realize that if my evidence proves of the slightest value I would not like any reference to be made to the fact that I was his guest tonight."

"I don't see how that can possibly enter into the matter, except in its bearing on this mysterious car."

Though Winter was taking the lead, Theydon was aware that Furneaux, who had given him scant attention hitherto, was now looking at him fixedly. He imagined that the queer little man was all agog to learn something about the automobile which had thrust itself so abruptly into the affair.

"Exactly," he agreed. "I visited Mr. Forbes tonight for the first time. We are mutually interested in aviation. That is why I went to Brooklands today, and the invitation to dinner was the outcome of a letter of introduction given me by Professor Scarth."

Then, thinking he had said enough on that point, he described the gray car and its stolid-faced chauffeur to the best of his ability. He told of the brief chat with the taxi driver and its result.

"Good!" nodded Winter. "I'm glad you did that. It may help. I am doubtful of any information turning up, but you never can tell. The number plate, at any rate, is certainly misleading. Now, about last night? Try and be as accurate as possible with regard to time. Can you give us the exact hour when you returned home?"

"I happened to note by the clock on the mantelpiece that I came in at 11:35."

Winter compared the clock's time with his watch.

"You had been to a theater?" he said.

"Yes—Daly's."

"It was raining heavily. Did you take a cab?"

"Yes."

"Were you delayed? The piece ended at 11:05."

"My cab met with a slight accident."

"What sort of accident?"

Theydon explained.

"In all likelihood you can discover the driver," he smiled, "and he will establish my alibi."

His tone seemed to annoy Furneaux, who broke in:

"Don't you write novels?"

"Yes."

"Sensational?"

"Occasionally."

"Then you ought to be tickled to death, as the Americans say, at being mixed up in a first-rate murder. This is no ordinary crime. Several people will be older and wiser before the culprit is found and hanged."

"What Mr. Furneaux has in mind," purred Winter cheerfully, "is the curious habit of some witnesses when questioned by the police. They arm themselves against attack, as it were. You see, Mr. Theydon, we suspect nobody. We try to ascertain facts, and hope to deduce a theory from them. Over and over again we are mistaken. We are no more astute than other men. Our sole advantage is a wide experience of criminal methods. The detective of romance—if you'll forgive the allusion—simply doesn't exist in real life."

"I accept the rebuke," said Theydon. "I suppose the gray car was still rankling in my mind. From this moment I start afresh. At any rate, the man who brought me from the theater might check my recollection of the time."

Winter nodded. He was evidently pleased that Theydon was inclined to share his view of the difficulties Scotland Yard encountered in its fight against malefactors.

"Did you see or meet any one in particular while your car approached these mansions, or when you ascended the stairs?"

"No," said Theydon.

He perceived intuitively that if the detectives found the driver of the taxi which brought him from the theater it was possible the man might have noticed Forbes, who had certainly been scrutinized a few minutes later by a policeman, so he hastened to add:

"You said 'any one in particular.' I did see a tall, well-dressed gentleman at the corner of the street, but there is nothing remarkable in that."

"Which way was he heading?"

"In this direction."

"Then it is conceivable that he might be the man who called on Mrs. Lester?"

"Yes."

"Aren't you pretty sure he was the man?"

Theydon permitted himself to look astonished.

"I?" he said. "How can I be sure? If you mean that, judging from the interval of time between my seeing him at the corner and the sound of footsteps on the stairs, followed by the opening of the door at No. 17, it could be he, I accept that."

Winter nodded again. Apparently he was content with Theydon's correction.

"As the weather was bad, you probably hurried in when your cab stopped?" he said.

"That is equivalent to saying you credit me with sense enough to get in out of the wet," smiled Theydon.

"Just so. And you wore an overcoat, which you removed on entering your hall?"

"Yes," and Theydon's tone showed a certain bewilderment at these trivialities.

"Then if you paid no special heed to the movements of the tall gentleman you have mentioned, why did you open one of these windows and look out soon after Bates went to the post?"

Theydon flushed like a schoolboy caught by a master under circumstances which youth generally describes as "a clean cop."

"How on earth do you know I looked out?" he almost gasped.

"I'll tell you willingly. The discovery was Mr. Furneaux's, not mine. When we came here this morning, and ascertained that you had been out at a late hour last night, we asked your man if he could enlighten us as to your movements. He did so. To the best of his belief you dined at a club, and occupied a stall at Daly's Theater subsequently. He was sure, too, you had not walked home through the rain, so it was easy to draw the conclusion that you returned in a covered vehicle. Mr. Furneaux requested Bates to produce the clothes you had worn, which, owing to the uproar created by the news of the murder, had not been brushed and put away. As a consequence the silk collar and part of the back of your dress-coat bore the marks of raindrops. How had they got there? The only logical deduction was that you had thrust your head and shoulders through a window, and the time of the action is established almost beyond doubt, because you had changed the coat when Bates came from the pillar-box. It was either directly after you came in, or while Bates was absent. Of course you may have looked out twice. Did you? Whether once or twice, why did you do it?''

Theydon's feelings changed rapidly while Winter was delivering this very convincing analysis of a few simple facts. He had passed at a bound from the detected schoolboy stage to that of a man forcing his way through a thicket who finds himself on the very lip of a precipice.

He remembered hazily that Bates had said something at Waterloo with regard to the manner in which the detectives, especially

Furneaux, had questioned him. But it was too late to apply the warning thus conveyed. If he faltered now he was forever discredited. These men would read his perplexed face as if it were a printed page. In his distress he was prepared to hear Winter or that little satyr, Furneaux, say mockingly:

"Why are you trying to screen James Creighton Forbes? What is he to you? What matter his fame or social rank? We are here to see that justice is done. Out with the truth, let who may suffer."

But neither of the pair said anything of the sort. Furneaux only interjected a sarcastic comment.

"You will observe, Mr. Theydon, that even in a minor instance of deductive reasoning, such as this, the man who smells rather than the man who smokes tobacco solves the problem promptly."

Theydon threw out his hands in token of surrender. He thought he saw a means of escape, and took it unhesitatingly.

"I'm vanquished," he said. "You force me to admit that I do know a little, a very little, more than I have confessed hitherto about the man who visited Mrs. Lester's flat last night. I have said nothing about the matter thus far because I didn't want to be convicted of a piece of idle curiosity worthy of a gossip-loving housemaid. I noticed the

man I have described staring at the name
tablet of the street as my cab turned the
corner. I did not know him. I had never seen
him before last night, but he was of such
distinguished appearance and his face was of
so rare a type that I was interested and
wished to ascertain, if possible, on whom he
meant calling if, as it seemed, he was searching for an address in these flats. Therefore,
I did look out, and saw him enter the doorway beneath. In due course I heard him
arrive at Mrs. Lester's door—that is, I assume it was he. Five minutes later Bates
and I heard him depart. To make sure, I
looked out a second time. If you ask me why
I behaved in that way I cannot tell you.
I have occupied this flat during the past
five months, and I have never previously,
within my recollection, lifted a window and
gazed out to watch anybody's comings and
goings. The thing is inexplicable. All I can
say is that it just happened."

"Would you recognize him if you saw him
again?"

"Yes."

Theydon gave the assurance readily. It
was beyond credence that either detective
should put the one question to which he was
now firmly resolved to give a misleading
answer, and in this belief he was justified,
since not even Furneaux's uncanny intel-

ligence could suggest the fantastic notion that the man who walked through the rain the previous night and the man with whom Theydon had dined that evening were one and the same person.

"I don't blame you for adopting a policy of partial concealment," said the Chief Inspector, dryly. "You are not the first, and you certainly will not be the last witness from whom the police have to drag the facts. Now that we have reached more intimate terms, can you help by describing this stranger?"

Theydon complied at once. He drew just such a general sketch of Forbes as a skilled observer of men might be expected to formulate after one direct glance close at hand, supplemented by a view into a lamp-lit street from a second-storey window on a rainy night.

"So far, so good," said Winter. "You have contrived to fill in several details lacking in the description supplied by a policeman who chanced to be standing at the corner when Mrs. Lester's visitor posted a letter. Did you notice that?"

"Yes. Indeed, I believed that, whether intentionally or not, he held an open umbrella at an angle which prevented the constable from seeing his face."

"In fact, it's marvellous what you really do know when your memory is jogged," snapped Furneaux.

Theydon did not resent the sarcasm. He smiled candidly into the little detective's eyes.

"I suppose I deserve that," he said meekly.

"Why did you hide your knowledge of Mrs. Lester's visitor from your man Bates?"

"I was rather ashamed of the subterfuge adopted in order to get him out of the room while I opened the window the first time."

"That was understandable last night, but I fail to follow your reasoning for a policy of silence when we told you at Waterloo that Mrs. Lester had been killed."

"I was utterly taken aback by your news. I wanted time to think. I never meant to hide any material fact at this interview."

"You have contrived to delay and hamper our inquiry for twelve hours—twenty-four in reality. I can't make you out, Mr. Theydon. You would never have said a word about your very accurate acquaintance with this mysterious stranger's appearance had not last night's rainstorm left its legible record on your clothes. Do you now vouch for it that the man was completely unknown to you?"

"You are pleased to be severe, Mr. Furneaux, but, having placed myself in a false position, I must accept your strictures. I assure you, on my honor, that the man I saw was an absolute stranger."

Happily, Theydon was under no compulsion to choose his words. He met the detective's searching gaze unflinchingly. Fate, after terrifying him, had been kind. If Furneaux had expressed himself differently—if, for instance, he had said: "Had you ever before seen the man?" or "Have you now any reason for believing that you know his name?"—he would have forced Theydon's hand in a way he was far from suspecting.

"It may surprise you to hear," piped the shrill, cracked voice, "that there are dozens of policemen walking about London who would arrest you on suspicion had you treated them as you have treated us."

"Then I can only say that I am fortunate in my inquisitors," smiled Theydon.

Winter held up a massive fist in deprecation of these acerbities.

"You have nothing more to tell us?" he queried.

"Nothing!"

"Then we need not trouble you further tonight. Of course, if luck favors us and we find the gentleman with the classical features—the most unlikely person to commit a murder I have ever heard of—we shall want you to identify him."

"I am at your service at any time. But before you go won't you enlighten me somewhat? What did really happen? I have not even seen a newspaper account of the crime."

"Would you care to examine No. 17?"

61

It was Furneaux who put the question, and Theydon was genuinely astonished.

"Do you mean—" he began, but Furneaux laughed, almost savagely.

"I mean Mrs. Lester's flat," he said. "The poor woman's body is at the mortuary. If you come with us we can reconstruct the crime. It occurred about this very hour if the doctor's calculations are well founded."

Theydon rose.

"I shall be most—interested," he said. "By the way, Mr. Furneaux, yours is a French name. Are you a Frenchman, may I ask?"

"A Jersey man. You think I am adopting some of the methods of the French *juge d'instruction,* eh?"

"No. I cannot bring myself to believe that you regard me as a murderer."

The three passed out into the hall. Mr. and Mrs. Bates immediately showed scared faces at the kitchen door.

"It's all right, Bates," said Theydon airily. "I'm not a prisoner. I'll be with you again in a few minutes."

But Bates was profoundly disturbed.

"Wot beats me," he said to his wife when they were alone, "is why that little ferret wanted to see the guv'nor's clothes. I looked 'em over carefully afterwards, an' there wasn't a speck on 'em except some spots of rain on the coat collar. It's a queer business, no matter how you look at it. Mr. Theydon's manner was strange when he kem in last night. He seemed to be list'nin' for something. I don't know wot to make of it, Eliza. I reely don't.''

In effect, since no man is a hero to his valet, what would Tomlinson, butler at No. 11 Fortescue Square, have thought of his master if told that Mrs. Lester's last known visitor was James Creighton Forbes?

CHAPTER IV

THEYDON's journalistic experiences had been, for the most part, those of the "special correspondent," or descriptive writer. He had never entered one of those fetid slums of a great city in which, too often, murder is done, never sickened with the physical nausea of death in its most revolting aspect, when some unhappy wretch's foul body serves only to further pollute air already vile.

It was passing strange, therefore, that Winter had no sooner opened the door of No. 17 than the novice of the party became aware of a heavy, pungent scent which he associated with some affrighting and unclean thing. At first he swept aside the phantasy. Strong as he was, his nervous system had been subjected to severe strain that evening. He knew well that the mind can create its own specters, that the five senses can be subjugated by forces which science has not as yet either measured or defined.

Moreover, he was standing in a hall furnished with a taste and quiet elegance that

64

must surely indicate similar features in each room of a suite which, in other respects, bore an almost exact resemblance of his own apartments. In sheer protest against the riot of an overwrought imagination he brushed a hand across his eyes.

The chief inspector noted the action.

"You will find nothing grewsome here, I assure you," he said, quietly. "Beyond a few signs of hurried rummaging of drawers and boxes there is absolutely no indication of a crime having been committed."

"Mr. Theydon came prepared to see ghosts," squeaked Furneaux. "Evidently he is not acquainted with the peculiar smell of a joss stick."

Theydon turned troubled eyes on the wizened little man who seemed to have the power of reading his secret thought.

"A joss stick," he repeated. "Isn't that some sort of incense used by Chinese in their temples?"

"Yes," said Furneaux.

"Lots of ladies burn them in their boudoirs nowadays," explained Winter offhandedly.

"The Chinese burn them to propitiate evil spirits," murmured Furneaux. "The Taou gods are mostly deities of a very unpleasant frame of mind. The mere scowl of one of them from a painted fan suggests novel and

65

painful forms of torture. I've seen Shang Ti grinning at me from a porcelain vase, otherwise exquisite, and felt my hair rising.''

"I do wish you wouldn't talk nonsense, Charles," said Winter, frowning heavily.

"Am I talking nonsense, Mr. Theydon?" demanded Furneaux. "Didn't your flesh creep when that queer perfume assailed your nostrils, which are not yet altogether atrophied by the reek of thousands of rank cigars?''

"Stop it!" commanded Winter, throwing open a door.

"And they christened him Leander—Leander, who swam the Hellespont for love of a woman!" muttered Furneaux.

Theydon began to believe that both detectives were cranks of the first order. Furneaux, whose extraordinary insight he actually feared, was obviously an excellent example of the alliance between insanity and genius. In a word, he failed, and not unreasonably, to understand that when the Jersey man was mouthing a strange jargon of knowledge and incoherence, and Winter was inclined to be snappy with his subordinate, and each was more than rude to the other, they were then giving tongue like hounds hot on the trail.

Winter's Christian names were James Leander, the latter being conferred for no more classical reason than his father's association with a famous boating club, but the fact supplied Furneaux with material for many a quip. These things Theydon learnt later. At present he was giving all his attention to Winter, who led the way into a daintly furnished bedroom. The electric lights were governed by two switches. A pair of lamps occupied the usual place in front of a dressing table; a third was suspended from a canopy over the bed, and was controlled also by an alternate switch behind the bolster. Winter turned on all three lights, so the room was brilliantly illuminated.

Any place less likely to become the scene of a brutal crime could hardly be imagined. It looked exactly what it was, the bedchamber of a refined and well-bred woman, whose trained sense of color and design was shown by the harmony of carpet, rugs, wall paper and furniture.

Winter pointed to a slight depression on the side of the bed. A white linen coverlet was rumpled as though some one had sat there.

"That is where Ann Rogers, the maid, found her mistress at ten o'clock this morning," he said. "As you see, the bed had not been slept in. Indeed, Mrs. Lester was fully dressed. My belief is that she was pounced on the instant she entered the room—probably to retire for the night—strangled before she could utter a sound, and flung here when dead."

Again Theydon was aware of the subtle, penetrating, and not wholly unpleasing scent which Furneaux had attributed to the burning of a joss stick, but his mind was focused on the detective's words, which suggested a queer discrepancy between certain vague possibilities already flitting through his brain and the terrible drama as it presented itself to a skilled criminologist.

"But," he said, almost protestingly, "from what I have seen of Mrs. Lester she was a strong and active woman. It is inconceivable that the man who came here last night could have murdered her while I was writing two brief notes. I am positive he did not remain five minutes, and Bates or I, or both of us, must have heard some trampling of feet, some indications of a struggle. Moreover, you think she was about to retire. Doesn't that opinion conflict with the known facts?"

"What known facts?"

"Well—er—those I have mentioned. The brief visit, the open nature of the arrival and departure, the posting of a letter, which, by the way, may have been written in his presence."

"It was."

Theydon positively jumped. He would not

be surprised now if Forbes's name came out.

"How do you know that?" he asked.

"Mrs. Lester wrote to an aunt in Oxfordshire, a lady who lives in the village of Iffley, near the first lock on the Thames below Oxford. As it happened, this aunt, a Miss Beale, was lunching with a friend in Oxford today, and some one showed her an early edition of a London evening newspaper containing an account of the murder. Instead of yielding to hysteria, and passing from one fainting fit into another, Miss Beale had the rare good sense to go straight to the police station. One of our men has interviewed her this evening, and she is coming here tomorrow, but in the meantime the Oxford police telephoned the gist of the letter, which is headed 'Monday, 11:30 p. m.' The hour is not quite accurate, but near enough, since the context shows that 'a friend' had just called and given certain information which had determined the writer to leave London 'tomorrow'—meaning today—'or Wednesday at latest.' So you see, Mr. Theydon, if the unknown is an honest man, he will soon hear of the hue and cry raised by the murder, and declare himself to the police. Indeed, for all I know, he may have reported himself to the Yard already. In that event you will probably meet him again quite soon."

An electric bell jarred at the end of the

main passage. It smote on their ears with
the loud emphasis of a pistol shot. Even the
detectives were startled, and Winter said,
in a tone of distinct annoyance:

"Go and see who the deuce that is, Furneaux."

Furneaux returned promptly with Bates,
pallid and apologetic.

"Beg pardon, sir," said the intruder, addressing Theydon, but allowing his eyes to
roam furtively about the room as though he
expected to see something ghoul-like and
sinister, "Mr. Forbes has rung up—"

Theydon's voice literally quavered. For
the first time in his life he knew why a woman
shrieks in the stress of sudden excitement.

"Tell Mr. Forbes I am still engaged with
the gentlemen from Scotland Yard," he
gasped. "I'll give him a call the moment
I'm free. He will understand. Anyhow, I
can't explain further now."

"Yes, sir," and Bates disappeared.

"Mr. Forbes? The gentleman you were
dining with?" inquired Winter.

"Yes," said Theydon. He knew he ought
to add something by way of explanation, but
his heart was thumping madly, and he dared
not trust his voice.

"You told him, I suppose, that Scotland
Yard was worrying you, and he wants to
know the result?"

Then Theydon saw an avenue of escape, and took it eagerly.

"I spoke of the murder, of course," he said, "but Mr. Forbes was hardly interested. He had seen the newspaper placards, and that was all he knew of it. The truth is, he is wholly wrapped up in a scheme for reforming mankind by excluding airships and aeroplanes from warlike operations, and found me a somewhat preoccupied listener. He wants my help, such as it is, and I have no doubt the present call is a preliminary to another meeting tomorrow."

"Why not go to him? We'll wait. We can do nothing more tonight after leaving here."

"Speaking candidly, I am not in a mood to discuss such visionary projects. I shall be glad if Mr. Forbes has gone to bed when I do ring him up."

Winter shook his head.

"Excuse me, Mr. Theydon, but I am older than you, and may 'venture on advice,' " he said. "A writer who has his way to make in the world cannot afford to slight a man of Mr. Forbes's standing. Go to him at once. It will please him. Don't hurry."

Theydon realized that a continued refusal would certainly set Furneaux's wits at work, and he dreaded the outcome. He went without another word. When the outer door had

71

closed behind him Winter turned to Furneaux.

"Well?" he said.

For answer Furneaux waved a hand and tiptoed into the hall. Waiting until he heard the door of No. 18 slam he opened the latch of No. 17 so cautiously that no sound was forthcoming. Soon he had an ear to Theydon's letter box and was following attentively a one-sided conversation.

Now, Theydon had thought hard during the few strides from one flat to the other. His telephone was fixed close to the party wall dividing the two sets of apartments and he was not certain that, in the absolute quietude prevailing in Innesmore Mansions at that late hour, a voice could not be overheard. True, he did not count on Furneaux playing the eavesdropper at the slit of the letter box, but he resolved to take no risks and say nothing that any one could make capital of.

So, when he had asked the exchange to reconnect him with the caller who had just rung up, and he was put through, this is what Furneaux heard:

"That you, Mr. Forbes. Sorry I sent my man just now with a message that must have sounded rather curt, but the Scotland Yard people kindly excused me, so I can give you a minute or two. . . . No, I'm sorry, but I cannot come to luncheon tomorrow, nor go to

Brooklands again this week. You see, this dreadful murder which I spoke of will necessitate my presence at an inquest, and the police seem to attach much significance to the visit to Mrs. Lester last night of a man whom I saw in the street, and whom Bates and I heard entering and leaving the poor lady's flat. . . . Bates? O, he is my general factotum. He and his wife keep house for me. . . . Yes, I'll gladly let you know the earliest date when I'll be free. Then you and I can go into the flying proposition thoroughly. . . . No. The detectives have apparently not got any clew to the murderer, nor even discovered any motive for the crime. They have taken me into No. 17. In fact, I was there when your call was made. . . . The murderer ransacked the place thoroughly, but did not touch money or jewelry, I understand. The only peculiar thing, if I may so describe it, about the place, is the scent of a burnt joss stick. It clings to the passage and the bedroom in which the body was found. . . . Ah, by the way, Mrs. Lester wrote a letter, which her visitor posted, and the addressee, her aunt, is in communication with the police. The text tends to clear the man of suspicion. . . . Yes, if, by chance, I find myself at liberty tomorrow, I'll 'phone you at your city office. I'll find the number in the directory, of course? . . . O, thanks—I'll jot it down—00400 Bank. . . . Goodnight! Too bad that this wretched affair should interfere with our crusade, which, the more I think of it, the stronger it appeals. *Au revoir,* then.''

In reality, Forbes had not said one word about his peace propaganda, but he had evidently been quick to realize that Theydon was purposely giving their talk a twist in that direction. A muttered "I understand—perfectly," showed this, and he did not strive to conceal the alarm which possessed him when Theydon spoke of the joss stick. He murmured distinctly, "Great Heavens! Then I was not mistaken," and again voiced his distress on hearing of the letter.

But he made matters easy by pressing Theydon to come and see him on the morrow, either at his office in Old Broad Street or at his residence. On the whole, Theydon did not care who heard what he had said, but it was a relief to find that he had to ring for readmission to No. 17.

Furneaux opened the door.

"You soon got rid of your friend, then?" said the detective, while they were on the way to rejoin Winter.

"Yes. It was just what I imagined—a pressing invitation to plunge forthwith into Mr. Forbes's project for the regeneration of mankind. I had to tell him frankly that you gentlemen had first claim on me. I suppose I shall be wanted at the inquest?"

"Not tomorrow. The coroner will hear the medical evidence, and that of Ann Rogers, if she is in a condition to appear, and there will be an adjournment for a week."

"Ah, that reminds me. Didn't Mrs. Lester's servant admit the visitor last night?"

Theydon put the question advisedly. He was calmer now, and had made up his mind as to the course he should pursue. Although he had assured Winter that he would recognize the stranger if confronted with him, and, if Forbes was brought into the inquiry, the admission might prove awkward, he meant to say that he had, indeed, noticed a remarkable resemblance in the millionaire to the man he had seen looking up at the name tablet on the corner, but felt that the likeness was only one of those singular coincidences which abound in a cosmopolitan city.

The smartest cross-examiner at the bar could not shake him if he took that stand. The sheer improbability of Forbes being the mysterious visitor would justify his attitude, and the notion was so consoling that he faced the two detectives with new confidence and a self-possession that was exceedingly pleasant when compared with his earlier embarrassment.

"No," said Winter. "By a most remarkable

chance, Ann Rogers was given leave to spend
the night with her father, who lives in Cam-
den Town. He is an old man and was taken
ill last evening. He believes he asked some
one to telegraph to his daughter, asking her
to come to him. She certainly received a telegram and as certainly did visit him. Of
course, that phase of the affair will be cleared
up thoroughly, but the main facts are indispu-
table. Ann Rogers has her own latchkey. As
Mrs. Lester usually sat up late, being a lover
of books, and seldom stirred before ten o'clock,
the maid waited until that hour before bringing her mistress's cup of tea. That stain on
the carpet near the door shows where the
tray fell from her hands.''

Sometimes an artist obtains the strongest
effect by one deft sweep of the brush.
Winter, though he would have blushed if
described as an artist in words, had achieved
a similar result by his concluding sentence.
Theydon pictured the scene. He saw the
limp form thrown across the bed, the dis-
torted face, the hands and arms posed gro-
tesquely.

He heard the shrill scream of the terrified servant, an elderly woman whom Bates
described as ''a quiet body,'' and could
imagine the clatter of the laden tray as it
dropped from nerveless fingers. A sort of
fury rose within him. Mrs. Lester had been

done to death in a horrible and insensate way, and no matter who suffered, be he millionaire or pauper, the wretch who committed the crime should be made to pay the penalty of the law.

In that moment he forgot Evelyn Forbes, and thought only of the fair and gracious woman whose agonized spirit had taken flight under the compulsion of the tiger grip of some human brute now moving among his fellow-creatures unknown and unsuspected. It was inconceivable that Forbes should be guilty, but why should he not avow his acquaintance with the victim, and thus aid the police in their quest?

He glowered savagely at the telltale stain, and vowed to rid his conscience of an incubus. He would wait till the morrow and force Forbes to come out into the open. Otherwise—

"You wish you had the murderer here now?"

Furneaux spoke softly, and with no trace of his wonted irony, but Theydon was aware that once more the little detective had peered into his very soul.

"Yes," he said, and there was a new gravity in his tone. "I do wish that. I have never before been brought in contact with a crime of this magnitude. It conveys a sort of personal responsibility. To think that I was in my room, reading about aviation, while a woman's life was being choked out of her within a few feet of where I was seated! O, it is monstrous! Let me tell you two, here and now, that if I can do anything to bring Mrs. Lester's slayer to justice, you can count on me, no matter what the cost."

"I'm sure you mean what you say, Mr. Theydon," said Winter soothingly. "Well, I suppose we can do no more tonight. I have little else to tell you—"

"The skull—the ivory skull!" put in Furneaux.

For an instant an expression of annoyance flitted across the chief inspector's good-humored face. Theydon did not see it, because Furneaux's odd-sounding words caused him to look with astonishment at the man who uttered them.

"An ivory skull!" he cried. "What has an ivory skull to do with the murder of Mrs. Lester?"

"We cannot even begin to guess at its meaning yet," said Winter, who, after one fierce glance at his colleague, had recovered his poise. "That is why I did not mention it. I hate the introduction of bizarre features into an inquiry of this sort. But, now that the thing has been spoken of, I may as well state that when the medical examination was being made at the mortuary a tiny skull, not bigger than a pea, and made of ivory, was found inside Mrs. Lester's underbodice. The curious fact is that it was loose. Had it been attached to a cord, or secured in some way, one might regard it as a charm or amulet, because some women, even in the London of today, are not beyond the reach of superstition in such matters. But, as I say, it was not safeguarded at all, so we may reasonably assume that it was not carried habitually. Of course, Furneaux readily evolved a far-fetched theory that it is a sign, or symbol, and was thrust out of sight among the clothing on the dead woman's breast by the man who killed her. But that is idle guess-work. We of the Yard seldom pay heed to theatrical notions of that kind. Here is the article. I don't mind letting you see it, but kindly remember that its existence must not be made known. I must have your promise not to mention it to a living creature."

Furneaux chuckled derisively.

"That is precisely the sort of thing anybody would say who attached no importance to the exhibit," he piped.

Winter so nearly lost his temper that he repressed the retort on his lips. He contented himself, however, with producing a small white object from his waistcoat pocket, and handed it to Theydon. It was a bit of ivory, hollow, and very light, and fashioned as a skull.

Yet, it was by no means an ordinary creation. The artist who fashioned it had gratified a morbid taste by imparting to the eyeless sockets and close-set rows of teeth a malign and threatening grin. Wickedness, not death, was suggested, but the craftsmanship was faultless. A collector would have paid a large sum for it, while the average citizen would refuse to have it in his house.

"What an extraordinary thing," said Theydon, turning the curio round and round in his fingers.

"It's wonderfully well carved," agreed Winter.

"From that point of view it's a masterpiece, but what I meant was the astounding fact that it should have been discovered on the dead woman's body. Was it placed over her heart?"

"Why do you ask that?" came the sharp demand.

"Because—if it is a token of some vendetta —if the murderer wished to signify that he had glutted his vengeance—"

"O, you're as bad as Furneaux," cried Winter impatiently. "Give it to me. I must be off. The hour is long past midnight and I have a busy day before me tomorrow."

Back in the seclusion of his own rooms, Theydon debated the question whether or not he should endeavor to communicate with Forbes again that night. Somehow it seemed to him that Forbes would be most concerned at hearing of the gray car. And what of the ivory skull?

Suppose he knew of that! But a certain revulsion of feeling had come over Theydon since the sheer brutality of the murder had been revealed. He failed to see now why he should be so solicitous for Forbes's welfare. No matter what private purpose the man might serve by concealing his visit to Mrs. Lester, it ought to give way before the paramount importance of tracking a pitiless and callous criminal.

So Theydon hardened his heart and went to bed, and, being sound in mind and constitution, slept like a just man wearied. Nevertheless, the last thing he saw before the curtain fell on his tired brain was an ivory skull dancing in the darkness.

Greatly as the many problems attached to Mrs. Lester's death bewildered him, he would have been even more perplexed if he had overheard the conversation between Winter and Furneaux when they entered a taxi and gave Scotland Yard as their destination.

"Look here, Charles," began Winter firmly; but the other stayed him with a clutch of thin, nervous fingers on an arm strong enough to fell an ox.

"Listen first, James—lecture me afterward," pleaded Furneaux. "I can't help yielding to impulse. And why should I strive to help it, anyhow? How often has impulse led me to the goal when by every known rule of evidence I was completely beaten? That is my plea. That is why I brought that young fellow into No. 17, and watched the story of the tragedy reshaping itself in his imagination. That is why, too, I spoke of the ivory skull. Think what it means to one with the writer's temperament. The skull will never leave his mind's eye. It will focus and control his thoughts and actions. And I feel it in my bones that only by keeping in touch with Mr. Francis Theydon shall we solve the Innesmore Mansions mystery. I can't explain why I think this, no more than the receiver of a wireless message can account for the waves of energy it picks up from the void and transmutes into the ordered sequences of the Morse code. All I know is that when I am near him I am, as the children say, 'warm,' and when away from him, 'cold.' While he was examining the skull I was positively 'hot,' and was half inclined to treat him as a thought transference medium and order him sternly to speak. . . . No. Be calm! I even bid you be honest. When have you, ever before, admitted an outsider to your councils? And, if you make an exception of Theydon, why are you doing it?"

Winter bit the end off a cigar with a vicious jerk of his round head. He struck a match and created such a volume of smoke that Furneaux coughed affectedly.

"The real clew," he said at last, "rests with the gray car. What did you make of that?"

"That, my bulky friend, will figure in my memory as a reproach for many a year. When, if ever, I am tempted to preen myself on some peculiarly close piece of ratiocinative reasoning, I shall say: 'Little man, pigmy, remember the gray car.' "

"You think that some one had the impudence to follow us, watch us in Waterloo, and take up Theydon's trail when we had revealed it?"

"A-ha. It touched you, too, did it?"

"But why?"

"The some one in question wants to know that."

"You mean they are anxious to find out what we are doing?"

"Exactly."

Winter laughed cheerfully.

"Before long I shall begin to enjoy this hunt, Charles. I like to find originality in a felon. It varies the routine. At any rate, it is something new that you and I should be shadowed by the very people we are in pursuit of—O, I was nearly forgetting. Anything fresh in that telephone talk?"

"It seemed all right."

"Seemed?"

"Well, it was too straightforward. Theydon puzzles me. I admit it frankly. He also worries me. But let me handle him in my own way. Have no fear that he will use our material for newspaper purposes. With regard to the Innesmore Mansions affair, Theydon will lie close as a fish. Why? No use asking you, of course. You despise intuition. When you die some one should begin your epitaph: 'From information received.' But I'll stick to Theydon. See if I don't, even if I have to go up with him in one of Forbes's airships."

CHAPTER V

With the morning Theydon brought a mature and impartial judgment to bear on his perplexities. The average man, if asked to form an opinion on any difficult point, will probably arrive at a saner decision during the first pipe after breakfast than at any other given hour of the day. Excellent physiological reasons account for this truism. The sound mind in a sound body is then working under the most favorable conditions.

It is free from the strain of affairs. The cold, clear morning light divests problems of the undue importance, or, it may be, the glamour of novelty, which they possessed overnight. At any rate, Frank Theydon, clenching a pipe between his teeth, and gazing thoughtfully through an open window at the trees in Innesmore Gardens, reviewed yesterday's happenings calmly and critically, and arrived at the settled conviction that his proper course was to visit Scotland Yard and make known to the authorities the one vital fact he had withheld from their ken thus far.

It was not for him to assess the significance

of Mr. Forbes's desire to remain in the background. If the millionaire's excuse, or explanation, of his failure to communicate at once with the Criminal Investigation Department was a sufficiently valid one, Scotland Yard would be satisfied and might agree to keep his name out of the inquiry.

On the other hand, he, Theydon, might be balking the course of justice by holding his tongue. There was yet a third possibility, one fraught with personal discredit. Mr. Forbes himself might realize that a policy of candor offered the only dignified course.

Suppose he was minded to tell the detectives that he was the man who visited Mrs. Lester shortly before midnight, what would Winter and Furneaux think of the young gentleman who had actually dined with Forbes before they took him into their confidence—who heard with such righteous indignation how Mrs. Lester met her death— yet brazenly concealed the fact that he had just left the house of one whom they were so anxious to meet and question?

Of course, the radiant vision of Evelyn Forbes intruded on this well-considered and unemotional analysis; but Theydon resolutely shook his head.

"No, by Jove!" he communed. "You mustn't make an ass of yourself, my boy, because a pretty girl was gracious for an

86

hour or so. Be honest with yourself, old chap! If there were no Evelyn, or if Evelyn were harelipped and squinted, you wouldn't hesitate a second — now, would you?''

Yet he had given a promise. How reconcile an immediate call on Scotland Yard with the guarantee of secrecy demanded by Forbes? Well, he must put himself right with Forbes without delay—tell him straightforwardly that the bond could not hold. Theydon was no lawyer, but he was assured that an agreement founded on positive wrong was not tenable, legally or morally.

He would be adamant with Forbes, and decline to countenance any plea in support of continued silence. If Forbes's demand was reasonable, Scotland Yard would grant it. If justice compelled Forbes to come out into the open, no private citizen should attempt to defeat the ends of justice.

''So that settles it,'' announced Theydon, firmly if not cheerfully. ''I'll ring up Forbes, and get the thing over and done with. I'll never see his daughter again, I suppose, but that can't be helped. 'Tis better to have seen and lost than never to have seen at all.''

He turned from the window, walked to the fireplace, tapped his pipe firmly on the grate, and was about to go into the hall and call up the telephone exchange, when the door-bell rang. He was aware of a muffled conversation between Bates and a visitor. Then the valet appeared, obviously ill at ease.

"If you please, sir," he announced, "a lady, a Miss Beale, of Oxford, who says she is Mrs. Lester's aunt, wishes to see you."

Theydon was immensely surprised, as well he might be. But there was only one thing to be done.

"Show her in," he said.

Miss Beale entered. She was slight of figure, middle-aged and gray-haired. The wanness of her thin features was accentuated by an attire of deep mourning, but the pallor in her cheeks fled for an instant when she set eyes on Theydon.

"Pray forgive the intrusion," she faltered. "I—I expected to meet an older man."

It was a curious utterance, and Theydon tried to relieve her evident nervousness by being mildly humorous.

"I hope to correct my juvenile appearance in course of time," he said, smiling. "Meanwhile, won't you be seated? You are not quite unknown to me, Miss Beale. That is—I heard of you last night from the Scotland Yard people."

She sat down at once, but seemed to be at a loss for words. Her lips trembled, and Theydon thought she was going to cry.

"Have you traveled from Oxford this

morning?" he said, simulating a courteous nonchalance he was far from feeling. "If so, you must have started from home at an ungodly hour. Let me have some breakfast prepared for you."

"No—no," she stammered.

"Well, a cup of tea, then? Come, now, no woman ever refuses a cup of tea."

"You are very kind."

He rang the bell.

"I would not have ventured to call on you if I had not seen your name in the newspaper," she went on.

Miss Beale certainly had the knack of saying unexpected things. It was nothing new that Theydon should find his own name in print, but on this occasion he could not choose but associate the distinction with the crime in No. 17; that he should be mentioned in connection with it was neither anticipated nor pleasing. At the same time he realized the astounding fact that he had not even glanced at a newspaper during twenty-four hours.

"What in the world have the newspapers to say about me?" he cried.

"It—it said—that Mr. Francis Berrold Theydon, the well-known author, lived in No. 18, the flat exactly opposite that which my unhappy niece occupied. I—I have read some of your books, Mr. Theydon, and I pictured you quite a serious-looking person of my own age."

He laughed. Bates entered, and was almost shocked at finding his master in such lively mood.

"Oh, this lady has traveled from Oxford this morning; a cup of tea and some nice toast, please, Bates," said Theydon. Then when the two were alone together again, he brushed aside the question of his age as irrelevant.

"I assure you that since this time yesterday I have lost some of the careless buoyancy of youth," he said. "I had not the honor of Mrs. Lester's acquaintance, but I knew her well by sight, and I received the shock of my life last evening when I heard of her terrible end. It is an extraordinary thing, seeing that we were such close neighbors, but I believe you got the news long before I did, because I left home early and heard nothing of what had happened till my man met me at Waterloo in the evening."

"You have seen the—the detectives in the meantime?"

"Yes."

"Then you will be able to tell me something definite. I have promised to call at Scotland Yard at eleven o'clock, and the only scraps of intelligence I have gathered are those in the papers. I would have come to

London last night, but was afraid to travel, lest I should faint in the train. Moreover, some one in London promised to send a detective to see me. He came, but could give no information. Indeed, he wanted to learn certain things from me. So, after a weary night, I caught the first train, and it occurred to me, as you lived so near, that you might be kind enough to—to—"

The long speech was too much for her, and her lips quivered pitifully a second time.

"I fully understand," said Theydon sympathetically. "Now, I'm positive you have eaten hardly anything today. Won't you let me order an egg?"

"No, please. I'll be glad of the tea, but I cannot make a meal—yet. Is it true that my niece was absolutely alone in her flat on Monday night?"

Seeing that Miss Beale was consumed with anxiety to hear an intelligible version of the tragedy, Theydon at once recited all, or nearly all, that was known to him. The only points he suppressed were those with reference to the gray car and the ivory skull. The lady listened attentively and with more self-control than he gave her credit for.

Bates came in with a laden tray, on which a boiled egg appeared. Mrs. Bates had used her discretion, and decided that any one who had set out from Oxford so early in the day must be in need of more solid refreshment than tea and toast. Thus cozened, as it were, into eating, Miss Beale tackled the egg, and Theydon was glad to note that she made a fairly good meal, being probably unaware of her hunger until the means of sating it presented itself.

But she missed no word of his story, and when he made an end, put some shrewd questions.

"I take it," she said, "that the strange gentleman who visited my niece on Monday night posted the very letter which I received by the second delivery yesterday?"

"That is what the police believe," replied Theydon.

"Then it would seem that she resolved to come to me at Iffley as the result of something he told her?"

"Why do you think that?"

"Because I heard from her only last Saturday, and she not only said nothing about coming to Oxfordshire, but asked me to arrange to spend a fortnight in London before we both went to Cornwall for the Summer."

"Ah! That is rather important, I should imagine," said Theydon thoughtfully.

"It is odd, too, that you and the detectives should have noticed the smell of a joss stick in the flat," went on Miss Beale. "Edith—

92

my niece, you know—could not bear the smell of joss sticks. They reminded her of Shanghai, where she lost her husband."

Theydon looked more startled than such a seemingly simple statement warranted. He had realized already that the ivory skull was the work of an Oriental artist, and the mention of Shanghai brought that sinister symbol very vividly to his mind's eye.

"Mrs. Lester had lived in China, then?" he said.

"Yes. She was out there nearly six years. Her husband died suddenly last October—he was poisoned, she firmly believed—and, of course, she came home at once."

"What was Mr. Lester's business, or profession?"

"He was a barrister. I do not mean that he practised in the Consular courts. He was making his way in England, but was offered some sort of appointment in Shanghai. The post was so lucrative that he relinquished a growing connection at the bar. I have never really understood what he did. I fancy he had to report on commercial matters to some firm of bankers in London, but he supplied very little positive information before Edith and he sailed. Indeed, I took it that his mission was highly confidential, and about that time there was a lot in the newspapers about rival negotiators for a big Chinese loan, so I formed the opinion that he was sent out in connection with something of the sort. Neither he nor Edith meant to remain long in the Far East. At first their letters always spoke of an early return. Then, when the years dragged on, and I asked for definite news of their home-coming, Edith said that Arthur could not get away until the country's political affairs were in a more settled state. Finally came a cable-gram from Edith: 'Arthur dead; sailing im-mediately,' and my niece was with me within a few weeks. The supposed cause of her hus-band's death was some virulent type of fever, but, as I said, Edith was convinced that he had been poisoned."

"Why?"

"That I never understood. She never will-ingly talked about Shanghai, or her life there. Indeed, she was always most anxious that no one should know she had ever lived in China. Yet she had plenty of friends out there. I gathered that Arthur had left her well provided for financially, and they were a most devoted couple. Edith was the only relative I possessed. It is very dreadful, Mr. Theydon, that she should be taken from me in such a way."

Her hearer was almost thankful that she yielded to the inevitable rush of emotion. It gave him time to collect his wits, which had lost their poise when that wicked-looking little skull was, so to speak, thrust forcibly into his recollection.

"In a word," he said, at last, "you are Mrs. Lester's next-of-kin and probably her heiress?"

"Yes, I suppose so, though I was not thinking of that," came the tearful answer.

" Yet the relationship entails certain responsibilities," said Theydon firmly. " You should be legally represented at the inquest. Are your affairs in the hands of any firm of solicitors?"

"Yes—at Oxford. I contrived to call at their office yesterday and they recommended me to consult these people," and Miss Beale produced a card from a handbag. Theydon read the name and address of a well-known West End firm.

"Good," he said. "I recommend you to go there at once. By the way, was any one looking after Mrs. Lester's interests? Surely she had dealings with a bank or an agency?"

"Y—yes. I do happen to know the source from which her income came. She—made a secret of it—in a measure."

"Pray don't tell me anything of that sort. Your legal adviser might not approve."

"But what does it matter now? Poor Edith is dead. Her affairs cannot help being dragged into the light of day. She had some railway shares and bonds, some of which were left to her by her father, and others which came under a marriage settlement, but the greater part of her revenue was derived from a monthly payment made by the bank of which Mr. James Creighton Forbes is the head.''

Miss Beale naturally misinterpreted the blank stare with which Theydon received this remarkable statement.

'' I don't see why any one should wish to conceal a simple matter of business like that,'' she said nervously. ''May I explain that I have an impression, not founded on anything quite tangible, that Mr. Forbes was largely interested in the syndicate which sent Arthur Lester to China, so it is very likely that the payment of an annuity, or pension, to Arthur's widow would be left in his care. I do not know. I am only guessing. But that matter, and others, can hardly fail to be cleared up by the police inquiry.''

Theydon recovered his self-control as rapidly as he had lost it. He glanced at the clock—10:15. Within half an hour, or less, Miss Beale would be on her way to Scotland Yard. He must act promptly and decisively, or he would find himself in a distinctly unfavorable position in his relations with the Criminal Investigation Department.

''I happen to be acquainted with Mr. Forbes,'' he said, striving desperately to appear cool and methodical when his brain was seething. "Would you mind if I just rang him up on the telephone? A few words now might enlighten us materially."

"O, you are most helpful," said the lady, blushing again with timid gratitude. "I am so glad I summoned up courage to call on you. I was terrified at the idea of going to the Police Headquarters, but I shall not mind it at all now."

Soon Theydon was asking for "00400, Bank." He had left the door of his sitting room open purposely. No matter what the outcome, he no longer dared keep the compact of silence into which he had entered with Forbes. But the millionaire was not at his office. In response to a very determined request for a word with some one in authority, "on a matter of real urgency," the clerk who had answered the call brought "Mr. Forbes's secretary," a Mr. Macdonald, to the telephone.

"It is important, vitally important, that I should speak with Mr. Forbes within the next few minutes," said Theydon, after giving his name and address. "Do you expect him to arrive soon? Or shall I try and reach him at Fortescue Square?"

"Mr. Forbes will not be here till midday," came a voice with a pronounced Scottish intonation. "I'm doubtful, too, if ye'll catch him at home. Can I give him a message?"

"Do you know where he is?"

"Well, I cannot say."

"But do you know?"

"I'll be glad to give him a message."

"It will be too late, then. Please understand, Mr. Macdonald, that I am making this call at Mr. Forbes's express wish. It is, as I have said, vitally important that I should get in touch with him without delay."

Scottish caution was not to be overcome by an appeal of that sort.

"I cannot go beyond what I have said," was the reply. "If you like to ask at his house—"

"O, ring off!" cried Theydon, who pictured the secretary as a lanky hollow-cheeked Scot, a model of discretion and trustworthiness, no doubt, but utterly unequal to a crisis demanding some measure of self-confident initiative. In reality, Mr. Macdonald was short and stout, and quite a jovial little man.

After an exasperating delay, he got into communication with the Forbes mansion in Fortescue Square.

"I'm Mr. Frank Theydon," he said, striving to speak unconcernedly. "Is Mr. Forbes in?"

"No, sir."

"Is that you, Tomlinson?"

"Yes, sir."

"Can you tell me where I can find Mr. Forbes at once?"

"Isn't he at his office, sir?"

"No. He will not be there till 12 o'clock."

A pause of indecision on Tomlinson's part. Then, a possible solution of the difficulty.

"Would you care to have a word with Miss Evelyn, sir?"

"O, yes, yes."

Theydon blurted out this emphatic acceptance of the butler's suggestion without a thought as to its possible consequences. He was racking his brain in a frenzy of uncertainty as to how he should frame his words when he heard quite clearly a woman's footsteps on the parquet flooring, and caught Evelyn Forbes's voice saying to Tomlinson: "How fortunate! Mr. Theydon is the very person I wished to speak to, but I simply dared not ring him up."

The slight incident only provided Theydon with a new source of wonderment. Why should Evelyn Forbes want speech with him at that early hour? Perhaps she would explain. He could only hope so, and trust to luck in the choice of his own phrases.

"That you, Mr. Theydon?" came the girl's voice, sweet in its cadence yet ominously eager. "How nice of you to anticipate my unspoken thought! I have been horribly anxious ever since I read of that awful affair at Innes-

more Mansions. That poor lady's flat is next
door to yours, is it not?"

"Yes, but—"

"O, you cannot choke off a woman's curiosity quite so easily. You see, I happen to
know that Mrs. Lester's sad death affects my
father in some way, and I realize now that
you two were just on pins and needles to get
rid of me last night so that you might talk
freely."

"Miss Forbes, I assure you—"

"Wait till I've finished, and you will not
be under the necessity of telling me any
polite fibs. You men are all alike. You think
the giddy feminine brain is not fitted to cope
with mysteries, and that is where you are
utterly mistaken. A woman's intuition often
peers deeper than a man's logic. I—"

"Do forgive me," broke in Theydon
despairingly, "but I am really most anxious
to know how and where I can get a word
with your father. I would not be so rude as
to interrupt you if I hadn't the best of ex-
cuses. Tell me where to find him now, and
I promise to give you a call immediately
afterward."

"He's at the Home Office."

"At the Home Office!"

Some hint of utter bewilderment in Theydon's tone must have reached the girl's alert
ear.

"Ah! *Touché!*" she cried. "Now will you be good and tell me why Dad should receive a little ivory skull by this morning's post?"

Theydon knew that he paled. His very scalp tingled with an apprehension of some shadowy yet none the less affrighting evil. But he schooled himself to say, with a semblance of calm interest:

"What exactly do you mean, Miss Forbes?"

She laughed lightly. Theydon was so flurried that he did not realize the possibility of Evelyn Forbes being as quick to mask her real feelings as he himself was.

"Dad and I make a point of breakfasting together at nine o'clock every morning," she said. "We were talking about you, and he told me of the dreadful thing that happened to Mrs. Lester. I was reading the account of the tragedy in a newspaper, when I happened to glance at him. He was going through his letters, and I was just a trifle curious to know what was in a flat box which came by registered post. He opened it carelessly and something fell out and rolled across the table. I picked it up and saw that it was a small piece of ivory, carved with extraordinary skill to represent a skull. Indeed, it was so clever as to be decidedly repulsive. I was going to say something when I saw that the letter which was in the same box had alarmed him so greatly that, for a second or two, I thought he would faint. But he can be very strong and stern at times, and he recovered himself instantly, was quite vexed with me because I had examined the ivory skull, and forbade my going out until he had returned from the Home Office. Tomlinson and the other men have orders not to admit any one to the house, no matter on what pretext, and I'm sure the letter and its nasty little token are bound up in some way with Mrs. Lester's death. Won't you let me into the secret? I shan't scream or do anything foolish, but I do think I am entitled to know what you know if it affects my father.''

A sudden change in the girl's voice warned Theydon of a restraint of which he had been unconscious hitherto. He tried to temporize, to whittle away her fears. That was a duty he owed to Forbes, who was clearly resolved not to take his daughter into his confidence— for the present, at any rate.

''I really fail to see why you should assume some connection between the crime which was committed here on Monday night and the arrival of a somewhat singular package at your house this morning,'' he said reassuringly.

''Like every other woman, I jump at conclusions,'' she answered. ''Why should this crime, in particular, have worried my father? Unfortunately, the newspapers are full of such horrid things, yet he hardly ever pays them any attention. No, Mr. Theydon, I am not mistaken. He either knew Mrs. Lester, and was shocked at her death, or saw in it some personal menace. Then comes the letter, with its obvious threat, and I am ordered to remain at home, under a strong guard, while he hurries off to Whitehall. You have met my father, Mr. Theydon. Do you regard him as the sort of man who would rush off in a panic to consult the Home Secretary without very grave and weighty reasons?"

"But you can hardly be certain that a wretched crime in this comparatively insignificant quarter of London supplies the actual motive of Mr. Forbes's action," urged Theydon.

The girl stamped an impatient foot. He heard it distinctly.

"Of course I am certain," she cried. "Why won't you be candid? You know I am right—I can tell it from your voice, and your guarded way of talking—"

An inspiration came to Theydon's relief in that instant.

"Pardon the interruption," he said, "but I must point out that both of us are acting unwisely in discussing such matters over the telephone. Really, neither must say another word, except this—when I have found your father I'll ask his permission to come and see you. Perhaps we three can arrange to meet somewhere for luncheon. That is absolutely the farthest limit to which I dare go at this moment."

"O, very well!"

The receiver was hung up in a temper, and the prompt ring-off jarred disagreeably in Theydon's ear. If he was puzzled before, he was thoroughly at sea now. But he took a bold course, and cared not a jot whether or not it was a prudent one.

The mere sound of Evelyn Forbes's voice had steeled his heart and conscience against the dictates of common sense. Let the detectives think what they might, the girl's father must be allowed to carry through his plans without let or hindrance.

"Miss Beale," said Theydon, gazing fixedly into the sorrow-laden eyes of the quiet little lady whom he found seated where he had left her, "I'm going to tell you something very important, very serious, something so far-reaching and momentous that neither you nor I can measure its effect. You heard the conversation on the telephone?"

"I heard what you were saying, but could not understand much of it," said his visitor in a scared way.

"I have been trying to communicate with Mr. Forbes, but his daughter tells me that the murder of your niece seems to have affected

him in a manner which is incomprehensible to
her, and even more so to me, though I am
acquainted with facts which her father and
I have purposely kept from her knowledge.
Mr. Forbes has gone hurriedly to the Home
Office. I suppose you know what that means?
He is about to give the Home Secretary
certain information, and it is not for you or
me to interfere with his discretion. Now, if
you tell the Scotland Yard people what you
have told me, namely, that Mr. Forbes was
the intermediary through whom Mrs. Lester received the greater part of her income,
he will be brought prominently into the inquiry. You see that, don't you?"

"Yes. I suppose that something of the
sort must happen."

"Well, I want you to suppress that vital
fact until we know more about this affair.
It will not be for long. Each of us must tell
our story without reservation at some future
date—whether this afternoon, or tomorrow,
or a week hence, I cannot say now. But I
do ask you to keep your knowledge to yourself until I have had an opportunity of
consulting Mr. Forbes. I undertake to tell
you the exact position of matters without
delay, and I accept all responsibility for my
present advice."

"I know little of the world, Mr. Theydon,"
said Miss Beale, rising, and beginning to

draw on her gloves, "but I shall be very greatly surprised if you are advising me to act otherwise than honorably. I shall certainly not utter a word about Mr. Forbes at Scotland Yard. When all is said and done, my statement to you was largely guesswork. You must remember that I have never seen Mr. Forbes, nor hardly ever heard his name except in connection with public matters in the Press. O, yes. I make that promise readily. I trust you implicitly!"

CHAPTER VI

CLOSE QUARTERS

Theydon escorted Miss Beale downstairs. As they passed the closed door of No. 17, the lady shivered.

"To think that within the next few days I would have been staying there with Edith, and planning evenings at the theater before going to Newquay!" she murmured; there was a pitiful catch in her voice that told better than words how the remainder of her existence would be darkened by the tragedy.

At best she was a shrinking, timid little woman, for whom life probably held but narrow interests. Such as they were, their placid content was forever shattered. The death of her niece had closed the one chief avenue leading to the outer world. She would retire to the quiet back-water of Iffley, to become more faded, more insignificant, more lonely each year.

Theydon commiserated with her deeply and did not hesitate to utter his thoughts while putting her into a cab.

"Have you no friends in London?" he inquired. "I don't like the notion of sending

107

you off alone into this wilderness. London is the worst place in the world for any one in distress. The heedless multitude seems to be callous and unsympathetic. It isn't, in reality. It simply doesn't know, and doesn't bother.''

"I used to claim some acquaintances here, but I have lost track of them for years," she said. "In any event, I shall have more than enough to occupy my mind today. The inquest opens at three o'clock, and I must face the ordeal of identifying Edith's body. The detective told me that this should be done by a relation, while the only other person who could act—Ann Rogers—has been nearly out of her mind since yesterday morning.''

"Where are you staying?''

She mentioned a small hotel in the West End.

"I used to go there with my people when I was a girl," she added, sadly.

"Then I'll get my sister to call. You'll like her. She's a jolly good sort, and a chat with another woman will be far more beneficial than the society of detectives and lawyers and such-like strange fowl. Keep your spirits up, Miss Beale. Nothing that you can say or do now will restore the life so cruelly taken, but you and I, each in our own way, can strive to bring the murderer to justice. I am convinced that a distinct step in that direction will be taken this very day. You can count on seeing or hearing from me as soon as possible after I have discussed matters with Mr. Forbes. Meanwhile, don't forget to have a lawyer representing you at the inquest.''

They parted as though they were friends of long standing. Theydon was genuinely sorry for this gray-haired woman's plight, and she evidently regarded him as a kind-hearted and eminently trustworthy young man. He stood and watched the cab as it bore her off swiftly into the maelstrom of London. He could not help thinking that seldom had he met one less fitted for the notoriety thrust upon all connected with a much-talked-of crime.

When the press interviewers, the photographers, the hundred and one officials with whom she must be brought in contact, were done with her, poor Miss Beale would retire to her Oxfordshire nook in a state of mental bewilderment that would baffle description. In one of his books Theydon had endeavored to depict just such a middle-aged spinster confronted with a situation not wholly unlike that which now faced Miss Beale.

He smiled grimly when he realized how far fiction had wandered from fact. The woman of his imagination had acted with a strength of character, a decisiveness, that outwitted and confounded certain scheming personages in the story. How different was the reality! Miss Beale, rushing across London in a taxi, reminded him of nothing more masterful than a cage-bird turned loose in a tempest.

He was about to reënter the mansions, meaning to telephone to both the Fortescue Square house and the Old Broad Street offices, and ask for instant news of Mr. Forbes in either locality. He was so preoccupied that he failed to notice an approaching taxicab, though the driver was signaling, and even tooted a motor horn loudly in the endeavor to attract his attention.

He did, however, catch his own name, and halted.

"Beg pardon, sir, but you are Mr. Theydon, aren't you?" said the man.

Then Theydon recognized Evans, the taxi-driver, who had brought him from Fortescue Square.

"Hullo!" he cried. "Any news of the gray car?"

"Yes, sir, I think so," was the somewhat surprising answer. "When I dropped you last night I got a fare to Euston. Then I took a gentleman to the Langham, an', as I felt like a snack, I pulled into the nearest cab rank. I was having some corfee an' a sandwich when I 'appened to speak about the gray car to one of ahr chaps. 'That's odd,' he said. 'Quarter of an hour ago I had a theater job to Langham Plice, an' a gray landaulette stopped in front of the Chinese Embassy. It kem along from the east side, too.' He didn't notice the number, sir, so there may be nothink in it, after all, but I thought you might like to hear wot my pal said.''

"Was the car empty? Did it call for some one at the Embassy?"

"That's the queer part of it, sir. I axed pertic'ler. This gray car brought a gentleman, a small, youngish man, 'oo skipped up the Embassy steps like a lamplighter, and went in afore you could s'y 'knife.' Somebody might ha' bin watchin' for him through the keyhole, the door was opened that quick. Then the car went off. My friend wouldn't ha' given a second thought to it if the gentleman hadn't vanished like a jack-in-the-box. That's w'y he remembered the color of the car.''

Theydon tried to look as though Evans's statement merely puzzled him, whereas his mind was already busy with the extraordinary coincidences which the haphazard events of a few hours had produced. Was the Far East bound up in some mysterious way with Mrs. Lester's death? Did the crime possess a political significance? If so, an explanation by Forbes was more than ever demanded.

"Your informant was not mistaken about the Chinese Embassy, I suppose?" he said.

"No, sir. He's always in that district.

111

His garage is at the back of Great Portland Street. He knows most of them there Chinks by sight."

"Then that gray car can hardly have been our gray car," commented Theydon, deeming it wise to prevent the sharp-witted taxi-driver from jumping at conclusions.

"I'm afraid not, sir. Still, I just took the liberty—"

"I'm very much obliged to you, of course. I said half-a-crown, didn't I? Here you are. Keep an eye open for XY 1314 and let me know if you hear or see anything of it."

"Thank you, sir." Then Evans lifted his eyes to the block of buildings. "A nasty business this murder which was done 'ere the other night, sir," he went on. "One 'ud hardly b'lieve it possible for such things to tike plice in London nowadays."

Much as he was disinclined for gossip of the sort at the moment, Theydon saw that he must endeavor to dissociate the gray car and the crime from their dangerous juxtaposition in the man's mind, so he spoke about Mrs. Lester's attractive appearance, harped on the apparent aimlessness of the deed, hinted darkly at clews in the possession of the police, and finally got rid of the well-meaning chauffeur. Back he went to his telephone, and having ascertained that Mr. Forbes was fully expected to put in an appearance at the city office before noon, settled down to read the newspapers.

They contained sensational but fairly accurate accounts of the tragedy. One enterprising journal had published an interview with Bates, whom the reporter described as "a typical British man-servant," which was amusing, since Bates had "retired noncommissioned officer" written all over his square frame and soldierly features.

The same journalist spoke of Theydon himself, and had even ferreted out the fact that Mrs. Lester was the widow of an English barrister who had died at Shanghai. On reflection, Theydon saw that there was nothing unusual in this statement. The connection between the metropolitan press and the bar is old and intimate, and scores of junior barristers must remember Arthur Lester's beginnings.

Resolved to possess his soul in patience till twelve o'clock, the hour being yet barely 11:30 a. m., Theydon tackled a page of reviews, since there is always consolation for a writer in learning at second hand what sheer drivel others can produce.

He was growling at the discovery that some hapless essayist had appropriated a title which he himself had marked down for his next book, when the door-bell rang. He did not give much heed, because so many tradesmen called during the course of each morning, so he was surprised and startled when Bates announced:

"Mr. Forbes to see you, sir."

Had a powerful spring concealed in the seat of his chair been released suddenly, Theydon could not have bounced to his feet with greater speed. Forbes came in. He was pale, but self-contained and clear-eyed.

"Forgive an unceremonious visit," he said. "I'm glad to find you at home. I meant to arrive here sooner, but I was detained on business of some importance."

By this time Bates had closed the door; Theydon explained his presence in the flat by saying that within a few minutes he would have been telephoning again to Old Broad Street.

" Ah! Did you speak to Macdonald? " said Forbes, dropping into a chair with a curious lassitude of manner which did not escape Theydon.

"Yes. I have been most anxious to have a word with you—"

Forbes broke in with a short laugh.

"You would get nothing out of Macdonald," he said. "He knows that my visits to the Chinese Embassy are few and far between and generally have to do with—but what is it now? Why should you be so perturbed when I mention the Chinese Embassy?"

Theydon was literally astounded, and did not strive to hide his agitation. But he was by no means tongue-tied. Now, most emphatically, was he determined to have done with pretense. Whether by accident or design, Forbes had placed himself with his back to the window.

The younger man deliberately crossed the room, pulled up the blind, thus admitting the flood of light which comes only from the upper third of a window, and sat down in such a position that Forbes was compelled to turn in order to face him.

"Before you utter another word, Mr. Forbes," he said gravely, "let me tell you that in my efforts to trace your whereabouts I also called up Fortescue Square. Miss Forbes came to the telephone. She said you had gone to the Home Office. By some feminine necromancy, too, she divined the link which binds you with the death of Mrs. Lester. She was distressed on your account, and I was hard put to it to extricate myself from the risk of saying something which I might regret. I—"

"What do you imply by that remark?" interrupted Forbes, piercing the other with a look that was strangely reminiscent of his daughter's candid scrutiny.

"I imply the serious fact that I know who visited Mrs. Lester before she met her death.

I not only heard her visitor's arrival and departure, but saw him at the corner of these mansions while on my way home from Daly's Theater, and again when he posted a letter in the pillar box on the same corner. If such unwonted interest on my part in the movements of one who was then a complete stranger surprises you, let me remind you that only a few minutes earlier I had stood by his side at the door of the theater and heard him telling his daughter that he intended to walk to the Constitutional Club.''

Forbes smiled, but uttered no word. His expression was inscrutable. His pallor reminded Theydon of the tint of ivory, of that waxen-white Dutch grisaille beloved of fifteenth century illuminators of manuscripts. His silence was disturbing, almost irritating, his manner singularly calm.

These negative indications conveyed absolutely nothing to Theydon, who for the second time in their brief acquaintance found himself in the ridiculous position of one explaining a fault rather than, as he imagined, arraigning a man under suspicion.

"So we had better dispense with ambiguities, Mr. Forbes," he went on, speaking with a precision that sounded oddly in his own ears. "It was you who called on Mrs. Lester on Monday night, you who posted the letter she wrote to Miss Beale at Iffley, Oxfordshire, you for whom the police are now searching. I have contrived thus far to keep your secret, but the situation is passing out of my control. I would help you if I could— "

"Why?"

The monosyllable, sharp and insistent, was disconcerting as the unexpected crack of a whip, but Theydon answered valiantly:

"Because of the monstrous absurdities with which Fate has plagued me during the past two days, I appeal now for outspokenness, so I set an example. Had it not been for your daughter's remarkably attractive appearance I should not, in all likelihood, have given a second glance at my neighbors on the steps of the theater. But I cannot forget that I did see both her and you—indeed, Miss Forbes herself recalled the incident—and the close questioning of the Scotland Yard men who were here last night showed me the folly of imagining that I could deny all knowledge of you. I recognize now that some impish contriving of circumstances forced this knowledge upon me. The sudden downpour of rain, and the fact that I was delayed by a slight accident to my cab, conspired with the apparently simple chance which led me to overhear the conversation between Miss Forbes and yourself. I tried hard to baffle the detectives—"

"Again I ask 'Why?'"

Theydon was rapidly being wound up to a pitch of excited resentment.

"Why?" he cried. "Was I not your guest? How could I come from a house where I had been admitted to a delightful intimacy and tell the representatives of the law that my host was the man they were looking for?"

During some seconds Forbes bent his eyes on the floor, seemingly in deep thought.

"Theydon," he said at last, looking up in his direct way, "I am your senior by a good many years—am old enough, as the saying goes, to be your father. I may venture, therefore, to give you a piece of sound advice. Pack a kit-bag, catch the afternoon boat train for Boulogne, and go for a walking tour in Normandy and Brittany. When I was your age and a junior in a bank I had to take my holidays in May; each year I tramped that corner of France. I recommend it as a playground. It will appeal to your literary instincts, and it has the immeasurable advantage just now of being practically as remote from London as the Sahara."

It must not be forgotten that Theydon was a romancer, an idealist. The "lounge suit" of the modern tailor hampers the play of such qualities no more than the beaten armor of the age of chivalry.

"If my departure for France will relieve Miss Forbes of anxiety on your behalf, I'll go," he vowed.

Forbes regarded him with a new interest.

"I believe you mean that," he said.

"I do."

"But I cannot send you out of the country on a false pretense. It was your safety and well-being, not my daughter's, that I was thinking of."

"What have I to fear?"

"I do not know. I am like a man wandering by night in a jungle alive with fearsome beasts and reptiles."

"Yet you had some reason for suggesting my prompt departure."

"Yes. It is an absurd thing to say, but I believe I am putting you in danger of your life by coming here this morning."

"Can't you speak plainly, Mr. Forbes? What good purpose do you serve by holding forth these vague terrors? If, as Miss Forbes told me, you have visited the Home Office, I take it you made yourself clear to the authorities—assuming, that is, you went there in connection with the amazing conditions which seem to be bound up with this crime."

"There is a certain class of knowledge which is in itself dangerous to those who possess it, no matter whether or not it affects

them in any particular. I recommend you, in
good faith, to leave London today."

"If my own safety is the only consideration
I refuse as readily as I agreed before."

Theydon's tone grew somewhat impatient.
He really fancied that Forbes was trifling
with him. Indeed, a queer doubt of the man's
complete sanity now peeped up in him. Forbes
was regarded as a crank by a large section
of the public on account of his peace propaganda; if that opinion were justified why
should he not be eccentric in other respects?

It was fantastic, almost stupid, to look
upon him as responsible for Mrs. Lester's
murder, but there was always a possibility
that he might be utilizing the chance which
led him to her apartments shortly before the
crime was committed to cover himself and his
movements with a veil of spurious mystery.
In a word, though Theydon had likened his
visitor's face to a mask of ivory he had
momentarily forgotten the ominous token
found on Mrs. Lester's body and duplicated
in Forbes's own house by the morning's post.

Forbes spread wide his hands with the air
of one who heard, but was allowing his
thoughts to wander. When next he spoke it
was only to increase the crazy inconsequence
of their talk.

"Later—perhaps today—perhaps it may
never be necessary—I may explain myself to

your heart's content," he said slowly. "At present I am here to ask a favor. In the first place, is Mrs. Lester's flat in charge of the police?"

"I suppose so," said Theydon.

"Is there a detective or constable on duty there now?"

"I am not sure. I imagine there is not. When the Scotland Yard men and I came out after midnight they locked the door and took away the key. The—er—body is at the mortuary, awaiting the opening of the inquest at three o'clock."

"Ah! I hoped that would be so. Can you ascertain for certain?"

"But why?"

"Because I wish to go in there. And that brings me to the favor I seek. The secretary of these flats, even the hall porter, should have a master key. Borrow it on some pretext. They will give it to you."

"Really, Mr. Forbes—" gasped Theydon, voicing his surprise as a preliminary to a decided refusal. He was interrupted by the insistent clang of the telephone—that curt herald which brooks no delay in answering its demand for an audience.

"Pardon me one moment," he said. "I'll just see who that is."

The inquirer was Evelyn Forbes.

"I've waited patiently—" she began, but

he stopped her instantly by saying that her father was with him.

"Please ask him to come to the phone," she said.

Forbes rose at once. He merely assured the girl that he was engaged in important business and would be home soon after the luncheon hour. Meanwhile, she was not to go out, and his orders must be obeyed to the letter.

"Now, Theydon," he said, coming back to the sitting room, "what about that key?"

The most extraordinary feature of an extraordinary case was the way in which the mere sound of Evelyn Forbes's voice stilled any qualms of conscience in Theydon's breast. He knew he was acting foolishly in conducting a blind inquiry on his own account, an inquiry which might well arouse the anger and active resentment of the police, but he offered a sop to his better judgment by consulting Bates.

Then came a veritable surprise.

" The fact is, sir," admitted Bates nervously, "we have Ann Rogers's key in the kitchen. When she went away on Monday she left it here, bein' afraid of losin' it. Of course, she took it on Tuesday mornin', and after goin' from one fit of hysterics into another she gev it to us again."

Theydon's face was eloquent of the serious view of this avowal.

"Did you tell the police?" he said.

"No, sir. My missus an' me clean forgot all about it."

"So, while Mrs. Lester was being killed, the key of her flat was actually in your possession?"

"I suppose it might be put that way, sir."

By this time Theydon was becoming exasperated at the veritable conspiracy which fate had engineered for the express purpose, apparently, of entangling him in an abominable crime.

"Why on earth didn't you mention such an important fact to the detectives?" he almost shouted. "Don't you see they are bound to think—"

"O, a plague on the detectives and on what they think!" broke in Forbes imperiously. "It doesn't matter a straw what they think, and very little what they do. This affair goes a long way beyond the four-mile radius, Theydon. The vital point is that your man has the key. Where is it? Let us go in there at once!"

"You offered me some advice, Mr. Forbes," said Theydon firmly. "Let me now return it in kind. If you wish to examine Mrs. Lester's flat why not seek the permission of Scotland Yard?"

"My good fellow, I have spent a valuable hour this morning in persuading the Home

Secretary that the less Scotland Yard inter-
feres in my behalf the more effectually shall
I be protected. I don't want any detective
within a mile of my house or office. But, as
I have told you already, explanations must
wait— You, Bates, look a man who can hold
his tongue. Do so, and with Mr. Theydon's
permission I'll make it worth your while
when this storm has blown over— Now, give
me that key."

Theydon was silenced, if not convinced.
He realized, of course, that he must make a
full confession to the Criminal Investigation
Department before the sun went down, but
argued that he might as well see the present
adventure through.

Soon he and Forbes were standing at the
door of No. 17. Forbes curbed his impatience
sufficiently to permit of any one who happened to be in the interior answering the sum-
mons of the electric bell. Of course, no one
came. The police had no reason to remain
in charge of the place, and Ann Rogers would
have become a raving lunatic if left alone
there for one half-hour.

The aromatic odor of the burnt joss stick
still clung to the suite of apartments, and
Forbes noticed it at once.

"Where was the body found?" he asked.

Theydon led the way to the bedroom. He
related Winter's theory of the crime, and

124

pointed out its seeming aimlessness. So far as the police could ascertain from the half-crazy servant, none of Mrs. Lester's jewels was missing. Even her gold purse, containing a fair sum of money, was found on the dressing-table.

He did not know that the detectives had taken away a few scraps of torn paper thrown carelessly into the grate and had carefully gathered up a tiny snake-like curl of white ash from the tiled hearth, which, on analysis, would probably prove to be the remains of the joss stick.

Forbes gazed at the impression on the side of the bed as though the body of the woman whom he had last seen in full possession of her grace and beauty were still lying there. The vision seemed to affect him profoundly. He did not speak for fully a minute, and, when speech came, his voice was low and strained.

"Tell me everything you know," he said. "The Scotland Yard men took an unusual step in admitting you to their conclave. They must have had some motive. Tell me what they said, their very words, if you can recall them."

Theydon was uncomfortably aware of a strange compulsion to obey. His commonplace, everyday senses cried out in revolt, and warned him that he was tampering dangerously with matters which should be left to the cold scrutiny of the law, but some subconscious instinct overpowered these prudent monitors, and he gave an almost exact account of his talk with Winter and Furneaux.

Then followed questions, eager, searching, almost uncanny in their prescience.

"The little one—who strikes me as having more brains than I credit the ordinary London policeman with—spoke of the evil deities of China. How did such an extraordinary topic crop up?"

"In connection with the joss stick."

"Yes, yes. But I don't see the inference."

"Mr. Winter alluded to the habit some ladies have of burning such incense in their houses, whereupon Furneaux remarked that the Chinese use them to propitiate harmful spirits."

"Was that all?"

Theydon felt insensibly that his companion was hinting at something more definite, but he was bound in honor to respect the confidence reposed in him.

"I don't quite understand," he temporized.

"Was nothing said as to the finding of some object, such as a small article obviously Chinese in origin, which might turn an inquirer's thought into that channel?"

"The conversation I am relating took place the moment after we had entered the flat. We were standing in the hall. It was wholly the outcome of the strange smell which was immediately perceptible.''

Forbes passed a hand over his eyes.

"I wonder,'' he breathed.

Then, turning quickly on Theydon, he repeated the question.

"Are you quite sure they did not mention the discovery in this room of any object which could be regarded, even remotely, as a sign or symbol left by the murderer to show that his crime was an act of vengeance, or retaliation?''

Theydon hesitated. Unquestionably he was in a position of no ordinary difficulty. But his doubts were solved by an interruption that brought his heart into his mouth, because a thin, high-pitched voice came through the half-open door:

"Are you thinking of a small ivory skull, Mr. Forbes?''

CHAPTER VII

EVEN the boldest may flinch when confronted with that which is apparently a manifestation of the supernatural. Theydon and Forbes were standing in a chamber of death. To the best of their belief they were alone in an otherwise empty flat, and those ominous words coming from some one unknown and unseen blanched their faces with terror.

But Theydon was a healthy and athletic young Englishman, and Forbes was of the rare order which combines a frame of exceptional physique with a mind accustomed to think imperially; two such men might be trusted to display real grit if surrounded by a horde of veritable spooks.

The door was thrown wide as they turned at the sound of the words, and Theydon recognized in a strange little figure—wearing a blue serge suit, a straw hat and brown boots —Furneaux, the man whom he had looked on as somewhat of a crank and visionary during their talk of the previous night.

"You?" he gasped, and the note of rec-

ognition was sharpened by a sudden sense
of dismay, almost of alarm, because of the
overwhelming knowledge that now all his
scheming had collapsed, while the representatives of Scotland Yard would regard him as
nothing more than a poor sort of trickster.

But Forbes was not in the habit of yielding
to any man, no matter what his status, or
howsoever awe-inspiring might be the department of state which he represented.

"Who the devil are you, at any rate?" he
cried angrily. "And what right have you to
spy on gentlemen in this manner, listening to
their conversation, and breaking in with a
cheap stage effect obviously intended to
startle?"

Furneaux remained motionless, his feet set
well apart and his hands thrust into his
trousers pockets. The trim, natty figure, the
spruce and Summer-like attire, the small,
wizened face with its cynically humorous and
wide-awake aspect—above all, a certain jaunt-
iness of air and cocksure expression—certainly did not suggest a comedian fresh from
the boards.

"You tell," he said, nodding to Theydon.

"This is Mr. Furneaux of Scotland Yard,"
said the latter nervously. He imagined he
could detect in Furneaux's glance a mixture
of amusement and contempt, amusement at
the notion that any amateur should harbor

129

the belief that the two best men in the "Yard" could be egregiously hoodwinked, and contempt of one who so far forgot himself as even to dare attempt such a thing in relation to a police inquiry into a murder.

"I don't know, and care less, who Mr. Furneaux of Scotland Yard may be," went on Forbes hotly. "I resent his intrusion, and wish to be relieved of his presence."

"Why?" said Furneaux.

"I have given my reasons to the Home Secretary. That mere statement must suffice for you."

"Really, I must ask you to be more explicit."

"I visited the Home Office this morning, and placed such evidence in the hands of the Home Secretary that Scotland Yard will be requested to suspend all further investigation into the death of Mrs. Lester."

"Do you mean that the Home Secretary has sanctioned the breaking off of this inquiry."

"In the conditions—"

"Because, if that is what your words imply, Mr. Forbes, I may tell you at once that I don't believe you. It is more than any Home Secretary dare do, and if you harbor any lingering doubts on the point, go to Mr. Theydon's telephone, ring up the Home Office,

and tell the gentleman at the other end of
the wire exactly what I have said. Of course
you really don't mean anything of the sort.
By virtue of some special and inside knowledge of certain facts communicated to the
Home Secretary, you may have persuaded
him to promise that, provided the ends of
justice are not defeated thereby, every pre-
caution will be taken to keep the main lines
of the inquiry secret until the whole position can be laid before the law officers of the
Crown. The Home Secretary may have gone
that far, Mr. Forbes, but not one inch farther,
and you know it."

The two antagonists, so singularly dis-
proportionate in size, were yet so perfectly
matched in the vastly more important qualities of brain and nerve that the contest lost
all sense of inequality. Theydon felt himself
of no account in this duel. He was like an
urchin watching open-mouthed a combat of
gladiators.

Forbes, not without a perceptible effort,
choked down his wrath and recovered his
poise.

"You have gaged the state of affairs accurately enough," he said, speaking more
calmly. "May I, then, recommend you to
consult your direct superiors before carrying
your investigations any furthur, Mr.—"

" Furneaux—Charles François Furneaux."

" Just so, Mr. Charles François Furneaux."

"I give you my full name, because one of the peculiar features of this case is the inability of some persons mixed up in it to recall names, or even the mere salient facts," and the detective's glance dwelt for an instant on Theydon, who, again, in his own estimation, shrank into the boots of a fourth-form boy detected by a master in an overt breach of college rules.

But the little man was speaking impressively, and Theydon compelled his wandering wits to pay attention.

"It will clear the air, perhaps," went on Furneaux, "if I point out that if any one here is playing the spy—carrying on some underhanded game, that is—it is not I. These apartments are in charge of the police. The manager of the whole block of flats and the porter of this particular section have been warned that no one can be allowed to enter No. 17, on any pretext, until our inquiry is closed. Now, Mr. Forbes, kindly explain how you contrived to get possession of a key."

An experienced man of the world like Forbes could hardly fail to see that he was in a false position, and that any persistent attempt to browbeat the detective would not only meet with utter failure but might possibly compromise him gravely.

"That was a simple matter," he said. "Mrs. Lester's servant left her key in Mr. Theydon's establishment. Bates surprised both his master and me by producing it when I expressed a wish to examine the place."

"But why adopt such a clandestine method?"

Forbes's face, usually so classic in outline, assumed a certain rigidity, and his firm chin grew markedly aggressive.

"I don't answer questions put in that way," he said.

Furneaux laughed sardonically.

"You meet with greater respect in Capel Court, I have no doubt," he snapped. "There you stand on a pedestal, with one hand flourishing a check-book and the other resting gracefully on the neck of a golden calf. Here, you are simply an ordinary citizen behaving in a suspicious manner. If the uniformed policeman on the neighboring beat knew what I know of your recent movements he would arrest you without ceremony, and charge you with being concerned in the murder of Mrs. Lester. Between you and Mr. Theydon, the work of my department has been hindered and burked most scandalously. Don't glare at me like that! I don't care tuppence for your millions and your social position. What I do care about is the horrible risk you and each member of your family are incurring.

You know why, and while you are still alive I mean to force you to speak. Tell me now why Mrs. Lester was killed. Tell me, too, why the same hand which thrust a little ivory skull into the dead woman's underbodice caused a similar token to be delivered to you by this morning's post. Ah, that touches you, does it? Now, my worthy financier and philanthropist, step down from your pedestal and behave like a being of flesh and blood!''

Forbes positively wilted under that extraordinary attack. His white face grew wan, and his eyes dilated with surprise and terror. The detective's words seemed to have the effect of a paralytic shock. Thenceforth he was under dog in the fight.

"How do you know," he gasped, "that I received an ivory skull this morning? Have you been to my house? Did my daughter tell you?"

Furneaux chuckled.

"You're ready to listen, eh? Well, I don't mind telling you that I have not stirred out of this flat since seven o'clock this morning, and I question if your letters were delivered in Fortescue Square at that hour."

"I give in," said Forbes curtly. "Need we remain here? The smell of that cursed joss stick oppresses me."

Then Theydon found his tongue.

"If Mr. Furneaux cares to abandon his vigil, my flat is entirely at your disposal," he said.

"My vigil, as you accurately describe it, has ended for the time being," said Furneaux, apparently mollified by the millionaire's surrender. "I was sure that if I remained here long enough I would clear away some of the fog attached to a case which promises to be one of the most remarkable I have ever investigated. Come, gentlemen, let us be amiable to one another. I'm sorry if I lost my temper just now, but I regard myself as being the only detective in existence who uses other sections of his brain than those governed by statutes made and provided, and it riles me when men of superior intelligence like yourselves treat me as though my mission in life was to direct the traffic and keep a sharp eye on mischievous juveniles. . . . Mr. Theydon, can that soldier-servant of yours make coffee?"

"His wife can," said Theydon.

"Will you be good enough, then, to set her to work? Thus far, since the sun rose, I have stayed the pangs of hunger with an apple and a glass of water."

By this time, Theydon had thoroughly revised his first estimate of the diminutive detective. Indeed, he was beginning to look on him as a quite noteworthy person, a man whose mental equipment it was most unwise to assess at any lower valuation than the somewhat exalted one which Furneaux himself had set forth with such refreshing candor.

As for Forbes, the millionaire seemed to have sunk into a species of stupor since Furneaux spoke of the ivory skull. He uttered no word until the three were seated in Theydon's room, and his expression was so woebegone that it stirred even the mercurial Jerseyite to pity.

"I imagine that a cup of coffee will do you also a world of good," he said. Then, whirling round on Theydon, he stuck a question into him as if each word was a stiletto.

"Where do you get your coffee?"

"At the grocer's," was the surprised answer.

"Is that all you know about it?"

"Yes."

"Singular thing, isn't it?" mused the detective aloud, "how idiotic men and women can be in their attitude to the supreme things of life. What is of greater importance than the food we eat and the liquors we drink? Through them the body reconstitutes itself hourly and daily. Providence gives us a perfect engine, yet we clog and choke its shafts and cylinders by supplying it haphazard with any sort of fuel and lubricant, no matter how unsuited either may be to its purpose. Take coffee, for instance. The physiological action of coffee depends on the presence of the alkaloid caffeine, which varies from 0.6 percent in the Arabian berry to 2 percent in that of Sierra Leone. Again, the aromatic oil, caffeine, which is developed by roasting, increases in quantity the longer the seeds are kept. Unfortunately, coffee beans lose weight during storage, so you have a clear commercial reason why grocers should not sell the best coffee, unless under compulsion of an enlightened public opinion. Now you, Mr. Forbes, would never dream of putting your money into a investment without full and careful inquiry into the history and scope of the proposed undertaking, while our young friend here would snort furiously at a split infinitive or a false rhyme, yet, when I submit the vital problem of the sort of coffee you imbibe—the very essence and nutriment of your brains and bodies—you hear the kind of answer I receive."

All this, of course, was excellent fooling, intended to dispel the brooding horror which had suddenly descended upon Forbes since it was borne in on him that the demoniac wrath wreaked on Mrs. Lester was now directed with equal ferocity against his family and himself.

To an extent, Furneaux's scheme succeeded. A gleam of interest shot from the mil-

lionaire's eyes. They lost their introspective
look. He even smiled wistfully.

"You are a man after my own heart, Mr.
Furneaux," he said. "I had no idea that the
Criminal Investigation Department employed
philosophers of your caliber. I suppose that
you and I are about to swallow coffee containing indeterminate percentages of the chief
constituents you named."

"One does not look at gift coffee in the
cup," grinned the little man, obviously well
pleased with himself. "But, if ever you two
gentlemen favor my obscure dwelling with a
visit, and partake of a meal, you will have
a strict analysis with every bite and sup.
There is a grocer in Battersea who used to
tremble at sight of me. Now he has learned
wisdom, and has quadrupled his trade by
publishing learned disquisitions on the nature
and quality of each principal article he sells.
You ought to read his treatise on butter. He
is an authority on the dietetic value of jam.
The nutritive properties of his cheese are
ruining the local butchers."

Furneaux's efforts were rewarded when the
really excellent beverage provided by Mrs.
Bates was disposed of. Forbes seemingly
atoned for his earlier secretiveness by placing
every fact in his possession fully and fairly
before his auditors.

"Nearly seven years ago," he said, "I

made a very large sum of money by amalgamating certain shipping interests at a favorable moment. Thus, as it happened, I had at command practically unlimited resources when I was asked to finance the cause of reform in China. The wretched lot of the Chinese Nation had always appealed to my sympathies. Some hundreds of millions of the most industrious and peace-loving people in the world have been exploited for centuries by a predatory caste. Given a chance to expand, freed from the shackles of the Manchus, the Chinese, in my opinion, contain the elements which go to form a great race. But the Manchus held them in bondage, body and soul, and, so powerful is self-interest, there has never been an Emperor or statesman who strove to elevate the masses who was not mercilessly assassinated as soon as he allowed his intent to become known. The only path to freedom lay through revolution, and I had reason to believe that the ruling faction could be overthrown by a well-organized and properly financed movement without the appalling bloodshed which often accompanies such dynastic changes. At any rate, I entered the conspiracy, heart and soul. But I met with two difficulties at the outset. I could not exercise efficient financial control in London, and I could neither go and live in the Far East nor transact my business through ordinary banking channels. So I had to find a substitute, and my choice fell on a rising young barrister named Arthur Lester, whom I had known since he was a boy who had married the daughter of an old friend. He had a taste for adventure, and was alive to the magnificent career which lay before one who helped materially in the rebirth of China. In a word, he went to Shanghai as my agent, and the outcome of his work there is the present Chinese constitution. Of course, as holds good in all human affairs, events did not follow the precise track mapped out for them. But, on the whole, he and I were satisfied. China is awake at last. The giant has stirred, and, if his first uncertain steps have deviated from the open road of reform, he will never again sink into the torpor of the past centuries. Manchu arrogance and domination, at any rate, are shadows of the past, but unhappily, the conquerors who have been so effectually thrust aside have now embarked on a secret campaign of vengeance and reaction. A society which calls itself the 'Young Manchus' is inspired by one principle, and one only, and that is 'death to the reformers.' I don't suppose you gentlemen follow closely the trend of affairs in China, but you must have read of the assassinations of prominent men reported occasionally in the newspapers.''

Furneaux clicked his tongue so loudly that

Forbes stopped speaking and looked at him, thinking, apparently, that the little detective meant to say something. He did, but it was Theydon whom he addressed.

"I'd give a week's pay if Winter was here now, and I could see those big eyes of his bulging out of his head," he cackled.

Theydon nodded. He understood perfectly. Then he caught Forbes's inquiring glance, and explained matters.

"Mr. Furneaux hinted last night at some such development as that which your present statement conveys, and his colleague, Mr. Winter, pretended to scout it," he said.

"Pretended!" shrieked Furneaux, instantly in a rage.

"That was how it struck me," said Theydon coolly.

"Didn't I drag the Chinese aspect of the crime out of him with pincers?" came the indignant demand.

"Unquestionably. I only remark that your large-sized friend had it tucked away all the time at the back of his head."

Furneaux pounded the table so viciously that the cups rattled.

"Of course, he has a nose to smell joss sticks, and eyes to see an ivory skull, but didn't he say I was talking nonsense when I spoke about Shang Ti scowling from a porcelain vase?" he shrilled.

"Yes. For all that, I don't think he missed the least hint of your meaning."

Furneaux gazed at Theydon fixedly.

"Sorry," he said, with an acid tone that was almost malicious. "I imagined you were so busy throwing dust in our eyes that you wouldn't have noticed such fine shades of perception on Winter's part."

But Theydon was now able to measure this strange little man with some degree of accuracy; he only smiled.

"As a thrower of dust I was a most abject failure," he said.

Furneaux smiled and turned to the millionaire.

"Pardon the interruption," he said. "Like every artist, I am pained when my best efforts are scoffed at by heedless mediocrity. You, at least, will understand what a big thing it was to deduce even the vaguest outline of the truth from the facts at my command."

"I certainly do," agreed Forbes. "Until this morning I was convinced that Mrs. Lester's death removed the one person in England who knew of my connection with the revolution in China. To revert to the Young Manchus—they have secured far more victims than the world at large is aware of. I am sure that they poisoned Arthur Lester, and his wife held the same view. They aim at nothing less than the extinction of the democratic cause by the murder of every prominent man connected with it. But they never yet have been able to obtain a full and authentic list of the reform leaders. They suspected poor Lester of complicity in the movement, and killed him. It was through Mrs. Lester that I first became aware of their existence as an active organization, and I hoped that when she had returned to England, and was living quietly in London, she would be lost sight of—ignored, in fact. Nevertheless, both she and I thought it prudent that our acquaintance should cease until the turmoil in China had subsided. For that reason I never visited her, nor did I permit the growth of friendship between her and my wife and daughter—a friendship which, in happier conditions, would have been natural and inevitable. But we were woefully mistaken. An Oriental vendetta neither slackens nor dies. By some means wholly unknown to me, the Young Manchus must have discovered, or guessed, that in leaving Lester's widow out of their reckoning they had lost a promising clew. Be that as it may, they followed her to London, and, by a singular fatality, I was the first to know of it. Last Monday, while driving home from the city, my car was held up in Piccadilly for a few seconds. Looking idly out at the passing crowd, I saw a Chinaman in European clothes.

He was waiting to cross the road, so I was able to scrutinize him carefully, and, owing to a scar on the left side of his face, recognized him. His name is Wong Li Fu, a Manchu of the Manchus, a mandarin of almost imperial lineage. Some years ago he was a young attaché at the Chinese Embassy here. Suddenly, while on the way to my house, I recollected that certain members of the Revolutionary Committee had spoken of this very man as being one of the ablest and most unscrupulous adherents of the Manchu faction in Pekin. Somehow, his presence in London was disconcerting and menacing. Who more likely than he, I argued, to be a leading spirit among the Young Manchus? In any event, London was not big enough to hold both Mrs. Lester and him, and I decided to visit her that very night, tell her I had seen Wong Li Fu, and advise her to go away into the country, leaving no record of her whereabouts. I happened to be taking my daughter to Daly's Theater, and contrived to slip away on some pretext after the performance. I found Mrs. Lester alone in her flat, and she fell in with my views at once, because she, too, had heard of this very man, and the mere sound of his name terrified her. I was half inclined to urge that she should go to an hotel for the night, but the lateness of the hour and the seeming fact that if danger threatened she was safe at least till the morrow, prevented me.''

Furneaux, sitting on the edge of a chair, his head bent forward, his piercing black eyes intent as those of a hawk, a hand resting on each knee, his attitude curiously suggestive of a readiness to spring forward at any instant, now leaned over and tapped the millionaire decisively on the shoulder.

"You couldn't have saved her, Mr. Forbes," he said gravely. "She was marked down as the first warning. Didn't the letter you received this morning tell you something of the sort?"

Agitation gave place to utter astonishment in Forbes's face.

"In Heaven's name, how do you know anything of any letter?" he cried.

"I will tell you later. But am I not right?"

"Yes, you are."

"Where is it? May I see it?"

Forbes took a creased and soiled document from a small, flat cardboard box which he carried in the breast pocket of his coat. But first he withdrew from the box a little object, and placed it on the table. It was an ivory skull, and the very presence of such a sinister token brought some hint of the charnel-house into the cozy and sunlit room.

Furneaux, a creature oddly constituted either of all nerves or of no nerves, disregarded the skull. He had eyes only for the few words typed on a single sheet of note-paper. They ran:

"James Creighton Forbes: If you are willing to come to terms, announce the fact by advertisement in Thursday's *Times*. Address your reply to Y. M., and sign it 'J. C. F.' Yield, and you will hear further. Refuse, and no other warning will be given."

CHAPTER VIII

FURNEAUX apparently made up his mind with reference to the contents of a somewhat enigmatic message after one quick, unerring perusal.

"The man who wrote that took a great many things for granted," he said. "He assumed, firstly, that you knew of Mrs. Lester's death and understood its significance; secondly, that you are aware of the nature of the 'terms' he will offer; thirdly, that you may hesitate between compliance and threatened death. 'Y. M.,' of course, can be read as 'Young Manchus.' Even there, the writer exhibits artistic reticence. . . . Frankly, Mr. Forbes, I wish you had come straight to Scotland Yard on Monday evening instead of wasting those precious hours at Daly's Theater."

Forbes was moved to energetic protest.

"How was I to deduce the true nature of these hell hounds' mission from a casual glance vouchsafed of one who may or may not be their leader?" he cried.

"Yet you treated your discovery as serious enough to warrant a prompt visit to the woman with whom association was dangerous?"

"Yes; I wanted to act secretly."

"Just so. You were afraid the police would bungle the job. Between you and Mr. Theydon, you have exhibited remarkable skill in heading us off the scent. Fortunately, we were able to dispense with your assistance, having other matters to occupy our brains. You two were ripe nuts waiting to be cracked and have the contents extracted at leisure. There were a few freshly broken shells lying about which invited immediate attention. For instance, some four months ago, a well-known and reputable firm of private inquiry agents was instructed from Canton to secure all possible information about Mrs. Lester and you—yes, you, Mr. Forbes—your household, friends, methods of living, servants, tradesmen,—every sort of fact, indeed, which might be useful to a thoroughgoing and well-organized society of cutthroats like the Young Manchus. The inquiry agents did their work well, and were handsomely paid for it. I haven't the least doubt that Wong Li Fu knows what brand of cigars you favor, and what you eat for breakfast. His informants sent us a copy of their notes an hour after the murder was announced in the newspapers. Mr. Lester is 'removed' in Shanghai. His widow comes home. The inquiry agents receive instructions. They forward their report to Canton, and Wong Li Fu turns up in London. The program is a tribute to the excellence and regularity of the mail service between England and the Far East."

While the detective was speaking, Forbes's face, already haggard, had grown desperate.

"I care little for my own life," he said, "but I shall stop short of no measures to protect my wife and daughter."

"I certainly recommend that an armed guard should be on duty day and night in any house where you may happen to be living at the moment," replied Furneaux airily. "I really think that if your safety alone were at stake I would do you a good turn by arresting you on suspicion."

"On suspicion of what crime?"

"Of killing Mrs. Lester, to be sure."

"I regard you as a clever man, Mr. Furneaux, so may I remind you that this is neither the time nor the place for a display of gross humor?"

Theydon expected that Furneaux would flare into anger at this well-deserved rebuke; but, much to his surprise, the detective treated the matter argumentatively.

"Personally, I have looked on you from the outset as an innocent man," he said placidly. "But, just to show how circumstantial evidence may be twisted into plausible error, let me point out that nearly all the known facts conspire against you. Have you considered how dexterously a prosecuting counsel would treat your admission that Mrs. Lester was the one person in England who knew of your connection with the revolutionary party in China? And how would you set about convincing a stolid British jury that you were acting in the interests of law and order in concealing your visit to No. 17 on the night of the murder? These fine-drawn speculations, however, are a sheer waste of breath. Suppose we concoct an advertisement for the *Times*? "

"Do you mean that I am to parley with these ruffians?"

" Of course you are."

"But the Home Secretary agreed with me that no action should be taken until the Chinese Legation had considered the matter."

"And, pray, what can the Legation do?"

"They have their own sources of information. When all is said and done, Orientals are best fitted to deal with Orientals."

Furneaux laughed sarcastically.

"If I remember rightly, the way in which the Chinese Embassy dealt with one of your pet reformers some years ago did not win general approval. No, Mr. Forbes, we must try and circumvent the wily Chinese by other methods than torture and imprisonment. Of what avail will it be if this fellow, Wong Li Fu, is laid by the heels? Isn't it more than certain that he has plenty of determined helpers? Do you imagine that he killed Mrs. Lester? Not a bit of it. He will be able to produce the clearest proof that he was miles away from Innesmore Mansions on Monday night. Now, let's see how we can get him to show his hand a little more openly. How would this be? 'Y. M.—Terms can be arranged. J. C. F.' The terms are, of course, that the whole gang be hanged or sent to penal servitude and deported.''

"One moment," struck in Theydon. "I have something to say before you decide on any definite action. I need hardly inflict on you, Mr. Furneaux, an explanation of my silence hitherto. I don't even apologize for it. Faced by a similar dilemma tomorrow I should probably take the same line. But, to adopt your own simile, now that Mr. Forbes has come out of his shell, and admits his presence here on Monday night, my self-imposed restrictions cease. In the first place, then, Miss Beale came here this morning—"

"Excellent! I wondered who the lady was," put in Furneaux.

"And, secondly, the gray car which pursued me on Monday seems to have been partly identified later. A car resembling it in every

detail deposited some one at the Chinese
Legation in Portland Place, at an hour which
corresponds closely with its presence here.''

"Ah, that is important! I like that! I
wasn't far wrong when I sensed you as an
absolute carrier of clew-germs in this affair,"
cried Furneaux.

"The Chinese Embassy!" gasped Forbes.
"What car? And why should any car pursue you? Do you mean that you were followed on leaving my house?"

It was lamentable to watch the inroad which
each successive shock was making on Forbes's
physical resources, but Theydon affected to
ignore the new fright in his eyes, and told
him what had happened. Although he could
see that Furneaux was in a fever of impatience to learn the later news, he thought that
Forbes should know the facts in view of the
remarkable statement that he had visited the
Chinese Embassy that morning.

In one respect, the recital was a test of the
millionaire's professed readiness to deal candidly with the police. Theydon was half
inclined to believe that the other was still
wishful to conceal that part of the day's
doings. But he was mistaken. When he had
finished his own story, and given the taxi-
man's version of the gray car's appearance
in Portland Place, Forbes threw out his hands
in a gesture of despair.

"If the Embassy people are playing me false I do not know whom to trust," he said brokenly; "I have just come from there, and they assure me that if Wong Li Fu and his gang are in London they are absolutely ignorant of the fact."

"Pooh!" cried Furneaux, snapping a thumb and forefinger. "Don't worry about that! Put yourself in the position of the Chinese Ambassador. He can't even guess who may be the ruler of China from one day to another. Yesterday it was an old woman, today a dictator, tomorrow the mob; who can foretell what shape the lava erupted from a volcano will take? Bet you a new hat, Mr. Forbes, that the minute the embassy heard of Mrs. Lester's murder they put two and two together and kept a sharp eye on these mansions and on your house. That gray car is nothing more nor less than a red herring accidentally drawn across the trail. Some cute Chinaman said 'Hallo! that murdered woman is the wife of Forbes's agent in Shanghai. Now, let's see what Forbes is doing, and who visits him, and perhaps we'll learn something.' Want a bet?"

Forbes could not help but recover some of his shattered nerve in view of the detective's airy optimism. Still, he was shaken and dubious.

"Don't forget that the Chinese Ambassador

has no knowledge whatsoever of my share in the revolution," he said.

"And don't forget that for ways which are dark and tricks which are vain the heathen Chinee is peculiar," retorted Furneaux. "How can you be sure that there is not in the Embassy at this moment a full statement of your payments into the reformers' funds, as well as the list of conspirators which our friend Wong Li Fu is in search of?"

"I think that such a thing is almost impossible."

"Is there anything really impossible? We used to believe that once a man was dead he could not be brought to life again. A Frenchman has just demonstrated that by a judicious application of galvanism to the heart and salt water to the veins any average corpse can be revived."

Evidently Furneaux was enjoying himself. He sat there, absorbing new impressions and irradiating scraps of irrelevant knowledge in a way that would have been full of significance to Winter had he been present. Furneaux was never so mercurial, never so ready to jump from one subject to another, as when his subtle brain was working at high pressure.

He actually reveled in a crime which lay on the borderland of the exotic and the grotesque. Like the French philosopher in

Poe's "Tales of Mystery and Imagination," the savant who read his newspaper in a dingy Paris room, and solved by sheer force of intellect extraordinary criminal problems which baffled the shrewdest official minds, he felt in relation to this particular tragedy that he required only to be brought in touch with certain contingent forces bound up with it— Forbes, for instance, and, in a minor degree, Theydon—and in due course he would be able to go forth and find the master wrongdoer.

Suddenly the millionaire seemed to cast off the cloak of despair which clogged his energies and impaired his brilliant intellect. He rose to his feet and involuntarily squared his shoulders.

"Surely we are wasting valuable hours which should be given to action," he cried. "I am going to the city and shall arrange for a prolonged absence from my office. Then I'll hurry home, perfect my defenses, and defy these murderous curs. My wife must come to London. In a crisis like this I must have my loved ones under my own personal supervision. I can still shoot straight and quick, and woe betide any man, white or yellow, who enters my house unbidden. As for this infernal symbol—!"

He raised a clenched fist, and would have pounded into fragments the thin fabric of the ivory skull still lying where he had placed it on the table had not Furneaux snatched it into safety.

"No, no!" protested the detective. "I want that for purposes of comparison. Kindly give me that typed note, too, Mr. Forbes. It may bear finger-marks. You never can tell. The cardboard box in which it was posted also. Thank you. Now, a few more questions before you go. How much money did you provide for the revolutionaries?"

"Two millions sterling."

"As a gift or a loan?"

"If they failed, I lost every farthing, of course. If they succeeded, I was to recoup myself by financing the new government."

"But I gather that they have neither failed nor succeeded. China has a constitution, but the Presidential election was conducted on lines suspiciously akin to those recently adopted in Mexico."

"Nevertheless negotiations are now on foot for a big loan."

"If you died, what would become of the two millions?"

"They would be lost irretrievably."

Furneaux sat back in his chair.

"That gives one furiously to think," he said. "The gray car comes back into the picture."

"What do you mean?"

" I don't know. But I'll tell you what—the

man who first spoke of a Chinese puzzle as a metaphor for something downright bewildering knew what he was talking about."

Forbes put a hand to his forehead in an unconscious gesture of hopelessness.

"My brain is reeling," he muttered. "To think that in the London of today we should live in abject terror of a band of Mongolian ruffians! Why do you remain here, man? You vaunt the prowess of your department—why are you not scouring every haunt of Chinamen in the East End? Spread your net widely enough, and you will surely get hold of some minor scoundrel who will talk for fear or money. Bribe him to the point where he cannot refuse to speak. Wong Li Fu is the only man I fear. Put him where he can accomplish no mischief, and the rest of his crew will be powerless!"

"When you come to count up the achievements of my friend Winter and myself—in the face of stupid but none the less disheartening obstacles—we have not done so badly in two days," said Furneaux complacently.

"Can I drive you anywhere? My car is waiting."

"No, thanks. The truth is, Mr. Forbes, I look on you as a disturbing influence. A man who can talk as calmly as you about dropping two millions on a crazy project to introduce Western methods into China is not fitted for the phlegmatic and judicial atmosphere of Scotland Yard. If I want any money I'll come to you. If not, and all goes well at No. 11 Fortescue Square, the next time I'll trouble you will be when you are asked to identify Wong Li Fu, dead or alive.''

Forbes seemed hardly to be aware of Furneaux's words. He went out. Theydon accompanied him, and, as they descended the stairs together, the older man said brokenly:

''It is my wife and daughter for whom I fear. I can hardly control my senses when I think of these yellow fiends contemplating vengeance on me through them. Theydon—do you believe in that detective? He is either a vain fool or a genius. By the way, I forgot to ask him how he found out that I had received the warning delivered by this morning's post.''

''I'll try and worm an explanation out of him. If he tells me I'll telephone you later. He is an extraordinary creature, but abnormally clever at his work, I am sure. For my own part, I feel disposed to trust him implicitly. I wish you had met his colleague, Chief Inspector Winter. He is the sort of man whose mere presence inspires confidence.''

Forbes halted on the step of the automobile and glanced at his watch.

''I shall be home in an hour,'' he said. ''After that I shall not stir out all day.

Telephone me if you have any news. Why not dine with us tonight?"

Theydon's eyes sparkled. He was longing to meet Evelyn Forbes once more, but a wretched doubt diminished the glow of gratification which the prospect brought. Should he, or should he not, tell the girl's father of the rather indiscreet admissions she had made during their brief talk that morning?

That minor worry, however, was banished suddenly and forever. Furneaux, taking the three steps which led from entrance hall to pavement with a flying leap, cannoned right into Forbes, whom he grasped with both hands, quite as much by way of emphasis as to check the impetus of his diminutive body.

" In with you! " he piped. " Tell your chauffeur to obey my orders, no matter what they are!"

Action, determination, were as the breath of the millionaire's nostrils. He aroused himself instantly.

"You hear, Downs!" he said to the chauffeur.

Downs was one of those strange beings who have been evolved by the age of petrol, an automaton compounded, seemingly, of steel springs and leather. He had long ago lost the art of speech, having cultivated delicacy of hearing and quickness of sight at the

expense of all other human faculties. The
old-time coachman possessed a certain fluent
jargon, which enabled him to chide or encourage his horses and exchange suitable comments with the drivers of brewers' drays and
market carts, but the modern chauffeur is all
an ear for the rhythm of machinery, all an eye
for the nice calculation of the hazards of the
road fifty yards ahead.

At any rate, Downs mumbled something
which resembled "Yes, sir," Forbes sprang
in and slammed the door, Furneaux raced
round the front of the car and perched himself beside Downs, and the heavy automobile
was almost into its normal stride before it
had traveled twice its own length.

Theydon was left gaping on the pavement.
He saw that the car turned west, and caught
a glimpse of Furneaux's outstretched hand
with forefinger pointing like the barrel of
a pistol.

"Fool!" he cried, in bitter self-apostrophe.
"Why didn't I jump in after Forbes? Now I
am out of the hunt! I wonder what the deuce
Furneaux saw or heard?"

That concluding thought sent him back to
the flat, two steps at a time.

"Bates!" he shouted. "Has Mr. Furneaux
used the telephone, or did any one ring up?"

"No, sir," said Bates, coming hurriedly at
that urgent call. "Fust thing I knew was he

was tearin' out, an' runnin' downstairs like mad."

"O, double-distilled idiot that I am!" growled Theydon again. "Why didn't I go with them!"

As though the gods heard his plaint and meant to crush him with their answer, the telephone bell sounded at his elbow. Mechanically, he lifted the receiver off its hook, and immediately became aware of Tomlinson's voice, with some element of flurry and distress in its unctuous accents.

"That you, Mr. Theydon?" said the butler.

"Yes."

"Have you had any news of Mr. Forbes, sir?"

"Yes. He has just left me."

"Ah, if only I had known, and had given you a call before ringing up the city!"

"What is it? Can I do anything?"

"It's Miss Evelyn, sir."

"Yes, what of her?"

"She's gone, sir."

Theydon's heart apparently stopped for a second, and then raced madly into tumultuous action again.

"Gone! Good Lord, man, what do you mean?" he almost groaned.

"A telegram came from Mrs. Forbes, at Eastbourne, saying she was ill and wanted Miss Evelyn. I tried all I knew to persuade

Miss Evelyn to wait until she had spoken to her father, but she wouldn't listen—she just threw on a hat and a wrap, and took a taxi to Victoria."

Some membrane or film of tissue which might have served hitherto to shut off from Frank Theydon's cheery temperament any real knowledge of the pitfalls which may beset the path of the unwary seemed in that instant to shrivel as though it had been devoured by flame.

He knew, how or why he could never tell, that the girl had been drawn into the plot which had already claimed so many victims and sought so many more. All doubt vanished. He spoke and acted with the swift certainty of a man tackling an emergency for which he had prepared during a long period of training and expectation.

"Mr. Forbes may arrive at any moment, Tomlinson," he said. "Tell his office people to let you know if he goes first to the city. When you hear from or see him, say that I have either accompanied or followed Miss Evelyn to Eastbourne. If I do not catch the same train I shall take prompt measures in other respects. Got that?"

"Yes, sir."

It was easy to distinguish the relief in Tomlinson's utterance, relief mingled, doubtless, with astonishment that a comparative stranger should display such an authoritative and prompt interest in the family affairs.

"That is all. Write down my message, lest you omit any part of it."

Theydon rang off.

"Come!" he said to Bates, who had not retired to his den, but was listening, discreet yet rabbit-eared, to these queer proceedings. Followed by the manservant, he darted into the sitting room and did several things at once.

He unlocked a drawer and took from it a considerable sum of money which he kept there for emergency journeys, also pocketing an automatic pistol. Pouncing on an A B C time table, he looked up the trains for Eastbourne. A fast train left Victoria at 1:25 p. m. The hour was now 1:05.

Meanwhile he was talking.

"Bates," he said, "I promised Miss Beale, the lady who came here this morning, that my sister, Mrs. Paxton, would visit her this evening, say about six. Miss Beale is staying at Smith's Hotel, Jermyn Street. Go to Mrs. Paxton, and see her, waiting at her house if she happens to be out. Tell everything you know about Mrs. Lester's death, and ask her to take care of Miss Beale this evening. She will understand. I'll wire her at Smith's Hotel before the dinner hour, if possible. If anybody calls here, I leave it to your discretion and

your wife's whether or not they should be informed of my movements. Mr. Forbes or the
police, of course, must be told everything.
Miss Forbes is probably in the 1:25 p. m.
train for Eastbourne, and I am going with
her. Do you understand?"

"Yes, sir."

"I'll wire or 'phone you later."

Grabbing a straw hat and a bundle of
telegraph forms, Theydon vanished, not even
waiting to slam the outer door. Bates, who
had seen service, knew that men in time of
stress and danger acted just like the detective and his own employer.

"By Jingo!" he muttered, beginning to as-
semble the empty coffee-cups on a tray.
"Things is wakin' up here, an' no mistake!"

Theydon was fortunate in finding a taxicab
depositing a fare at a neighboring block. Just
before he reached the vehicle a gentleman hurried out of the building and forestalled him.
Theydon dashed up, and caught the other man
by the arm.

"My need is urgent," he said. "Let me
have this cab."

The stranger smiled good-humoredly. He
was an American and had not the least objection to being hustled by a Britisher; indeed
he rather appreciated this exhibition of haste
as a novel experience.

"I'm on a hair-trigger myself," he said,

164

pleasantly. "I want to make Victoria pretty quick. Can I give you a lift?"

"In with you!" cried Theydon. "Now, cabby, half a sovereign if you get us to Victoria, Brighton line, in 15 minutes. I'll pay all fines."

Then they were off, and the Trans-Atlantic cousins were banged against one another as the cab whirled round in a sharp semicircle.

"Say!" cried the American, "this reminds one of home. I've been here a week, an' had a kind of notion that London air was half fog, half dope. But you're awake all right. Bet you a five spot you're after a girl!"

"I pay," said Theydon, his eyes glistening. "And such a girl! Her portrait on the paper wrap of a 50-cent novel would sell it in millions!"

"Gee whiz! Is it like that? Go right ahead, Augustus! Never mind me. Take this old bus all the way to Paris. I'll find the fares and hold your hat. But kindly shift that gun into your opposite pocket. You've dug it into my thigh quite often enough. If you want to get first drop on the other fellow, shove it up your sleeve!"

CHAPTER IX

The American's easy-going badinage provided the best sort of tonic. Theydon laughed as he transferred the pistol from one pocket to the other.

"My motto is 'Defense, not Defiance,'" he said. "I hope sincerely that I shall not be called on to shoot, or even threaten any one. Using firearms, although for self-protection, is a very serious matter in this country. May I ask your name? Mine's Theydon. I live in those mansions we have just quitted."

"And I'm George T. Handyside, 21,097 Park Avenue, Chicago," was the answer.

"Is that your telephone number?"

"No, sir. It's my home address."

"Well, Mr. Handyside, if ever I come to Chicago, I'll travel along Park Avenue and give you a call. How many days' journey are you from the center of the city?"

"Say, Mr. Theydon, I'm real glad to make your acquaintance. I haven't been joshed in that way since I left the steamer. This little island of yours is all right as a beauty spot, but I do wish your people wouldn't carry such a grouch agin' life generally. Great Scott! It'll do 'em a heap of good to try a real chesty laugh occasionally."

"Tell me where I can drop across you in London later in the week, and I'll see if we can't find a smile somewhere."

The American scribbled the name of a Strand hotel on a card, which Theydon disposed in his pocketbook, at the same time producing one of his own cards.

"You'll hear from me," he said. "Now, Mr. Handyside, pardon me for the next few minutes. I have to write telegrams."

The first was to Forbes, addressed in duplicate to Old Broad Street and Fortescue Square. It ran:

"If this message is not qualified by another within a few minutes I am in the 1:25 train for Eastbourne."

Then to Winter:

"Young lady summoned to Eastbourne by telegram stating that her mother is ill. Suspect the message as bogus and emanating from Y. M. See Furneaux. He will explain. Am hoping to travel by same train. If disappointed will wire again immediately.—Theydon."

He read each slip carefully, to make sure that the phraseology was clear. The speed at which the cab was traveling rendered his handwriting somewhat illegible, but he

thought he saw a means of circumventing that
difficulty.

"Which place are you going?" he inquired
of his unexpected companion.

"To a place called Sutton."

"What time does your train leave?"

"Guess it's about 1:30."

"You have five more minutes at your disposal than I have. Will you hand in these
three messages at the telegraph office? I'll
read them to you, in case the counter clerk
is doubtful about any of my words."

"Sure thing, Mr. Theydon. You've interested me. I don't care a row of beans if
I drop out Sutton altogether."

" I'm greatly obliged, but that is not necessary. You'll have loads of time. We're in
the Park already, and our driver has a clear
run to Victoria. Now, listen!"

Mr. Handyside did listen, and pricked his
ears at the mention of Scotland Yard.

"Gosh!" he exclaimed, "this is better'n a
life-line movie! For the love of Mike, let
me in by the early door! Now, how's this for
a proposition? You send those telegrams, and
I'll fix the cab an' buy the transportation
to Eastbourne for the pair of us. I'm not
heeled, but I may be useful, an' I'll jab any
fellow in the solar plexus at call."

Theydon gazed at this self-avowed knight-
errant in surprise. Handyside was a man of

forty, whose dark hair was flecked with gray. He was quietly dressed, a wide-brimmed high-crowned hat of finely-plaited white straw providing the sole note of markedly American origin in his attire. The expression of his well-moulded features was shrewd but pleasing, and the poise of a spare but sinewy frame gave evidence of active habit and some considerable degree of physical strength.

" 'Pon my honor," said the Englishman. "I'm half inclined to take you at your word, except in the matter of expenses, which, of course, I must bear. You see, if my services are called for, and prove effective, I may need help."

"Go right ahead," said the other calmly. "Tell me as much or as little as you like. Where's this place, Eastbourne? On the south coast, I guess."

"Yes."

"I thought it would be. A man on the steamer asked me to come and see him at Westgate, which is about as far east as you can go in England without wetting your feet. I'm getting the hang of things here by degrees. Southport, of course, is away up north, and Northamptonshire in the midlands."

Theydon grinned, but the taxi was passing Buckingham Palace, and the hour was 1:17 p. m.

"I cannot give you any sort of an explanation now, Mr. Handyside," he said. "Later in the week, perhaps, I may have a big story for your private ear. All I can say at the moment is this—I have reason to believe that a young lady, a daughter of Mr. James Creighton Forbes, a well-known man in the city of London, is being decoyed to Eastbourne in the belief that her mother is ill. Now, I may be wholly mistaken. Her mother may be ill. If that is so, I am making this trip under a delusion. At any rate, my notion is to try and fall in with Miss Forbes accidentally, as it were, and watch over her until I am quite sure that she is with her mother. You follow me?"

"Seems to me," said the American imperturbably, " it's the most natural thing in the world that Mr. Theydon should want to show his friend, Mr. Handyside of Chicago, England's most bracing and attractive seaside resort, if that's the right way to describe Eastbourne."

"Both the plan and the description are admirable."

"The plan sounds all right. As for the description I have been looking up a selection of posters, and those seven words apply to every half-mile strip of beach in the island. When it comes to a real show-down, your poster artists have got our real estate men skinned a mile. How much did you promise the taxi-man?"

"Half a sovereign."

"Two-fifty. Gee! That's the nearest thing to New York I've struck yet. And the railway tickets—first-class, of course?"

"Yes."

The cab stopped. Theydon sprang out and raced to the telegraph office, where, as he anticipated, there was a slight delay. Handyside awaited him at the correct barrier, and together they walked down a long platform, Theydon peering into every carriage, though convinced that Evelyn Forbes would not travel other than first class. Thus, not being a detective, but only a very anxious and perplexed young man, he had eyes only for such ladies as were already seated in the train, and failed to note the immediate interest his appearance aroused in a man who occupied a window seat, and who was watching unobtrusively every one who passed. Oddly enough, after the first wondering glance, this observer was more closely taken up with Handyside. It was as though he said to himself:

"Theydon I know, but who in the world is his companion, and why are they traveling by an Eastbourne express—today of all days?"

The train was well filled; there were only

a few seconds to spare when Theydon came across Evelyn Forbes in a compartment which held two other passengers—a lady and a gentleman.

Recognition was mutual, and Theydon flattered himself that he betrayed just the right amount of pleasurable astonishment.

"Miss Forbes!" he cried, raising his hat. " Well, of all the unexpected meetings! Don't say you are going to Eastbourne!"

"But I am," she said, and, though she smiled, her eyes were heavy with unshed tears. She was deeply attached to her mother, and the thought that the loved one was too ill even to communicate with her by telephone was distressing beyond measure.

"Just imagine that!" went on Theydon, determined to rush his fences and travel with her unless openly forbidden. "I'm taking an American friend there for the afternoon. May we come in your carriage? Is there room for two?"

Now, although Evelyn Forbes had been attracted to Theydon during their vivacious conversation overnight, she would vastly have preferred the comparative solitude of a journey with strangers.

Still, she could hardly refuse such a request, and common sense told her that a pleasant chat with a man who could talk as well as Theydon offered a better means of

SHARP WORK

whiling away two and a half hours than brooding over the nature and extent of her mother's
unknown illness.

"There's plenty of room," she said.

Without further ado, Theydon entered and
Handyside followed. The compartment held
six seats, while a door led to a side corridor
running the length of the coach. The two
remaining occupants were worthy Britons
who neither invited nor received any special
attention.

Mr. Handyside was introduced, and
promptly said the right thing.

"I guess I knew what I was doing when
I forced Mr. Theydon to take me out of
London today," he said, with a smile which
left the girl in no doubt as to the nature
of the implied compliment.

"But it is hardly an hour since I spoke to
my father at Mr. Theydon's flat," she said.
"Were you there, too, Mr. Handyside?"

"No, in the next block. That was the
nearest I got to Mr. Theydon before we met
and took a cab for Victoria."

Theydon was pleased with his ally. No
diplomat, trained during long years to conceal
material facts, could have headed the girl off
more deftly, while every word was literally
true.

"Ah!" she said, glancing meaningly at
Theydon, "we are all the sport of fortune,

173

then. How strange! Of course, Mr. Theydon, you don't know why I am here. I have had a telegram from my mother, or one sent in her name. She has been taken ill suddenly.''

''That is bad news,'' was the sympathetic answer. ''If the message has not come direct from Mrs. Forbes may it not be rather exaggerated in tone? Some people can never write telegrams. The knowledge that each word costs a halfpenny weighs on them like a nightmare.''

As he hoped and anticipated, she produced the message itself from her handbag.

''This is what it says,'' she said, and read: '' 'Mrs. Forbes ill and unable communicate by telephone. Come at once. Manager Royal Devonshire Hotel.' '' Then she added, with a suspicious break in her voice: ''That sounds serious enough, in all conscience.''

''Is it addressed to you personally?'' said Theydon, racking his wits for some means of lessening the girl's foreboding without tickling the ears of the other people in the compartment by suggesting that she might have been brought from her home by some cruel ruse of her father's enemies.

''Yes.''

''But isn't that somewhat singular in itself? One would imagine that such a significant message would have been sent to your father.''

''Why?''

''Well, men are better fitted to withstand these shocks, for one thing. It was heartless, or, to say the least, thoughtless, to give you such news with the brutal frankness of a telegram.''

''I cannot understand it at all. Mother wrote this morning telling me that she was going to Beachy Head this afternoon with a picnic party.''

''I am convinced,'' said Theydon gravely, ''that some one has blundered. It may be the act of some stupid foreigner. I shall not be content now, Miss Forbes, until I have gone with you to the Royal Devonshire, and learnt what the extent of the trouble really is. Then, if Mrs. Forbes needs your presence, perhaps you will allow me to telephone to your father, as he will be greatly disturbed when he returns home and learns the cause of your journey.''

''But I can't think of allowing you two to break up your afternoon on my account. I'm sure, when we reach Eastbourne, I shall see an array of golf clubs among your luggage.''

''No,'' smiled Theydon. ''My friend here refuses to play until he has seen something of the country. He knows that the golfer's vision is bounded by the nearest bunker.''

Handyside took the cue.

"That's the exact position, Miss Forbes," he said. "I was warned by the horrible experience of a friend of mine. He left Newark, N. J., on a sightseeing tour of Europe, but unfortunately took his clubs with him. Now, if you ask him what he thought of Westminster Abbey or the Wye Valley he tells you he hadn't time to look 'em up, but that the fifth hole at Sandwich is a corker, while the thirteenth at St. Andrews has been known to restore the faculty of speech to a dumb man. You see, some poor mute had either to express his feelings or bust."

Evidently Miss Evelyn Forbes would not be allowed to mope during the run to Eastbourne.

As between Theydon and herself, the situation was curiously mixed. On the one hand, Theydon had now a remarkably close insight into the peril which threatened Forbes and each member of his family; the girl, on the other, knew well that her father was bound up in some way with the tragedy at No. 17 Innesmore Mansions.

Nevertheless, an open discussion was out of the question, and the two accepted cheerfully the limitations imposed by circumstances, so that the strangers in the compartment little suspected what grave issues lay behind an apparently casual meeting between a pretty girl and two men that summer's afternoon in the Eastbourne express.

The American played his part admirably. When not passing some caustically humorous comment on British ways and manners he was being even more critical of his fellow-countrymen.

As he himself put it, he guessed New York society was mighty like London society with the head cut off, and proved his contention with many wise saws and modern instances.

Thus the journey south passed pleasantly enough. When they alighted the girl reverted to the topic uppermost in her mind.

"You gentlemen will have to look after your luggage," she said. "I'm sure you will forgive me if I hurry to the hotel. If you come there, Mr. Theydon, I'll take care that I see you at once. It is exceedingly kind of you to bother with my affairs."

But Theydon had a scheme ready, having foreseen this very difficulty.

"Mr. Handyside will attend to everything," he said glibly. "Please let me come with you. I shan't have a moment's peace until assured that Mrs. Forbes is suffering from little more than a slight indisposition."

Evelyn looked puzzled, but was willing to agree to anything so long as she reached her mother quickly. Handyside, too, made matters easy by lifting his hat and walking off in the direction of the luggage van.

"Well," she said, "I really don't care what happens if only I lose no time."

Suiting the action to the word, she hurried toward the exit, and was murmuring something that sounded like an apology for her seeming brusqueness as they passed the ticket collector. Here a momentary difficulty arose. Theydon had forgotten to ask Handyside for his ticket. The girl, of course, had her own ticket, but her companion was not allowed to pass the barrier. He began an explanation to which a busy official paid no heed. In desperation, he produced a sovereign, and his card.

"Here," he said, "you can hold this as a guarantee that my ticket will be given up. This lady has been called to the bedside of her mother, who is said to be dangerously ill, and I simply must be allowed to take her to the Royal Devonshire Hotel."

Luckily, the railwayman had the wit to see that this earnest-eyed passenger was speaking the truth.

"That's all right, sir," he said. "We have to be very particular about tickets, you know."

Evelyn Forbes was a few yards in advance, and impatiently awaiting her escort, when a gentleman approached and spoke to her.

178

"Miss Forbes, I believe," he said, raising his hat.

"Yes," she answered breathlessly, because the man's garb suggested, before he uttered another syllable, that he was a doctor. He had a curiously foreign aspect, and spoke with a pronounced lisp.

"I am assistant to Dr. Sinnett," he said, "and he has sent me to take you to the hotel. This is his car. Will you come, quick?"

He pointed to a smart limousine drawn up near the exit, and, in his eagerness to be polite, almost pushed the girl toward the open door. Insensibly, she resisted, and turned to explain matters to Theydon, who had just placated the Cerberus at the gate, and was running after her.

"Mr. Theydon—" she began.

"There ith no time to wathe, I athure you," said Dr. Sinnett's assistant imperatively. At that instant Theydon came up. His temper was ruffled, and he did not scrutinize the doctor's appearance as closely as might be looked for in one who was actually on his guard against foul play.

"What is it now?" he asked.

"This gentleman has been sent by Dr. Sinnett to take me to the hotel," said Evelyn. "Now, Mr. Theydon, perhaps it will be better that you wait for Mr. Handyside and come on at your leisure."

"I'm a stiff-necked person," said Theydon, trying to smile unconcernedly. "I've made up my mind to see you safely to your destination, and I refuse to leave you on any account. I am sure the doctor will let me sit beside the chauffeur."

Then, for the first time, he glanced at the newcomer, and was almost stupefied to discover that the man, despite his faultless professional attire, was a Chinaman. Moreover, this Chinaman bore a livid scar down the left side of his face, and his eyes were set horizontally, a sure sign of Manchu descent, because all Southern Chinese have the oblique Mongolian eye. Though prepared for treachery of some kind, the very simplicity of this scheme almost disconcerted him, and he blurted out the first words that rose to his lips.

"Is your name Wong Li Fu?"

Half unconsciously, a hand dropped to the pocket containing the revolver. For answer, he was struck a violent blow in the throat and sent sprawling. The attack was so sudden that he was nearly unprepared for it— nearly, not quite, because a flicker of baffled spite in the dark eyes gave him the ghost of a warning.

It was fortunate that he saved himself by a slight backward flinching, since he learnt subsequently that his assailant was a master of jiu jitsu, and that vicious blow was intended to paralyze the nerves which cluster around the cricoid cartilage. Had he received the punch in its full force he would at least have been disabled for the remainder of the day, while there was some chance of the injury proving fatal.

The Chinaman instantly seized the terrified girl in an irresistible grip, and was about to thrust her into the automobile when a big, burly man flung himself into the fray and collared the desperado by neck and arm.

"Stop that!" he said authoritatively. "Let go that young lady or I'll shake the life out of you!"

By this time Theydon was on his feet again, and rushing to the assistance of Chief Inspector Winter, who seemed to have miraculously dropped from the skies at the right moment. The Chinaman, seeing that he was in imminent danger of capture, released Evelyn, wrenched himself free by another jiu jitsu trick, swung the girl into Winter's arms, thus impeding him, and leaped into the car, which made off with a rapidity that showed how thoroughly the chauffeur was in league with his principal.

Naturally, the people coming out from the station, reinforced by the mob of semi-loafers always in evidence in such localities, gathered in scores around Evelyn Forbes and her two protectors. Such an extraordinary scuffle was bound to attract a crowd; few had seen the commencement of the fray, because nothing could be more usual and commonplace in a fashionable place like Eastbourne than the sight of a frock-coated and top-hatted gentleman handing a well-dressed lady into a motor car.

The first general intimation of something bizarre and sensational was provided by Theydon's fall. After that, events traveled rapidly, and the majority of the onlookers imagined that it was Winter who had knocked Theydon off his balance, while the rush made by the latter to intercept Wong Li Fu was actually stopped by a well-intentioned railway porter.

Worst of all, Theydon was quite unable to speak. He indulged in valiant pantomime, and Winter fully understood that the Chinaman's escape should be prevented at all hazards. But the chief inspector accepted the inevitable.

The limousine was equipped with a powerful engine, and the only vehicles available for pursuit were some ancient horse-drawn cabs. He noted the number on the identification plate, and that was the limit of his resources for the moment.

Moreover, Evelyn Forbes, finding herself clutched tightly by a tall, stout man whom she had never seen before, was rather more indignant than hurt.

Disengaging herself from the detective's hands, she looked to Theydon for an explanation.

"Has everybody suddenly gone mad?" she said vehemently. "What is the meaning of this? Did you know who that man was? And why did he try to force me into the car?"

Theydon, slowly regaining his breath, stammered brokenly that he would make things clear in a minute or so. Then he gasped to Winter:

"That is Wong Li Fu—the man wanted—at No. 17!"

"We'll get him all right," was the grimly curt answer. "Meanwhile, are you and Miss Forbes going to the hotel?"

Hardly less surprising than Winter's appearance on the scene was his seeming knowledge of the purpose of their journey.

"We must get out of this," he went on, gazing around wrathfully at the ring of curious faces. "Here, you!" he cried, singling out a policeman who was forcing a passage through the crowd, "clear away this mob and get us a cab!"

The policeman seemed inclined to resent the masterful directions, but a word whispered in his ear when he reached Winter acted like magic, and he soon had the gapers scattered.

A cab was called, and Evelyn Forbes was already inside when Theydon remembered the American. He looked around, but could see nothing of him.

"Where is—Mr. Handyside?" he said, still finding a good deal of difficulty in articulating his words.

"Is that the man who came with you from London?" inquired Winter.

"Yes. He's—an American."

"Well, he may have been scared, and made a bee-line for the States. He is not anywhere in sight."

"O, please, Mr. Theydon, do let us go to the hotel," pleaded Evelyn. She was pale, and yielding to reaction after the excitement of the fracas.

Unwillingly, since he was certain now that there was absolutely no ground for the girl's alarm on her mother's account—at any rate, so far as illness was concerned—Theydon entered the cab, and Winter followed.

"The first thing to do," said the chief inspector, when they were *en route,* "is to assure this young lady, whom I take to be Miss Forbes, that she has probably been brought to Eastbourne by a lying telegram, and that her mother is quite well in health. Secondly, why should Wong Li Fu be described as the man wanted in the Innesmore Mansions inquiry; and, thirdly, how does Mr. Handyside come into the picture?''

"I can't—talk—just yet," wheezed Theydon hoarsely. "In a few minutes—I'll—tell you everything."

Evelyn had not realized earlier that her self-appointed champion had been seriously hurt. She was deeply concerned, and wanted to take him straight to the nearest doctor.

But he smiled and essayed to calm her fears by whispering that he would soon be fully recovered. It was pleasant to know that he had succeeded in rescuing her from some indefinable though none the less deadly peril, yet the insistent question in his subconscious mind was not connected with Evelyn's escape, or the flight of her assailant, or the mysterious presence of the chief inspector, but with the vanishing of Mr. Handyside.

What had become of him? It was the maddest of fantasies to imagine that he could be bound up in some way with the Young Manchus. Yet why did he fail to turn up at the station?

Theydon could not even guess at a plausible explanation. He leaned back in the cab and closed his eyes. Really, there were times in life when it would be a relief to faint!

CHAPTER X

THOUGH Theydon was in first-rate athletic trim, that blow on the throat had nearly stunned him. The effort to rise promptly and bear a hand in the imminent capture of one whom he regarded as something akin to a homicidal maniac had imposed a further strain on his resources, and it was possible that he did actually lose his senses during a couple of seconds.

In all likelihood, too, he changed color slightly, because the next thing he was aware of was the note of alarm in Evelyn's voice when she cried excitedly:

"Mr. Theydon is really very ill. I'm sure we ought to try and revive him."

At that he reopened his eyes and looked at her whimsically. Nature, in fact, had put forth a supreme effort; from that moment he recovered rapidly.

Winter took a calmly professional view of the younger man's collapse.

"There's nothing to worry about, Miss Forbes," he assured the agitated girl. "Our friend has just escaped being knocked insensible, if not killed. He was hardly prepared for such a vicious attack, I fancy. Most certainly that scoundrel took me by surprise, or he would not have slipped through my fingers like an eel. Next time, either Mr. Theydon or I may be trusted to balance matters.''

Theydon grinned and nodded. He signaled with his eyes that Winter was to make Evelyn Forbes understand that she had just escaped being the victim of an extraordinary outrage. Muddled as his thoughts were, he grasped the essential fact that Scotland Yard was better posted in the secret history of the Innesmore Mansions crime than he had given the department credit for before the dramatic meeting with Furneaux that morning.

And, indeed, the chief inspector lost no time in justifying that belief.

''You must have imagined that the world had suddenly turned topsy-turvy,'' he said, smiling at the mystified and distraught Evelyn, as though the whirl of events outside the station were part and parcel of the humdrum routine of life. ''When Mr. Theydon regains his speech he will tell us how he came to suspect that an attempt would be made to kidnap you today. In my own case, intervention was the outcome of sheer and simple logical deduction. You see, I repre-

sent the Criminal Investigation Department—
or Scotland Yard, as it is familiarly described
—and I have reason to believe that your father
is, and has been for some time, the object of
unpleasant attentions by a political society in
China, whose members are nothing more nor
less than criminal fanatics. Probably this is
the first you have heard of the matter, Miss
Forbes. Your father would wish, no doubt, to
keep any such disquieting knowledge from you
and your mother. But the policy of concealment must cease now. Today's daring attack
is a warning. Other efforts may be forthcoming. If you are to be protected efficiently
the police must have your loyal coöperation.
I admit candidly that I myself, with all
my experience, was taken off my guard a
few minutes ago. If Mr. Theydon had not
delayed that Chinaman—whose name he has
got hold of from Mr. Forbes, I expect—I
don't think I could have reached you in
time.''

''Is that the meaning of the little ivory
skull which my father received at breakfast
this morning?'' said Evelyn, breathlessly.

Winter's eyes twinkled. No question could
have thrown a more vivid light into the
somber depths of a crime which promised to
transcend in interest and importance any
similar occurrence in Great Britain during
the previous decade.

"Doubtless," he said. "Of course, I have not yet seen Mr. Forbes, but we have a mine of information here,"-and he laid a friendly hand on Theydon's arm. "So far as I am concerned, I have had your house unobtrusively watched—for the protection of the inmates, I hope you understand—and I arranged also that anything unusual in the shape of telegrams or telephonic messages"— here he glanced amusedly at Theydon— "should be communicated to the Yard. I heard, therefore, of Mrs. Forbes's sudden illness almost as soon as you did, and I traveled with you to Eastbourne, intending to reach the hotel at the same time as you, and ascertain whether or not your mother was really ill. I saw you on the platform at Victoria and guessed your identity. But, in my profession, we never take anything for granted, so I left that matter until I could interview the hotel manager. And here we are. I advise you not to say a word about Mrs. Forbes being ill. If, as I firmly believe, you find that she is in the best of health, you can explain your sudden visit by saying that Mr. Theydon and I have something of importance to communicate, which will be perfectly accurate, as I mean to urge strongly that we all return to London by the next train."

The cab stopped. To show that "Richard was himself again" Theydon, nearest the door, opened it, got out, and helped Evelyn to alight.

Reassured on his account, the girl smiled, and a wave of color leaped to her cheeks. Any one happening to watch their arrival would put them down as ordinary visitors. Evelyn Forbes was just a charming young woman, plainly but expensively dressed; Theydon an attentive cavalier, and Winter a prosperous city man, probably with a taste for coursing and pheasant shooting.

Subtly observant, indeed, would be the theorist who gathered from their demeanor that they had just emerged practically un-scathed from a situation rife with the elements of tragedy.

Nevertheless, Winter kept a sharp eye on Theydon after Evelyn Forbes had run up the steps of the hotel, and was relieved at seeing that he could walk without assistance.

"Keep nothing back," he said under his breath as they followed the girl with sedater pace. "These women must be frightened into complete obedience. Did Furneaux get hold of Forbes?"

Theydon nodded.

"That's right. Don't talk. I can pretty well guess what took place. But, look here. Who's Handyside—a mere acquaintance?"

Another nod.

"You just contrived to pick him up, and

used him as an excuse for coming to East-bourne? I see. That removes a troublesome pawn off the chessboard."

"But it doesn't," wheezed Theydon. "He ought to be here. Can't make out—what has become of him."

"He will turn up—an American, isn't he? I thought so. The indications were slight but certain—features, walk, figure. You can buy clothes, but the genuine citizen of God's own country is as distinct a type as a Highlander —all wool and a yard wide."

Inside the hotel they came on Evelyn Forbes talking to the manager. She hailed them at once.

"Mother has gone to Beachy Head," she cried. "She and her friends are expected home about six o'clock. Shall we have some tea? There is no use in following her. She will be starting back before we could get there."

"Mrs. Forbes is quite well, I hope?" put in Winter, casually.

"Yes, sir, in the best of health," said the manager, indicating, with a flourish of both hands, that nothing else was to be expected as to the condition of any among the numerous patrons of the Royal Devonshire Hotel.

Evelyn asked that tea should be served in her mother's sitting room. When they were screened by the closed door Winter examined Theydon's throat. Beyond a slight swelling and external soreness, the cricoid cartilage—known to the multitude as Adam's apple—was seemingly uninjured, while Theydon himself now made light of the blow, though a certain hoarseness was perceptible in his voice, and he deemed it advisable to speak in a low-pitched tone.

Evelyn Forbes listened with ill-repressed bewilderment while he related the day's doings. At first, she hardly grasped the significance of the story, but Winter's occasional questions and comments, and a parenthetical sentence or two introduced by Theydon for her benefit, quickly revealed the astounding nature of the plot of which her father was the chief object.

At this crisis she displayed a self-control and reticence which were admirable. She seemed to realize intuitively that any gaps in the recital could be filled in later, whereas it was all-important that the detective should be made acquainted as speedily as possible with the developments brought about by the morning's fuller disclosures.

As for Winter, he was keenly interested in Furneaux's behavior at the moment of Forbes's departure from Innesmore Mansions. Glancing at his watch, he rose when Theydon's revelations came to an end.

"I'll just go and ring up the Yard," he said. "There may be news. When Furneaux starts off in full cry it is a wary fox that escapes him. I only wish you and I had traveled from Victoria in company, Mr. Theydon; Wong Li Fu would now have been in custody. However, we'll get him. If, as I imagine, he is making for London in that car, there is even a chance of intercepting him in the suburbs. I'll see to it."

Left alone with Evelyn Forbes, Theydon suddenly grew tongue-tied. This man who could invent all manner of glib conversation for the characters in his novels now cudgeled his brains vainly for something to say that would dwell in her memory when they parted. And he knew why a cloud was thus effectually befogging his wits. He had only seen Evelyn three times in as many days, had spoken to her but twice, yet was hopelessly and irrevocably in love with her.

He, who had so often and so thrillingly described the grand passion of a man's life, had now fallen a victim to it, only to feel how unutterably ridiculous and impossible was the wild longing that had sprung up in his heart. Here, by his side, wistfully sympathetic and friendly in manner, sat the "one woman in the world," yet he felt awkward and constrained, and took refuge in a vague expression of anxiety on behalf of Handyside, a man who at least might be trusted to extricate himself safely from the labyrinth of Eastbourne!

The girl, of course, attributed these disjointed remarks to physical suffering. In reality, he was contrasting her wealth and his own comparative poverty, and bidding himself fiercely not to be a vain fool!

"Don't you think you ought to call in a doctor?" she inquired, tenderly.

"No, no," he hastened to assure her. "The effects of the blow are passing rapidly. In another hour I shall hardly feel it at all. I'm afraid, Miss Forbes," he ventured to add, "that when this piratical gang is broken up, as certainly will be the case now that the English police are tackling it, you will associate our brief acquaintance with the only dark days in your existence."

"Why do you say that?" she demanded.

"Because I am bound to admit that if I had not dined at your house on Monday evening, many, if not all, of the amazing events of the past thirty-six hours could not have happened."

"I don't agree with you—not one little bit," she protested emphatically. "Why, the detective-man himself said that the Young Manchus have been searching ever since the beginning of the year for proof of Dad's connection with the revolutionaries, and he was candid enough to tell us that if it hadn't been for you that horrid Wong Li Fu would have got me into the car. No, Mr. Theydon, our meeting has proved most fortunate for me. Suppose I had really been captured! Would he have gagged me and taken me away to some lonely place, where I would be kept a prisoner, or even killed?''

Theydon had no desire that her mind should dwell on such a harrowing topic. He shuddered to think of her fate if ever she fell into the hands of the miscreants who had not scrupled to murder Mrs. Lester. She evidently regarded the crime in No. 17 Innesmore Mansions as the sequel to some political disturbance in far-off Shanghai. It had not occurred to her that a hapless woman had been done to death merely as a warning to her father of the fate in store for him and his if he did not yield to the demand of the reactionary party in China, and deliver over to their vengeance some hundreds of the leading men in that distressed country.

''I doubt whether Wong Li Fu and his associates would have dared to offer you any real violence,'' he said. ''At the worst, I suppose, they might have retained you as a hostage.''

''A hostage for what?''

''For their claim against Mr. Forbes.''

"But what has he done? He has never been in China.".

"He is a power in the financial world. If the reform party cannot borrow money the movement will collapse. At any rate that is what the Manchus believe, and they will strain every nerve to effect their purpose."

"But why did they kill poor Mrs. Lester?"

Theydon felt that he was getting into deep water. This clear-sighted girl would soon have the various threads of the enigma in her hands, and then she could not fail but discover the true meaning of Edith Lester's death.

"That phase of the problem has yet to be solved," was his noncommittal reply.

Winter rejoined them somewhat hurriedly. He looked puzzled and rather irritated.

"Furneaux has made an arrest," he said. "A Chinaman, described as Len Shi, is lodged in the cells at Bow Street, on a charge of being concerned in the Innesmore Mansions murder. Furneaux is out, and that is all they know at the Yard. What I cannot understand is why no inquiry has been made by telephone or otherwise concerning Miss Forbes's flight to Eastbourne."

The words had hardly left his mouth when the bell of a telephone on the table jangled. The coincidence was so peculiar that Winter laughed.

"Some other person shares my opinion, I fancy," he said. "May I answer, Miss Forbes?"

"Please do," said the girl, and the chief inspector lifted the receiver from its hook.

"Trunk call from London; you're through," announced the hotel operator. After a slight pause, an agitated voice said: "Is that you, Evelyn?"

"Miss Forbes is here," said Winter. "Who is speaking?"

"Her father," was the reply.

"Oh, I'm Chief Inspector Winter of Scotland Yard. Your daughter is quite safe, Mr. Forbes. Mr. Theydon and I accompanied her from London. She will speak to you in an instant. Would you mind telling me what happened at one o'clock, when my colleague, Mr. Furneaux, jumped on to your car and went in pursuit of some one?"

"First, is Mrs. Forbes there, too?"

"She is out with a picnic party on Beachy Head. We expect her back before six o'clock. I propose bringing her and Miss Forbes to London tonight. They will be safer in your house than in Eastbourne, as you will probably agree when you hear what a narrow escape your daughter had this afternoon from being kidnaped by Wong Li Fu."

"Great Heavens! Evelyn in danger from that scoundrel!"

"Yes. But all is well, believe me. Owing
to Mr. Theydon's promptitude and pertinacity, Wong Li Fu's scheme was defeated.
Your daughter will make everything clear.
Give me the barest summary of events after
your departure from Innesmore Mansions, and
I'll get out of the way."

"We pursued a car which led us à pretty
dance nearly as far as St. Albans. It seems
that Mr. Furneaux, looking out of the window
of Mr. Theydon's flat while Theydon and I
were going downstairs, saw a Chinaman
watching us from a closed car standing in
the cross street at the end of the garden. He
gave chase instantly, but as soon as the man
realized that he had attracted notice he tried
to escape. At least, that was Mr. Furneaux's
first impression. Later, he convinced himself
that the supposed spy was little more than a
red herring drawn across the trail, and that
the man's real motive was to take me out
of London, or waylay or detain me in some
fashion, since it was manifestly impossible
that my presence in the Mansions should be
known to any one. I see now, of course,
what the project was. If, as I gather from
you, an attempt was to be made to capture
my daughter on arriving at Eastbourne, it
was all-important for the conspirators that
I should not know of her absence from home
until after the arrival of the train, so that

198

I could not communicate with the hotel and take measures to protect her. But that explanation was hidden from Mr. Furneaux, and the first glimpse of it vouchsafed to me was when I reached my office and was horrified to learn that she had gone away without my knowledge. However, in a desperate matter like this, I must not waste time by describing my agony and foreboding. As I have said, by some phenomenal method of reasoning beyond my comprehension, Mr. Furneaux did arrive at a sound conclusion. I suppose he was alive to the ridiculous aimlessness of the race across country. My car is powerful and speedy, but the Chinaman had a thoroughly up-to-date conveyance, too, and drove without paying the least heed to traffic conditions."

"There was only one man, then?"

"Yes. Didn't I make that clear? Perhaps not. But there can hardly be any doubt that this fellow was alone, and acting as a sort of scout or vedette. We had the utmost difficulty in following him along Oxford Street, and I am sure that my chauffeur has been reported by a score of constables on point duty for exceeding the speed limit and disregarding signals to halt. To come to the material facts, the chase took us up the Edgware road. We tore along at a tremendous rate after passing the Welsh Harp. Overhaul the fellow we could not, until on the

outskirts of St. Albans, when he deliberately
slowed up, as though to allow us to pass.
Mr. Furneaux flew at him like a terrier
grappling a rat, but the man made no resistance. He is undoubtedly a Chinaman,
though attired in a chauffeur's livery, and
he could handle a car in first-rate style, too.
His pidgin English was difficult to understand,
and Mr. Furneaux shared my view that he
did not try to render himself intelligible.
We gathered that he was obeying his
master's orders in trying the car, a new one,
before purchase, but Furneaux bundled him
off to the nearest police station, borrowed
handcuffs and brought him back to London,
leaving the car in a garage at St. Albans.
That is a bald but accurate summary of the
facts. I dropped Mr. Furneaux and his
prisoner at Bow Street and was on the way
to my city office, when I suddenly felt faint
for want of food, as I ate hardly any
breakfast this morning, and only drank a
cup of coffee in Mr. Theydon's place.
So I returned to the Carlton, where I
met a friend, a business associate, who remained for a chat while I had a meal. This
trivial accident prevented me from telephoning to my house, though, naturally, I
had no misgivings as to my daughter's well-
being. Even then I was detained unduly,
because my friend and I went to another

office in the city, and two more hours elapsed before I reached my own place. Then, and not until then, did I hear of Evelyn's journey and its cause."

"Thank you, Mr. Forbes," said Winter quietly. "We seem to have made a forward move today. Before calling Miss Evelyn to the phone I want to tell you that in disobeying your orders to remain at home she did my department a good turn. Wong Li Fu and I were brought face to face. He is not a myth."

"My word might be regarded as sufficient proof of that fact."

"Certainly, Mr. Forbes, if given earlier," was the inevitable retort. "But here is your daughter. She can plead her cause far better than I."

Evelyn took the woman's way. To defend she attacked.

"Dad, dear," she complained, "why didn't you give me your confidence? If I had had the least notion of the dreadful things that were going on I should certainly have telephoned to Eastbourne before starting. But don't you see the diabolical cleverness of the scheme? The telegram arrived just in time to allow me to catch the 1:25 p. m. train, and rendering it idle to think of making a trunk call if I would obey an urgent message from my mother. Then again, when I reached

Eastbourne, why should I suspect a foreign-looking gentleman who said Dr. Sinnett had sent his car to take me to the hotel? There isn't a Dr. Sinnett in Eastbourne at this date, but how was I to know that? Of course, both you and I have suffered a good deal, each in a different way, but all is well that ends well, and I shall have such a lot to tell you when we meet tonight. . . . What time? I don't know yet. I'll wire or phone when mother returns and we settle about the train. Goodby, darling! See you don't go anywhere alone until I come back."

For some reason Winter's manner was not so placid as usual. He looked so obviously perplexed and troubled that Theydon, searching for a cause, suddenly remembered that the chief inspector was a great smoker.

"Won't you have a cigar?" he said; "that is, unless Miss Forbes has any objection?"

"Me!" cried the girl. "I don't object in the least."

But the Royal Devonshire Hotel's best Havana did not wholly banish the frown from Winter's forehead. More than once he glanced at his watch and consulted a time table. At last he voiced one of his anxieties.

"What can have become of that American?" he said. "He knew what hotel you were making for?"

"Oh, yes," cried the others in chorus.

They laughed. Quite a cheerful air possessed two members of the little party, at any rate.

"Perhaps he has forgotten the name?" went on Evelyn.

"Americans never forget the names of hotels, or railway stations, or steamers," said Winter. "The average Englishman can tell you what will win the Derby, but the average American will be a good deal more accurate concerning next Saturday's mail steamer. . . . So, I frankly confess it—that man's prolonged absence supplies a riddle which I can't answer. What do you say if we give a look along the front? He may be shy, though I told the hall porter that any inquirer was to be shown up at once."

No; Mr. Handyside was not to be seen on Eastbourne's spacious marine promenade. A couple of well-dressed men caught sight of Winter, and decided that they had instant and urgent business elsewhere. But he only smiled. His quarry that day was not the swell mobsman, but much more dangerous game.

Lightning darted from a summer sky when the picnic party returned from Beachy Head in three cars, but without Mrs. Forbes.

Evelyn was hardly anxious at first. The hall porter informed her who the occupants of the cars were, and she watched the lively and chattering groups forming on the pavement and breaking up again to enter the hotel and dress for dinner.

At last, realizing that her mother was not among them, she singled out a lady whom she knew, and asked for an explanation. The lady, a Mrs. Montagu, was very much surprised.

"But, my dear Evelyn," she said, "didn't you yourself send for your mother?"

The girl blanched. Some premonition of evil gripped her very heart.

"What do you mean?" she said, and the other woman could not help noting the distress in her voice.

"If you didn't send, who did?" came the immediate response. "We were just going to have tea when a gentleman, a stranger, came and asked for Mrs. Forbes. We saw him arrive in a car which halted at the foot of the path—nearly a quarter of a mile away. Your mother answered, and he said that you were in Eastbourne, and had sent him to bring you to the hotel. He said the car belonged to a Doctor Somebody, but he himself looked like a foreigner."

A few others had gathered around, attracted by Evelyn Forbes's pallor and distress; Winter, too, had drawn near, and it was he who said:

"Did you see this stranger who brought the message?"

"O yes, plainly," said Mrs. Montagu.

"Had he a scar down the left side of his face?"

"Yes."

Then Evelyn Forbes, for the first time in her vigorous young life, fainted. Her mother was in the power of Wong Li Fu. All the terrors which imagination had painted in her own behalf were redoubled as to her mother's fate. Her brain reeled. Merciful oblivion came. Theydon and Winter were just able to catch her before she fell like a log.

CHAPTER XI

CONSTERNATION reigned for a while at the entrance to the Royal Devonshire. Men craned their necks and women uttered nervous little shrieks. But Evelyn Forbes was endowed with a vigorous frame and a splendidly vital spirit, and she recovered her senses before she could be carried into the vestibule.

The fact that she had fainted, too, brought to the aid of her waking senses the innate horror of her race and class for anything approaching a "scene," and she was almost unnaturally collected in speech and demeanor within a few seconds after her eyes had reopened.

"Did I give way like that?" she said, with a valiant smile, first at Theydon, and then at the ring of faces, each with its varying expression of curiosity or concern. "How stupid of me! How excessively stupid! That sort of behavior doesn't help at all—does it? . . . Thank you, I can walk quite well. . . . I'll just go to mother's room and telephone home. . . . There has been some silly mistake. By this time it will be rectified, I'm sure. . . . Come, Mr. Theydon. Where is Mr. Winter?"

"Here," said the detective. "I'll follow in a minute or so. Please don't communicate with London till I arrive."

His quietly insistent tone was meant rather for Theydon than for the half-demented girl, who was stumbling anywhere but in the right direction until Theydon caught her arm and led her to the lift. She contrived to remain outwardly calm until she reached the seclusion of the sitting room, when she broke into a flood of tears, while in disjointed and hysterical words she blamed her own rashness for the fate which had overtaken her mother.

If only she had used better judgment when the telegram came—if only she had hired an automobile and driven straight to Beachy Head—if only she had done a dozen other things which no one would possibly have dreamed of doing—she might have safeguarded her darling mother!

Theydon, meanwhile, was nearly frantic with the indecision of ignorance. Never had he felt so helpless, so utterly childish and unhinged in the face of disaster. He had heard that it was good for a woman to be allowed to cry when overwhelmed with misery. Again, he remembered reading some-

where that the feminine temperament should
not be allowed to yield to a too-tempestuous
grief, or the delicate and finely-balanced
female organism might suffer irreparable injury. Should she be given water or a stimulant? Should one leave her alone or endeavor to soothe her?

Heaven only knew—he didn't—so he did
exactly what any devout and despairing lover
might be expected to do—put an arm around
her shoulders, and murmured a frenzied assurance of his willingness to die several
times, and vanquish a horde of Young Manchus in the process, ere she could be allowed
to endure one needless hour of distress on
her mother's account.

Somehow, this sort of nonsense was helpful. The girl raised her swimming eyes to
his. She placed two appealing hands on his
shoulders, and said brokenly:

"Mr. Theydon—I am ready to trust you—
next to—my own father. . . . Where
shall we go? What can we do? I'll come
with you—anywhere—only—my dear one
must be rescued."

He believed afterwards that he answered
her by a kiss! He was not certain. The
delirium of the moment was such that he
could never recall its words or acts with that
precision which a well-regulated mind should
display even under the stress of intense emo-

tion. In any event, the crisis was interrupted by the clamor of the telephone bell.

Withdrawing from what was perilously near an embrace—so colorable an imitation of the real thing that Winter, entering at that instant, could make no distinction, and was secretly amazed at these strenuous methods of consoling the lady—Theydon lifted the receiver, and heard as one in a trance the telephone operator's conventional announcement:

"Trunk call from Croydon; you're through."

"Who is it?" demanded the chief inspector gruffly.

Even he, veteran fighter in the unceasing battle between the law and the malefactor, was feeling the strain of the Homeric struggle ushered in by the death of Edith Lester.

"I don't know yet," Theydon managed to say collectedly. "Some one from Croydon. Bend close. You'll hear."

A quiet, drawling voice reached them, the vibrating wire lending its measured accents a metallic accuracy.

"That you, Mr. Theydon?"

"Why, it's Mr. Handyside! Yes, I'm here. Where are you speaking from? Croydon?"

"That's so."

"Well, I don't understand, but I'm sure you'll pardon me. We are in a deuce of a fix at this end, so, if you'll arrange to call tomorrow—"

"You've lost Mrs. Forbes, I guess. Is that the lady's name? If it is, I've kept track of her. I—"

Theydon was so astounded that he looked at Winter in blank amazement, the pressure of his fingers on the circuit key relaxed, and the American's voice trailed abruptly away into silence. He put matters right at once and heard the continuation of a new sentence, whereupon he broke in excitedly:

"One second, Mr. Handyside. Miss Forbes is here. I must tell her your news!"

He turned to Evelyn.

"Hooray!" he almost yelled. "Your mother is all right. She is with Mr. Handyside. Some sort of miracle has happened. Come and listen."

Aroused from a stupor of grief as though she had received a galvanic shock, Evelyn sprang up. Naturally, she had to place an arm on Theydon's back to permit of her head approaching near enough to the telephone. Thus, the three heads were almost touching each other; if an artist had been present he would have obtained a study in facial expressions worthy of Phil May or Guerrido.

Handyside, of course, had heard Theydon's gleeful exclamation. He chuckled pleasantly:

"Your digest goes a little too far, Mr. Theydon," he said, "but compared with the newspaper placard facts in your possession, my story is a full-sized novel. Anyhow, I'll condense it, so here goes. I was back of the crowd when the circus started outside the Eastbourne depot. As I ante'd up your ticket and collected your deposit of a sovereign, I saw what took place, and sized up the result pretty accurately. The kidnaping proposition had failed, but the guy in the silk hat had got clear away in a bully good car—how good I know now. It seemed to me that, next to rescuing that charming young lady, it was important something should be known about the thug who wanted to carry her off, and, when my eyes lit on a workmanlike motor bicycle with a side-car rig standing close to the curb, and well clear of the arena, said I to myself: 'George T. Handyside, this is where you take a flier, and maybe Illinois will score one.' The man who owned the outfit was watching the commotion when I dug him in the ribs. 'Take me after that car,' I said, 'and I'll pay you a shilling a mile with five pounds on account if it's only a 100 yards.' I pressed a note into his hand—and, say, you Britishers wake up all right when you see real money! We were doing thirty per in less than ten seconds. No car on four wheels can lose any decent motorcycle on a switchback track, and Jackson, the owner of this one, says it's good enough for sixty on a fair stretch of road. Anyhow, we held the thug dead easy, but didn't press him any, as I had no call to butt in, had I?''

"Mr. Handyside," said Theydon. "I won't waste time now by telling you how grateful we all are. Get on with the knitting!''

"Sir, I've had the time of my life—a rip-snorting movie, with George T. on the film from A to Z . . . No! Go away, exchange. I'm renting this line for the next quarter of an hour. Well, we made a bee-line for Beachy Head—so Jackson told me—and, when the automobile pulled up, we got under a hedge and I did a bit of scout work on my feet. I saw Silk Hat pick out a lady from a bunch of people, who seemed to be taking the view with sandwiches, and it was simple as falling off a log to follow the position of affairs— Silk Hat urging lady to come with him, lady astonished, not able to size up exact bearings of the yarn, but finally yielding. Now, if Miss Forbes hadn't told us that her mother had written saying she was going to Beachy Head with a picnic party this afternoon I would have gotten off at the wrong address, because I could hardly have failed to believe that Silk Hat was picking up a female accomplice. But, as things stood, I suspicioned that, failing the daughter, he was putting up a bunco tale for the mother—a situation new, I believe, in the realm of romantic fiction. I

thought it was up to me to play a strong
hand, so I threw a few facts on the screen
for Jackson's benefit, and he straightway hit
the pike in pursuit. Where the country was
open we kept well in the rear, but crept closer
in villages and towns. We had to stop at
Tunbridge Wells for petrol, but that didn't cut
any ice, because Jackson knew the country like
a book, and we sighted the automobile within
five minutes, though the milestones were pretty
numerous during that run. After that, nothing
particularly happened, except to a hen and a
dog, until we came near Croydon—that is, I
knew it was Croydon because Jackson said so,
and I have considerable faith in him. In between whiles, where there was nothing doing,
he and I fixed up an automobile tour. Well,
outside Croydon, there's a new road, with a
half-built villa at the near end and a way-back
farmhouse at the other end. That villa was
the one thing needed when the thug made a
bee-line for the farm. I jumped out, told
Jackson to find something to do to his machine at the corner of the next block, and
hurried into the Alpine chalet. From a top
back room I watched Silk Hat carrying a lady
into the farm. Eh, what's that? Yes, he was
carrying her. I guess he'd given her a dope
so as to stop any cry for help. It made
me feel pretty mean to be standing there
without taking a hand in the deal, but

I forced myself to believe that another hour or two couldn't make such a heap of difference to the lady, while it would be better to leave things to the police. I waited just twenty minutes—I have all the times scheduled—until the car came back. By hurrying downstairs I was able to look inside as it passed, and Silk Hat was alone. He took the London road. I strolled out—didn't dare to hurry, you know, in case any one might be watching from the farm—and put in some hard thinking while walking to Jackson's stand. There were two courses open, either to send Jackson after the auto and try myself to get in touch with you and the police, or put Jackson on guard near the farm. Whether I decided rightly or not I haven't a notion, but I let the car go, and for this reason: We know where the lady is, and so does the thug; if the police put up a hard game they can rescue her without his knowledge and spread a web for the fly to walk into later. But they must get a move on. This phone is nearly a mile from the farm, and Jackson is tightening nuts outside the villa I spoke of. Now, what's the next item on the program?"

Winter grabbed the receiver unceremoniously.

"I am a representative of Scotland Yard, Mr. Handyside," he said. "If ever you want work come to me, J. L. Winter, and I'll find you some. Miss Forbes is vexed with me because I have stopped her from thanking you, but compliments must wait. Will you go as quickly as possible to the chief police station at Croydon? By the time you get there I'll be in touch with the inspector in charge, and he will do the rest. You understand? Goodby!''

Winter rang off. He smiled blandly at Evelyn.

''There's no opportunity now for sentiment,'' he explained. ''Our American friend will appreciate quick action far more than talk.''

Then he tackled the telephone again and asked to be put through to the Croydon police station.

''There must be no delay,'' he added. ''This is an official call.''

He was in touch with Croydon in a remarkably short space of time, and soon was in communication with a police inspector.

''What's your name?'' he demanded.

''Inspector Wilkins,'' came the surprised answer.

''Were you a sergeant at the time of the Surrey Bank robbery?''

''Yes; but what the—''

''I am Winter of Scotland Yard. Do you recognize my voice?''

215

"Well—er—"

"Do you remember that nip of old brandy I gave you while we were freezing in a drafty warehouse at three o'clock in the morning waiting for the Smasher to come for his plant?"

"Yes. You're Mr. Winter right enough, sir."

"Good! I want you to believe what I'm going to tell you, as there is a big job ahead. A gang of Chinese cutthroats have kidnaped a lady, wife of the London banker, Mr. James Creighton Forbes. In a few minutes an American, a Mr. Handyside, will be with you. He will point out the house near Croydon to which the lady has been taken in a motor car. Collect half a dozen plain-clothes men and two in uniform and go with Mr. Handyside—without attracting attention, of course. Surround the house and arrest any one, especially any Chinaman, who attempts to leave. Release the lady, and ask Mr. Handyside to escort her to her home, 11 Fortescue Square, Belgravia. If she is very ill, which is improbable, she should be taken to a hospital. In that event Mr. Handyside should telephone Mr. Forbes. Occupy the farm and arrest any one who comes there, no matter what the pretext, until Mr. Furneaux or I arrive. I'll be with you in two hours. Tell Mrs. Forbes that her daughter will set out from Eastbourne by the next train leaving after 6:30. Got all that?"

"Yes, sir! Are these Chinamen likely to show fight?"

"Better be prepared. But, after posting your sentries, I advise you and the uniformed constables to rush the place. By the way, it will save me some trouble if you phone the Yard and tell them exactly what I have told you. Ask for Furneaux. If he is not in, instruct them to leave a written record for him."

"I'll see to it, sir. Is that all?"

"Yes. Goodby! Meet you in two hours." He whirled round on Theydon.

"Tell the manager to supply at once the best car to be had in Eastbourne for love or money," he said. "I want something that is sure to go and go fast."

The chief inspector, with full steam up, was energy personified. His bulging eyes, his firm chin, his round fists, one clenching the telephone instrument, the other resting on the table, were eloquent of the man of action.

His pride had been sore stricken by the escape of Wong Li Fu when that master scoundrel was actually in his grasp. But those powerful hands of his were far-reaching, and it would go hard with the jiu-jitsu expert when next they gripped his lithe frame.

Almost before Theydon had quitted the room Winter snapped—there is no other word for it—literally snapped a question at Evelyn.

"What's your telephone number?"

She told him, and again the Eastbourne exchange was bidden exert itself.

"That you, Mr. Forbes?" said the chief inspector, after a short wait.

"Yes."

"I am Winter, of Scotland Yard. I want to assure you that your wife and daughter will be under your roof within the next three hours. Mrs. Forbes will probably be escorted by a gentleman named Handyside, an American. You owe him all possible thanks, because it is due to his action alone that Mrs. Forbes will soon be rescued from captivity. Yes, she was carried off from Beachy Head this afternoon by Wong Li Fu, but, by the rarest good fortune, this Mr. Handyside, a friend of Mr. Theydon's, was able to follow on the trail, and steps are now being taken to free her. Your daughter will speak to you. I intervened merely to vouch for it that an almost incredible story is true. By the way, let no one know that Mrs. Forbes is in London. Warn your servants not to speak of her return. One more word—have you heard anything of Furneaux?"

"I have not heard from or seen him since we parted outside Bow Street police station.

But, for Heaven's sake, what is this you tell me about my wife?"

"Miss Forbes will give you all the particulars we possess. Be calm and remain at home. You can best assist us by stopping within call. Mrs. Forbes and the American should arrive first, possibly before 7:30. If there is any hitch, which is unlikely, Mr. Handyside will telephone you. Your daughter will tell you the hour she and Mr. Theydon should reach Victoria. She will speak to you now. Excuse my abruptness. A lot of things may happen before I retire for the night, and I have no time to pick and choose my words.'"

Evelyn, able at last to pour out her soul in thanksgiving, nearly broke down when she heard her father's voice.

"Oh, Dad," she wailed, "I've passed through a dreadful time since I spoke to you shortly after five o'clock. I dropped as if I had been shot when Mrs. Montagu, who was one of the picnic party, told me that a man of foreign appearance, with a scar on the left side of his face, and who said he was a doctor, came to Beachy Head and told poor mother that I had sent for her."

She went on to relate such facts as were known to her, and was in the midst of a sensational narrative when Theydon announced that a high-powered touring car was in readiness.

219

"Won't you take us with you?" he said to Winter. "There is no train from here till 7:30, and in a motor we should be well on the way to London by that time."

Winter had anticipated some such request, and a prompt refusal was on the tip of his tongue, when he recalled that he would pass through Tunbridge Wells, whence an earlier train might be available. A glance at the time table showed that a train left Tunbridge Wells at 7:15.

"Yes," he said. "I'll take you part of the way. Tell your father, Miss Forbes, that you will arrive at London Bridge at 8:40. If you two reach London by a different route I think you should be tolerably safe."

"If any Chinaman shows up between here and Fortescue Square I'll shoot him at sight," Theydon said, producing an automatic pistol.

"I wouldn't do that," smiled Winter. "You might bore a hole in some perfectly innocent Celestial. But you won't be troubled. Wong Li Fu carries out his own plans, and at present he is congratulating himself on the possession of a valuable hostage. But, come along! How about a wrap for you, Miss Forbes? We'll create a breeze, you know."

She ran into her mother's bedroom and came out with a fur coat and motor veil, articles which, she had guessed correctly, her

mother would not be wearing for the short
run to Beachy Head. The hotel manager lent
coats to the men, and they started, not
without hearty congratulations from several
people in the porch, whose fears on Mrs.
Forbes's account Theydon had dissipated when
he went out to order the car.

Winter gave their thoughts a new direction
when Theydon inquired what means the authorities would adopt to rid the country of
the pestiferous gang which carried on its
vendetta with such scant respect for the law
and order of Great Britain.

"Once we have Mr. and Mrs. Forbes and
this young lady safely housed in Fortescue
Square, and protected, not only by their own
servants but by the Metropolitan Police, we
will devote ourselves to routing out the whole
crew," he announced. "My idea is that when
we lay hands on the ringleader, the rest will
be easy. Furneaux's prisoner, Len Shi, may be
got to talk when a Chinese interpreter tackles
him. Again, there is every prospect of an
important capture being made in the Croydon house. Most important of all is the prolonged absence from the yard of Furneaux.
He is busy, or he would have put in an appearance there hours ago, if only to get to
know my whereabouts. That means something. Furneaux never wastes time. Usually
we hunt in couples. Today, by the fortune of

war, we are separated, and perhaps fortunately so. It is all your fault, Mr. Theydon.''

"Mine?" was the astonished cry.

"Yes. We had to try all sorts of tricks on you before you would speak. Just imagine Scotland Yard being compelled to tap the telephone of a respectable and well-known author before he would own up to such knowledge as he possessed of the murder in No. 17!''

So that was how Furneaux had played the necromancer, and was able to mystify Theydon that morning.

The chief inspector, by raising the question, was touching on dangerous ground, as he was well aware, but he was determined now that all barriers should be thrown down. Evelyn Forbes was no bread-and-butter miss from whose cognizance the evil things of life must be sedulously averted. A woman of spirit and intelligence, who had already run the dreadful risk of sharing Mrs. Lester's fate, should be made to understand every phase of the difficulty with which the Criminal Investigation Department had yet to deal.

British law and Chinese anarchy would soon grapple in a life and death conflict, and it was idle folly to suppose that, no matter how reticent her friends might be, this sharp-witted girl would not find out for herself the exact nature of the link which bound the fortunes of her own family with those of the dead woman.

Theydon tried to pass off the detective's retort with a careless laugh, but Evelyn reverted to the topic when they were seated in the London-bound train after Winter had dropped them at Tunbridge Wells Station.

"What did the chief inspector mean when he said you refused to help him at first?" she inquired. "There are gaps in my history of this affair. How did you come to know that my father was acquainted with Mrs. Lester? Why did you seem, at one time, to be taking sides with my father against a public inquiry by the police?"

Then, seeing there was no help for it, Theydon began at the beginning and told the girl the full, true and unexpurgated story of events on the Monday night. Once or twice, when he hinted at the cause of his otherwise inexplicable actions—which, quite obviously, lay in his interest in the girl herself, she blushed a little and averted her eyes. But she listened in silence, and did not speak during many seconds after he had ceased.

Then she simply murmured:

"Poor, dear Dad! How worried he must have been! And how well he concealed it from me!"

After another pause, she added:

"We are deeply in your debt, Mr. Theydon.

When this ordeal is ended, and those horrid men have been put in prison or driven out of the country, our next difficulty will be to—to thank you adequately for what you have done.''

Surgit amari aliquid! Even in life's pleasantest hours something bitter arises. Theydon was in the company of the woman he loved, yet no word of love could rise to his lips. In the first place he dared not woo the daughter of a millionaire; in the second were his suit even possible, he was far too honorable minded to take immediate advantage of her disturbed state and the services he had undoubtedly rendered, and give the slightest hint of his passion.

So he sighed and looked out of the window at a fast-flying vista of a Kentish hillside, and contented himself by saying:

''For what little I have done, or attempted to do, I am already rewarded far beyond my wildest dreams.''

Even that was more than he meant to say. Glancing timidly at Evelyn to see whether or not she resented his words, he was astounded to find that she had blushed scarlet, and, in her turn, was absorbed in the landscape.

Then he remembered that in the frenzy of the moment following the report of her mother's capture by Wong Li Fu, he had kissed her. Had he, or had he not? If not, why not now? But that way lay madness.

And, wretched doubt, was she already the promised bride of another man? It was a relief when the train stopped at Sevenoaks.

When it moved on again, they were normal young people once more, and discussed various features of the Young Manchus' raid on society as though the extermination of political adversaries were a commonplace occurrence in modern England.

At last, after a journey which lived long in their minds, since even a prosaic train may follow the path to Wonderland, they arrived at London Bridge, and hummed in a taxi through streets of gaunt warehouses until the light of Westminster flashed on a Thames veiled in the blue mystery of a Summer gloaming.

The cab had hardly halted outside the Fortescue Square mansion when the door was thrown wide, and Tomlinson appeared, flanked by two stalwart footmen. The butler's face was aglow with pleasure.

"It's all right now you've come, Miss Evelyn," he said joyfully. "Mrs. Forbes arrived more than an hour ago."

But Tomlinson was in error. He did not know what tribulations loomed already through the haze of the future, or he would have laid to heart the time-honored advice to venturesome travelers:

"Never hallo till you're out of the wood!"

CHAPTER XII

NO SURRENDER

Mrs. Forbes, a slim, elegant woman, looked as if she were her daughter's elder sister. Although driven by hay fever to the seaside regularly at the beginning of the London season, she was far from being a *malade imaginaire*. She did not go willingly. Each year she hoped against hope that the annoying ailment would not make itself felt, yet no sooner was the month of May well established than for six or seven weeks she had either to drag her husband and daughter away from the metropolis or live by herself in some South Coast hotel.

She had tried Brighton, whence Mr. Forbes could travel to the city, but soon discovered that the daily train journey was not good for his health. After that, she insisted on adopting the self-denying ordinance of leaving Evelyn with her father in the town house from the middle of May till the end of June, when all three went to the Highlands.

She, of course, had not the remotest knowledge of the terrors threatening her household; a thunderbolt out of a Summer sky would have astonished her less than the indignities she endured when haled away from Eastbourne in the luxurious car which Wong Li Fu had at his command.

Theydon had been in the house nearly half an hour and was exchanging experiences with Forbes and Handyside—the latter, by virtue of his extraordinary share in the day's adventures, being admitted to the full confidence of the others—when Evelyn brought her mother into the library.

"Here is some one who positively refuses to retire for the night until she has met you, Mr. Theydon," said the girl, radiant with joy and relief, now that the shadow of death had passed, apparently forever, leaving her dear ones unscathed.

Mrs. Forbes, an aristocrat to the finger tips, greeted her guest with marked cordiality.

"I have been living during the past few hours like one of the characters one sees in the fearsome little plays produced on the stage of the Grand Guignol in Paris," she said, gazing at him with frank brown eyes singularly like her daughter's, "but I have contrived to gather one definite impression among the whirl of things, and ᴠhat is that were it not for Mr. Frank Theydon, my daughter and I would now be in as bad a predicament as two women could possibly face anywhere.''

''I was lucky enough to be of some little use, but Mr. Handyside is the lion of today's contest,'' said Theydon.

''I am grateful to both of you, how grateful I can never find words to tell, but Mr. Handyside rivals you in modesty, Mr. Theydon. He assured me that you were the *deus ex machina,* though he obtained the machine itself, and rode sixty miles to rescue me from my dragon. By the way, where is the motor cyclist—what is his name?''

''Jackson, ma'am,'' put in Handyside. ''He went back to Eastbourne—thought nothing of it. I fixed him all right. He's coming to London next week. I've hired him for a trip round the island.''

''In a side-car?'' laughed Evelyn.

''No; I guess we'll run to something more roomy.''

''Jim, dear,'' said Mrs. Forbes to her husband, ''get Mr. Jackson's address. Our thanks to him, at least, can take a tangible form. No, Evelyn, I'm not going to bed. I mean to sit up and talk. I want to hear everything. You men must smoke big strong cigars, please. If I breathe tobacco smoke I shall not fancy I want to sneeze.''

''I, for one, am simply aching to hear what happened to you,'' said Theydon.

Mrs. Forbes was equally ready to retail her trials.

"When a man who resembled a tall and well-built Japanese came to me on the Downs," she said, "I really believed him to be what he said he was—assistant to an East-bourne doctor. I never dreamed he was Chinese, not that it mattered at all where I was concerned, only one becomes quite accustomed to meeting well-dressed Japanese men in society, but hardly ever a Chinaman. I thought, too, I remembered his face, which is quite possible, since my husband tells me that this Wong Li Fu was once an attaché at the Chinese Embassy. He spoke excellent English, with a strongly marked lisp; when he said that my daughter wished to see me at the Royal Devonshire Hotel, and that a Dr. Sinnett had sent a car for my convenience, I was mainly concerned in getting him to admit the real cause of his presence, because I naturally assumed that Evelyn had met with an accident. No sooner had the car started than he seized my wrists, and gave them a queer twist, which seemer to render me powerless for a few seconds. 'If you scream or resist I hurt you—so—only very bad,' he said. I was that astonished I hardly realized what was taking place before he had my wrists and ankles strapped, tightly, but not painfully, and had placed a gag in my mouth.

'Now, you keep quiet,' he said, and showed me a horrible-looking knife, which he put on the seat between us. 'If you move at all when we pass through towns,' he went on, 'I stick this into you very deep.' Somehow, I knew that he meant to carry out his threats to the letter. At first I was more angry than hurt or even alarmed. Then I began to believe that I had fallen into the clutches of a lunatic, and grew horribly afraid. I saw that we were following the London road, and it oppressed me like a dreadful sort of nightmare to be speeding through a familiar district, a countryside dotted with the houses and estates of personal friends, and be unable to stir or utter a sound. It seemed to be almost stupid to see policemen in the streets of Tunbridge Wells, one of whom gazed into our car sharply, because, I suppose, we were traveling rather fast, and feel that no one could begin to guess at my predicament. You all appreciate the fact, of course, that I knew nothing whatever of any quarrel between my husband and a faction in China?''

"Your husband adopted the policy of the ostrich, Helena," said Forbes, grimly. "It may or may not be a fable as regards ostriches—I don't know enough about them to feel certain, but it is unquestionably too often true of mankind. I believed my head was hidden and imagined the remainder of my body was safe in consequence. Now I learn that my opponents have been tracking me steadily for half a year. The one fact which stands out clearly above all others during the past forty-eight hours is the phenomenal range and completeness of Wong Li Fu's plans.''

''I didn't mean my comment as a reproach, dear,'' and Mrs. Forbes gave him a look which told plainly that these two were lovers after many years of wedded happiness. ''Thank God, we have all escaped—thus far!''

''Oh, mother,'' laughed Evelyn nervously, ''you are not anticipating more horrors, are you?''

''A few hours ago I would have scoffed at any one who said that a handful of Chinese could tear aside our cloak of civilized security as though it were a spider's web,'' was the serious reply. ''But I have interrupted my own story. I began to think that I would be taken to some awful den in the East End, and held there till some huge sum of money was paid by way of ransom, when the car suddenly quitted the main road and bumped over a rough surface. I knew I was near Croydon—the last place I would have suspected as a brigands' stronghold. Then we halted, and that wretched man lifted me out, carried me into a back room of an old-fash-

ioned house, put me in a fairly comfortable
chair, tied me in with ropes, and left me. I
couldn't speak. I was looking at a blank wall
and smoke-stained ceiling. I was sure then
that he was after money, and began to calcu-
late the time which must elapse before my husband would hear from him and arrange for
my release. I wondered how much he would
ask—ten, twenty, fifty thousand pounds. How
much would you have paid, Jim?"

Mrs. Forbes took her trials so cheerfully
that they all laughed.

"That's hardly a fair question, is it?" she
continued, stealing another glance at her husband. "At any rate, being a banker's wife,
I knew how extraordinarily difficult it would
be to raise any considerable sum of gold at
such a late hour, and I resigned myself to remaining a prisoner all night. Then I think
I wept a little, but not for long, because I
felt that they meant to keep me alive, and as
I look more delicate than I really am, even
a Chinaman would see that he was taking
some risk by denying me food and all liberty
of movement. Then—very soon, it seemed—
I heard an outer door being forced off its
hinges and English voices, and the door of
my room was broken open, and I saw a
police inspector and some constables. Hitherto I have never properly appreciated our
policemen. From this day I become their most

ardent admirer and enthusiastic helper. I
could have gone down on my knees to those
big, kind-looking men in uniform. In fact I
nearly did. When they released me I could
hardly stand. After that, Mr. Handyside
came, and accompanied me here, with a detective sitting next the driver, and my husband and Evelyn have told me something of
the extraordinary things which have been going on in London while I was gadding about
at Eastbourne.''

''Was the detective a man named Furneaux?'' inquired Theydon.

Mrs. Forbes hesitated, and her husband
answered for her, as he alone, among the
members of the household, had met the Jersey man.

''No,'' he said. ''He belonged to the Croydon force, and was sent as an escort. Furneaux seems to have been swallowed alive
since three o'clock. Everybody is inquiring
for him, and no one appears to know anything
about him.''

''I wonder whether Wong Li Fu is aware
I have been liberated?'' said Mrs. Forbes.
''It's rather odd, is it not, that nothing has
been heard from him or his gang if I
was to be held a prisoner in order to extort
terms?''

''I fancy he meant to add significance to
his demand for a reply by advertisement in

tomorrow's *Times*," said Forbes. "You see, Helena, he meant to carry off Evelyn as well as you."

Mrs. Forbes smiled again at that.

"What in the world should each of us have thought if we had both been bound and gagged in that car?" she cried.

"I know what I think," said her husband emphatically. "You are going straight to bed now, and you'll take ten grains of bromide before lying down. Evelyn, I appoint you nurse. Don't leave your mother till she is sound asleep."

Mrs. Forbes rose at once. She admitted, though reluctantly, that a night's rest was necessary to steady her nerves.

"Ah!" she sighed, "I shall be so glad when all this turmoil is ended, and we are settled for the season in Sutherland."

"Sutherland, ma'am," inquired Handyside. "Isn't that in the far north of Scotland?"

"Yes."

"It would be, just as the North Foreland is in Kent."

Theydon explained his friend's theory of geographical names in the British Isles, and on that lightly humorous note the ladies disappeared. When they were gone Forbes quickly gave a sinister turn to their talk. He produced a letter from his pocket.

"Listen to this," he said.

"Y. M. is pleased to inform James Creighton Forbes that Mrs. Forbes is a prisoner,
and will remain, without food or drink and
unable to move, in an empty house until
Y. M.'s demands are granted."

His face was white with fury while he
read, and his fingers moved convulsively as
if he could feel them twining around Wong Li
Fu's throat. The other men maintained a
sympathetic silence. They understood why
that ghastly message had been withheld from
the cognizance of the lady who had just
quitted them.

"It was delivered by a messenger boy
shortly before you arrived, Theydon," said
Forbes, when his passion had subsided and
he could trust his voice again.

"Have you informed Scotland Yard?" said
Theydon.

"No. I dared not use the telephone. I
could not leave my wife. She is far more
shaken than she thinks. Ever since her return she has followed me if I even walked
across the room. It was pitiful. I had to
lie to her when the butler brought this infernal note. She saw it was typed, and believed my explanation that it was a mere
record of an office cablegram."

"Give it to me," said Theydon. "Mr.
Handyside and I must leave you now. We'll
take it to Scotland Yard. Mr. Winter ought

to know of it. In all likelihood he is arranging to remain in the Croydon house tonight, and, if Wong Li Fu is telling the truth, which is highly probable, the local police can watch the place adequately."

"Yes. You're right, of course. I should have seen that an hour ago, but my brain is on fire owing to the torture these fiends have devised."

"Are you quite safe here? It is an absurd question, but I would like to feel assured on that point. Shall I return, and strengthen your guard?"

"I'm exceedingly obliged to you, but, in addition to two of my servants, thoroughly trustworthy men, a detective sergeant and constable have come from Scotland Yard. They are now having supper. When the household retires for the night two will remain in this room, with the door open, and two in the butler's room, which commands the other staircase. Moreover a constable will patrol this side of the square, and a second one the back of the premises, until long after daybreak."

"Tell you what," said Handyside, when he and Theydon were in a taxi, and had made certain they were not being followed, "tell you what, son, you've struck a bonanza in this Chinese drama."

"What do you mean?" said Theydon.

"Well, I guess you're the curly-haired boy where Miss Evelyn is concerned."

"Like most Americans, you jump at conclusions," was the ungracious reply.

"And, like most Americans, I'm right nearly all the time," said Handyside dryly.

"Surely one can hardly discuss such a matter."

"Why not? If a proposition sounds hard, chew on it, and may be you'll get your teeth into it somehow."

Theydon nearly allowed himself to become angry. Was his hopeless admiration for Evelyn Forbes so patent that a sharp-eyed stranger could discern it after a brief hour in their company?

"Millionaires' daughters marry poor men only in novels and on the stage," he said bitterly. "In real life, and in England, they take unto themselves titles and landed estates."

"I guess Wong Li Fu will have to round you up some more," was the cryptic answer, and Handyside forthwith plunged airily into some wholly different topic.

At Scotland Yard they inquired for Furneaux, and were told he had not reported at headquarters since the early afternoon. So Theydon was introduced to another representative of the department, and handed over the typed note; the detective promised that its purport should be telephoned to Croydon without delay.

When the two reached the Embankment again, Theydon felt unaccountably tired, and was minded to take leave of his companion then and there. But Handyside placed an unerring finger on the cause of his weariness.

"Say, Mr. Theydon," he cried, "I don't know what food product arrangements you've made all day, but I couldn't have eaten less since breakfast if Wong Li Fu was sitting over me with a pistol. How about a square meal? Come to my hotel, and I'll start the chef on a nice little menoo while we're having a wash and a brush up."

"By Jove! Now I know what is the matter with me," was the astonishing answer. "I have lunched and dined on a cup of tea at Eastbourne."

"Guess I'm fifteen years older than you, so I knew my trouble all the time. Those people in Fortescue Square were so rattled that they never thought of asking us to eat. Come right along. It's only a step."

"I'll come with pleasure. I owe you some money, too, which I was nearly forgetting."

"What do you owe for?"

"Railway tickets, and taxis, and motor-cycles, to begin with."

"No, sir," said the American decisively. "I've had the cheapest day's amusement I've ever dreamed of. On balance I owe you one sovereign. As for those half-tickets from Eastbourne I wouldn't sell them for dollars and cents. When I get back to my home, 21,097 Park Avenue, Chicago, I'll have those bits of cardboard framed, and when some particular friend asks the reason I'll tell him, suppressing names of course, and he'll go away thinking that George T. Handyside is the biggest liar in the State of Illinois, which is some pumpkin, you bet.''

"What beats me," rejoined Theydon, "is how you remember where you live. You must have a marvelous head for figures.''

So they dined well, and wined moderately, and Theydon walked to Innesmore Mansions, thinking of little else in the world except of the moment when he held Evelyn Forbes in his arms, almost in an embrace, and he had dared nearly, if not quite, to kiss her.

As he drew near Innesmore Mansions, however, he kept his wits about him. One of the most remarkable features of a series of remarkable crimes was the thorough command of the resources of civilization exhibited by the Young Manchus. A few days earlier he would not have dared to introduce into a story of his own an association composed exclusively of Chinamen which adapted to its needs the motor car, the messenger boy, perhaps the telephone and telegraph, to say nothing of the advertising columns of the daily press.

It was monstrous to imagine that a number of Orientals—marked men, every one, no matter what disguises they might adopt— should dare bid defiance to the forces of the British Constitution in order that they might wreak vengeance on those more enlightened compatriots who wished to see their country rescued from the effete control of a puppet Emperor.

But Theydon was now some days older and many degrees wiser. He knew that the wildly improbable had become dogged fact, that Chinese fanaticism, tigerish in its crafty and utter cold-bloodedness, was setting at naught not only the ordinances of the law, but the brightest intellects whose duty it was to make that law respected.

It behooved him, therefore, to lend a sharp eye to his own safety, and never a vehicle or pedestrian came near while he traversed the quiet streets in the neighborhood of Innesmore Mansions that he did not give the closest attention to cab or wayfarer, as the case might be.

As it happened, that quarter of London was singularly deserted. The first flight of people homeward-bound from the theaters was well over; the later contingent, supping in restaurants, had not begun to arrive. Save for the slow-moving figure of a policeman the long front of the mansions themselves was devoid of life.

Nevertheless, it was with a feeling of relief that he turned the key in the lock of No. 18, and heard the scraping of a chair on the kitchen floor as Bates rose to meet him.

"Hello, Bates!" he cried wearily, "here I am again, you see! Anything new or interesting during my absence?"

"Mrs. Paxton—" began the valet, stopping when his master uttered a sharp exclamation. Theydon had completely forgotten Miss Beale and his sister.

"Yes," he said. "Sorry I interrupted you. What of Mrs. Paxton?"

"I saw her, sir, as you ordered, and she promised to call on Miss Beale. She kem here about an hour ago—"

"Who? My sister?"

"Yes, sir. She was anxious to see you. From what I could gather, sir, the two ladies had bin puttin' their heads together, and agreed that this Chinese business has a nasty look, an' you'd better keep out of it."

"What Chinese business, Bates?"

"Well, sir, Miss Beale will 'ave it that Mrs. Lester was killed by a Chinaman, an' one of the police on duty in this district told me

241

a little while ago that he saw no less than three Chinamen prowlin' round here last Monday between dusk and dark.''

Theydon drew a deep breath. If there was gossip going on about ''Chinamen'' in connection with the murder in No. 17 the newspapers would soon be getting hold of it. The arrest of Len Shi by Furneaux must be reported. Possibly some newspaper correspondent in Eastbourne would hear of the kidnaping exploit, and describe the Eastern aspect of its chief actor, Mrs. Forbes's name would ''transpire'' in the paragraph, and, by putting two and two together the lynx-eyed journalism of London would ferret out a good deal of the truth.

''Ladies very often talk nonsense about such things,'' he said sharply. ''Why should any Chinaman single out poor Mrs. Lester as a victim? I think the inquiry may be left safely to Scotland Yard. Have you seen the evening papers? I'll bet you sixpence nothing was said at the inquest concerning Chinamen?''

''No, sir. That's true. However, Mrs. Paxton wants you to ring her up.''

''Why?''

''She wants to be sure you are safe home.''

Theydon laughed. ''How can I?'' he cried. ''She is not on the telephone.''

''Mrs. Paxton left a number, sir. If you give them a call it will be taken to her.''

Theydon shook his head good-humoredly but obeyed. A voice at the other end answered:

"Will you oblige me by telling Mrs. Paxton that I took an American friend to Eastbourne this afternoon and returned by a late train?" he said.

"Who is it, please?"

"Mr. Theydon, Mrs. Paxton's brother."

"O, I have a message for you. Miss Beale is staying with Mrs. Paxton tonight. There was a Chinaman in her hotel, and she didn't like it."

Theydon controlled his feelings sufficiently to thank his informant. He really wanted to say something crude.

"Gad!" he muttered, when he had rung off, "these women have Chinamen on the brain. Look here Bates," he added emphatically, "I hope you won't lend an ear to this nonsense. You've seen no Chinamen, I suppose?"

"No, sir."

"If you do see one, tell me, and I'll get to know his business, pretty quick."

"Yes, sir."

"Any letters?"

"Three, sir, and a small parcel. I put them on your table. Shall I get you something, sir?"

"No, thanks. I've just had a huge supper. Goodnight."

"Goodnight, sir. Any orders for the morning?"

"Let me sleep as long as I like, unless I'm wanted."

Theydon entered the sitting room. He opened the letters. Two were of no moment; the third was a request from the editor of a magazine that the "copy" of his article on the "Forbes Peace Propaganda" should be forwarded as speedily as practicable. What a mad world it was, to be sure! Here was an important periodical waiting impatiently for the views of the millionaire on the best means of securing peace on earth and good will to all men, while that same master mind was obsessed with fear of a few Chinese bandits. Society was looking to Forbes for a promised panacea against war and its evils; Forbes himself was wondering whether bolts and locks and armed servants and policemen would protect him and his from the claws of the Young Manchus!

Theydon heard Bates locking and bolting the outer door of the flat with a certain thankfulness. He was thinking of the sheer impossibility of any marauder gaining access to No. 18, when he opened the small parcel which the valet had spoken of. He speculated idly as to the nature of its contents, because he could not remember having ordered any article which would be contained in so tiny a package.

He took out a piece of stout paper, folded twice, and a little white object fell to the table and rolled over several times, finally coming to rest with a curious suddenness. It was a small, carved, ivory skull!

CHAPTER XIII

THEYDON gazed fixedly at the skull for the best part of a minute. His state of mind was that of a man, utterly incredulous, who nevertheless thinks he sees a ghost. Then he recovered himself and laughed angrily, harshly, because he had not succeeded better in controlling his nerves.

He examined the paper. It bore no writing of any kind. It was precisely similar in color and texture to the two typed slips which Forbes had received, but the sender had evidently thought that the skull was symbolical enough of deadly intent without troubling to add a written threat.

The ivory skull was an exact replica of its predecessors. The set teeth, the scowling grin of the gaunt jawbones, the dull menace of the empty eye sockets, were equally convincing, equally disconcerting.

Lighting a cigarette, Theydon scrutinized the address and postmarks. In a sense, it was ludicrous to find "Francis B. Theydon, Esq., 18 Innesmore Mansions, W. C.," typed in plain script on the wrapper. What an unholy alliance of modern science and medievalism! The mind almost refused to focus itself on the tragic aspect of the affair, yet the hour at which the package was posted, 5:30 p. m. in the West Strand, showed conclusively that Wong Li Fu, at any rate, had not sent the death's head by his own hand, but had entrusted it to a confederate. The notion brought in its train the departure of Miss Beale from her hotel, "because she had seen a Chinaman there." "Every little helps," mused Theydon, "I must let Scotland Yard know."

He went straight to the telephone, and was pleased to hear that Mr. Winter had reached headquarters. The chief inspector was feeling grateful, and said so.

"It was very thoughtful on your part to deal so promptly with the message received by Mr. Forbes," he said. "I meant remaining in Croydon all night. No one came to the house, of course. Wong Li Fu's note explained why. Callous and calculating demon, isn't he?"

"Yes. Even more calculating than you are aware. He has included me in the count now. When I reached home ten minutes since, after gormandizing with Mr. Handyside, I found the totem of the tribe awaiting me."

"The what?"

"An ivory skull."

"You don't say!" and there was a genuine thrill in Winter's voice. "Anything else?"

"There was no written legend. I have no doubt the enemy believes that such a work of art speaks for itself. It does. I am to be exterminated, I suppose."

A marked pause ensued. When Winter spoke again his tone was grave.

"This is a very serious business, Mr. Theydon," he said. "The worst part of it is that it seems to be spreading in an ever-widening circle. If it goes much further we'll be obliged to run in every Chinaman in London, and sift out the decent ones from the heap until we reach the unpleasant residuum. Are you worried about things? If so, I'll send a man to mount guard tonight."

"Not at all, thanks. Bates and I will take care that there isn't even a joss stick in the flat before we go to bed. But I say, there's another matter. Have you met Miss Beale?"

"Yes. She came here this morning. She gave evidence at the inquest, I am told. What of her?"

"I asked my sister to spend the evening with her, and she was so alarmed at finding a Chinaman as a fellow-guest in her hotel that she is spending the night in my sister's house."

"A plague on all Chinamen!" cried Winter wrathfully. "After this I'm dashed if I don't drink Indian tea. However, we'll look him up. Sleep soundly. Your earlier sins of omission are forgiven you, because you have done us several good turns today. I'll tell your local police station that if any pigtail or squint eye is found within half a mile of Innesmore Mansions tonight it is to be jugged without the slightest hesitation. Keep the skull safely. Furneaux is collecting them."

"Have you seen him, then?"

"No. But I've heard from him. He has gone home suffering from opium poisoning."

"Great Scott!"

"O, that's only pretty Fanny's way. He means that he is sick of the reek of Chinamen. You know his peculiar views with regard to tobacco. If he has been prowling around among opium dens in the East End all the evening, I'm sorry for him. But he'll turn up all right in the morning, looking like a skinned weasel. By the way, it'll interest you to hear that we have cleared up one minor issue. You remember that Ann Rogers, Mrs. Lester's maid, was called away by a telegram saying that her father was ill?"

"Yes."

"The old fellow, who is a bit of a sponge, admits that he was given two pounds by 'a foreign gentleman' for sending that telegram and shamming illness during the night. I wish I could put the hoary old rascal in jail, but his action probably saved Ann Rogers from sharing her mistress's fate."

"Mr. Winter, has it struck you that the man who devised this scheme, beginning with the murder of Mrs. Lester and ending, Heaven alone knows when or where, is an organizing genius of a very high order?"

"You would be surprised if you knew the real extent and scope of this affair," said Winter. "Some day soon I'll be more outspoken. Goodnight. If you go out in the morning leave word with Bates where you can be found if wanted."

Theydon turned from the telephone and found Bates standing beside him. That stolid and worthy ex-noncommissioned officer was armed with a red-hot poker. Henceforth his employer saw pretense was useless.

"Beg pardon, sir," said the valet apologetically. "I couldn't help overhearin' what you were sayin', an' if there's any blinkin' Chinee hidden in this place I'll put a mark on him he won't forget in a hurry."

Theydon could not help laughing, but Bates was in earnest.

"Once I was stationed in Cork, sir," he said solemnly, "an' we had to stop a riot. It was then I learnt the reel vally of a red-hot poker. It's as good as a baynit any time. I've kep' this one handy since Mr. Furneaux ran out. I do believe he saw a Chinaman."

"He did, and, what is more, arrested him. Well, come on, Bates. There are not many hiding places in one of these flats. I only hope we find a Celestial. It would be the fitting finale to a busy day."

But their search was in vain, though they succeeded in scaring Mrs. Bates badly. It was almost inconceivable that two such men, one a powerfully-built athlete and the other an ex-soldier, should even imagine that any marauder could be secreted in the flat; but the European insensibly credits the Oriental with occult powers, and they took their task quite soberly.

Singularly enough it led to a discovery bearing directly on the problem of Mrs. Lester's death. Leading out of the kitchen was a narrow scullery; here a lift, worked by a wheel on the ground level, delivered coals by the sack and other heavy parcels.

Theydon glanced at the sliding panel which gave access to the lift. Obviously he seldom, if ever, visited this part of his domain.

"Can that thing be operated only from the ground?" he inquired.

"O, no, sir," said Bates. "I often pull it up when I want to lower the dust bin."

"Can you do it now?"

Bates looked surprised at first, then thoughtful. Theydon's words had suggested a new idea. He opened the panel, tugged vigorously at a rope, and soon the lift itself, a sort of large cupboard, open at the side, came in view.

"By gum!" he muttered, gazing at its spacious depths, "I never thought of that."

"You see what I'm driving at, then?"

"Why, of course, sir. A moderate-sized man could stow away inside there and hoist himself to any floor. It 'ud be perfectly easy an' safe as nails. A hundredweight of coal is nothing to it."

"I think we see now at least one method whereby the man who killed Mrs. Lester could have entered the flat without her knowledge?"

"Not a doubt about it, sir. Nearly noiseless, too, an' if you heard it working you'd imagine it was meant for the flat beneath, because there's a whistle to warn us when it's comin' here."

They surveyed the lift in silence for a little while. Then Bates caused it to descend again, and Theydon examined the rather flimsy device which fastened the panel.

"I'm not what you might describe as a nervous individual," he said, at last, "but it wouldn't be fair to your wife and yourself, Bates, if I didn't tell you I have just received an ugly reminder that the gang which killed Mrs. Lester has a grudge against me now. Wouldn't it be a reasonable thing if we drove a couple of screws into that door tonight?"

Bates stroked his chin. The long-dormant spirit of combat kindled in his eye.

"Better still, sir," he grinned, "let's drive a screw into any one who comes up in the lift."

"But how?"

"By tying your pistol firmly to the dresser, putting it on a hair-trigger—I know how to do that, of course—an' letting it plug a bullet into the right place when the panel is half open."

"Are we justified in taking the law into our own hands?"

"Is any one justified in tryin' to get in here an' cut our throats while we're asleep, sir?"

Theydon weighed the pros and cons of this thesis very carefully. He dreaded the possibility of taking a human life, even in self-defense. Yet against the wretches who had strangled Edith Lester, and coolly prepared to leave Mrs. Forbes to starve in an empty house until their revengeful scheme was perfected by full knowledge of the identity of every man in China, who had assisted in the downfall of an effete monarchy, what code of conduct would apply unless it were that which holds sway in the jungle?

"Couldn't we contrive matters so that if the pistol were fired it need not necessarily inflict a fatal wound?" he said.

"Let's see what we can do, sir," and Bates set to work gleefully on the arrangements. There was not the slightest difficulty in devising an efficient means of pressing a trigger with a reduced pull by opening the door. Any schoolboy could adjust a piece of string to act unfailingly. By measuring distances, and careful sighting of the pistol when fixed in position, they arrived at a line of fire which would strike a body crouched in the lift about the region of the right shoulder.

Then Bates locked the scullery door, put the key in his pocket, and assured his trembling wife that she might sleep like a top, since no bloomin' Chinaman could get at her that night. Theydon himself retired soon afterwards. He was as tired as though he had been trudging steadily along country roads since daybreak.

When he awoke, it was broad daylight. Around the corners of the drawn blinds in his bedroom he could see strips of golden sunshine. Glancing at a clock on the mantlepiece he was amazed to find that the hour was ten o'clock, so, not only had there not been a raid on the premises, but Bates had taken the overnight instructions literally, and allowed him to sleep far beyond the usual hour.

He rose hurriedly, raced to the bathroom and shouted for "breakfast in fifteen minutes." He was splashing in his tub when the telephone bell rang, and Bates answered. Within a few seconds the valet was knocking at the door.

"A Mr. Handyside has rung up, sir," was

the announcement. "I think he's an American.
He wants to know if there is anything doin'.
He said you would understand."

"Tell him I'm alive, and will call at his
hotel at 11:30."

"Yes, sir."

When Bates brought in the breakfast Theydon was glancing hurriedly through the morning papers. Some of them contained an allusion to the Eastbourne incident, but no names were mentioned.

A reference to "developments" in connection with the "Innesmore Mansions Murder," however, caught his eye. Appended to a brief account of the inquest were the following paragraphs:

"It may be taken as certain that the police are not altogether at sea as to the motive of this atrocious crime. Strange as it may seem —the victim being a young and attractive lady, living unostentatiously and taking little, if any, part in the social life of London—there is some probability that Mrs. Lester's death was the outcome of political revenge rather than an incident in an interrupted burglary.

"At first, every indication pointed to the act of some ghoul surprised by the unfortunate lady in her bedroom, but we have reason to believe that graver issues to the community-at-large will be revealed when Scotland Yard's inquiry is completed. It must not be forgotten

that her husband died 'suddenly' some six
months ago in Shanghai. Oddly enough, the
police are now keeping a close surveillance on
Chinese quarters in London, not only in the
neighborhood of the docks, but in the fashionable West. It may, or may not, be a mere
coincidence that a Chinaman was arrested yesterday at St. Albans and lodged in Bow Street.

"There are not wanting other similar 'coincidences' in places so far apart as a well-
known South Coast seaside resort and South
Croydon. At present, the whole matter is
nebulous, but striking developments may take
place at any hour, and the murder of Mrs.
Lester may yet figure as one of the most sensational crimes of recent years."

Theydon was reading these discreet but exceedingly well-informed sentences with much
care, when he noticed that Bates had closed
the sitting-room door before beginning to arrange the contents of the tray on the table.
Such an unusual action meant something.

"Well, what is it now?" he inquired, lifting
his eyes to the manservant's impassive face.

"When the milkman come this morning, sir,
he told me that a policeman was found lyin'
insensible on the road outside the mansions
shortly after three o'clock," was the answer,
conveyed in a low note that suggested a matter
better kept from the cognizance of Mrs. Bates.

"That's a bad job for the policeman; it is

nothing very remarkable otherwise," said Theydon.

"But the milkman heard he was set about by three swells, young gentlemen in evening dress, sir, who ran away when another constable appeared."

"Very likely. There was a row, and the law got the worst of it. Anyhow, we were not disturbed during the night."

"No, sir. I was only thinkin' of what might have happened if the police were not on the job."

"Look here, Bates"—and Theydon's manner was most emphatic—"if you and I begin seeing shadows we'll soon collect a fine show of Chinese ghosts. I'm astonished at you, a man who has been under fire."

"Sorry, sir. I thought you'd like to hear the lytest, that's all."

Theydon ate a hearty breakfast, thus proving that the marvels and portents of the previous day had not begun to undermine his constitution. Finding he had time, after attending to his correspondence, to walk to Handyside's hotel in the Strand, he did so. The American was awaiting him at the end of a long, thin cigar.

"Any noos?" said the Chicagoan, after a cheerful greeting.

"Yes. The feud continues. You heard about those ivory skulls yesterday?"

"Yes, sir. They reminded me of the tales of my youth."

"Well, I got mine last night. Here it is!"

"Gee whiz!"

Handyside took the small object which Theydon produced from a waistcoat pocket. He examined it with minute care.

"I've never crossed the Pacific," he said, after apparently satisfying himself as to the exact nature of the unpleasant token, "but one of my hobbies is the collection of ivories. In my home—"

"21,097 Park Avenue," interrupted Theydon.

"Just so—four doors short of 211th Street. Well, sir, when you blow in there you'll see a roomful of curios. I'm not exactly a connoisseur, but I know enough to tell Japanese work from Chinese. This was made by a Jap. And that reminds me. You said last night that Wong Li Fu put you off your balance by a jiu jitsu trick and handed that husky detective some, too. Very few Chinks have ever even heard of jiu jitsu. I've a notion that a bunch of Japs is mixed up in this business."

"Surely not?"

"It's possible. You good people here are crazy in your treatment of the Japanese. You think they're civilized because they dress in good shape, and can put up a mighty spry imitation of Western ways. But they ain't.

They're the greatest menace to Europe that
has yet come up on the tape. Do you believe
they want China to wake up and organize before they're ready to take hold? No, sir.
Anyhow, that skull was carved by a Japanese
artist, and a bully good one at that.''

The two were standing near the fireplace of
a square and spacious foyer. There were
plenty of people in the place, some conversing
with friends, others writing or doing business
at the various bureaus. It chanced that Theydon faced the two swing doors which led to
the street, and he was returning the bit of
ivory to his pocket when, somewhat to his surprise, Furneaux entered.

The detective saw him, too—of that he was
quite certain—but ignored him completely.
After one sharp, comprehensive glance around,
as though he were seeking some one who was
not visible, the little man went to a desk, scribbled a note, handed it in at the inquiry office,
walked swiftly in the direction of an anteroom
and restaurant, and disappeared forthwith.

Theydon was puzzled by Furneaux's behavior, but was quick to perceive that if the
latter had not wished to be left alone he
would at least have made some sign of recognition.

A page approached Mr. Handyside.

''Note for you, sir,'' he said.

The American opened the envelope and read

259

a few lines scribbled on a sheet of note-paper. He passed it to Theydon.

"The circus is now about to commence," he said, and the meaning of this enigmatical remark was made clear when Theydon saw what was written.

"Dear Sir," it ran, "take Mr. Theydon to your room. I'll join you there immediately.— C. F. Furneaux."

"If this is the little sleuth who was missing yesterday I guess we've gotten our call," commented Handyside, with an amused grin at the expression of bewilderment on his companion's face.

"I was just about to tell you that Furneaux had come in and crossed the hall."

"Well, let's beat it to the third floor. I have the key in my pocket."

They were walking through a long corridor when Furneaux appeared at the other end. Beyond the three men, not another person was visible in that part of the hotel, and in a few seconds they were behind the closed door of Handyside's room.

"So you're still on the map?" said the detective, surveying Theydon with an air of professional interest.

"Yes, but I have received notice to quit," was the retort.

"So I hear. The executioner was quick on the heels of the warrant, too. If it had not

been for the precautions Winter took last night
the newsboys would have been bawling a second Innesmore Mansions tragedy during the
past couple of hours.''

Theydon smiled.

"I'm not joking," snapped Furneaux. "In
fact, I feel rather bad about it. I woke up at
eight o'clock, and pictured you and Bates and
his wife lying about in No. 18 in very uncom-
fortable and ungainly attitudes. I was so
worried and miserable that I telephoned your
hall porter to learn the worst, and was quite
astonished when he said that Bates had just
been chatting with him. You don't understand, of course. I forgot to tell you about
the lift. Wong Li Fu's special delegate
climbed into No. 17 by that means and three
of 'em would have reached you last night in
the same way if a policeman hadn't met them
in the street."

"My man heard about the row. He guessed,
too, that it had something to do with us.
The policeman was badly injured, he was
told."

"Yes—nothing broken; he was put to sleep
by some confounded Japanese wrestling
trick."

"Japanese, you say?"

"Precisely. The Young Manchus are being
backed up by a second gang which calls itself
the 'Sons of Nippon.' I don't know what

London is coming to. We've entertained Anarchists, Nihilists and Dynamitards for years. Now we have the Yellow Peril with us. I wish I were King for a few days. There would be a bigger clearance of reptiles out of England than St. Patrick made in Ireland.''

"Mr. Handyside here told me only ten minutes since that he was convinced there were Japs in league with the Chinese.''

"How did you know?'' and Furneaux whirled round on the American instantly.

"By using the gray matter at the back of my head,'' was the reply. "No Chink ever taught Wong Li Fu how to put away two chesty individuals like Mr. Theydon and your partner, Mr. Winter. But I couldn't be sure till I had seen the ivory skull. Then I knew.''

"So did I know yesterday morning,'' said Furneaux, "and a deuce of a time the discovery gave me. Anyhow, the street fight outside Innesmore Mansions at daybreak today settles the matter. There were two Japanese and one Chinaman. The Japs outed the policeman. Fortunately he and another man made a five-minute point at each end of the mansions, and, as No. 1 failed to turn up, No. 2 went to look for him. He saw the end of the row, and ran to help, blowing his whistle for assistance. Unfortunately for us, two of the three confounded blackguards escaped.''

"O, you've got one, then?" cried Theydon.

"Yes, a Jap. The constable was wise enough to give him the point of his truncheon in the gullet, and that settled him."

"I wonder if he is the one who would have been shot had he broken into my flat," said Theydon musingly.

"Shot! Man alive, you'd never have heard him!"

"Not till he had a bullet lodged securely in his inside, it is true. Bates and I surveyed that lift last night, Mr. Furneaux, and regarded it as the weak part of our defenses, so we arranged that an automatic pistol should live up to its name, and fire at any one who opened the sliding panel."

"Did you now?" said Furneaux admiringly. "Whose brainy idea was that—yours or Bates's?"

"A joint effort," he said, with a self-satisfied smile.

"Well, I'm glad it didn't come off. British law is a fearsome and wonderful thing. You might both have got ten years for fixing a man-trap, to wit, a lethal engine. However, during the next few days you're going to change your abode. Tell Bates and his wife that they need a holiday, and ought to visit relatives in Yorkshire or North Wales. Pack what you need for a week, at least, and make straight for Fortescue Square."

"Are you joking?" said Theydon, genuinely astounded.

"Do I look it?" And, indeed, the detective did not. "Winter has just settled that program with Mr. Forbes. You see, you're in this affair now, neck and crop, and it's easier for us to safeguard one place than two. You're pleased, aren't you? Doesn't a pretty girl live there?"

"Sir," said Handyside, "he's tickled to death, and that's a fact. I'm the only one to make a kick. I kind of reckoned on being allowed to play a walking-on part in this drama, but I look like being cut out in the new shuffle."

"I can make use of you," said Furneaux promptly. "You've seen Wong Li Fu, and would know him again?"

"Yes, sir."

"And you can tell a Japanese from a Chinaman at sight?"

"Yes, sir."

"Good. You're enrolled. Next thing you'll be receiving an ivory skull, too. These beggars are the smartest crowd I've come across in twenty years. I think they would have beaten us if it hadn't happened that Mr. Theydon and you, each of you strangers to the Forbes family, were selected by fate to intervene at psychological moments. The Young Manchus and their allies had the ground surveyed thoroughly. They even had us of the Yard marked down. Oh, it's a plot and a half, I can assure you, and the worst thing is that the real struggle is yet ahead. All that has happened before is mere skirmishing compared with what's to come.''

"Is that why you covered up your tracks, even in this hotel, before you came to my room?'' inquired Handyside.

"It is, and let me tell you that you're a living example of a contradiction in terms. You use your brains, Mr. Handyside, yet you smoke a cigar calculated to atrophy the keenest intellect. You, an American, chewing a vile Burmese Cheroot! *Cré nom d'un pipe!* When this bubble has burst I must reason with you!''

CHAPTER XIV

FURNEAUX, with that phenomenally clear mind of his, had perceived and expressed in one trenchant sentence the outstanding and almost unique feature of the tragic mystery which centered around the death of Edith Lester. Theydon's connection with either international finance or the rebirth of China was remote as that of the man in the moon. Yet he had been pitchforked by fate into an active and, indeed, dominating influence over those phases of both undertakings which were peculiar to London.

Theydon mused on this element in an unprecedented situation as he sat in the taxicab which bore him swiftly to Innesmore Mansions. Another quite abnormal condition was the ignorance of London with regard to the fierce struggle now being waged in its midst.

On the one hand, a few Oriental fanatics— most of whom were probably less swayed by racial enthusiasm than by good payment for services rendered—were carrying out the orders of a master criminal with a sublime indifference to the laws framed by the "foreign devils" whom they despised; on the other were ranged the three members of the Forbes family and Theydon himself, supported by the forces of the Crown, it was true, but singularly isolated from the knowledge and sympathy of their fellow-citizens.

Miss Beale hardly counted. The servants in Fortescue Square shared with Bates and his wife a sort of territorial interest in the fight. When Fortune picked an occasional warrior for the fray she chose a man from Chicago, a motorcyclist from Eastbourne, a policeman in Charing Cross road.

How portentous had been that hand raised to stem the traffic at a congested corner on the Monday night! Into what a vortex of crime and passion had it not pointed, all unknowing! If the cab in which Theydon was hurrying home from Daly's Theater had not been delayed by the dispute between driver and policeman, he would never have known that the millionaire visited Innesmore Mansions, and the subsequent course of the night's history might have left him wholly unaffected.

Then his wayward thoughts took to brooding on the gray car which shadowed him from Waterloo to Fortescue Square, and again from the square to his own abode. If it held some member of the Embassy staff, why had no more been heard of it? And what had Win-

ter and Furneaux meant by hinting that far
wider issues were bound up with the affair
than the authorities were yet at liberty to
divulge? The attack on Forbes, sinister and
malevolent in its scope and purpose, was,
in a sense, open warfare. But it was impossible to guess what part, if any, the official
representatives of China filled in the fray.
Were they active allies of Scotland Yard or
did they hold what is known in the law courts
as a watching brief? He could not tell.
He only knew that each successive period of
twenty-four hours broadened the area covered
by the struggle, and there, at least, he found
solid backing for the little detective's demand
that the threatened people should dwell under
one roof. His pulses quickened at the notice
that this new departure implied constant association with Evelyn Forbes. Yet, what did it
avail? Why should he dream of fanning into
a fiercer fury the flame of his love? As matters stood, he had about as much chance of
marrying Evelyn Forbes as of becoming Emperor of China!

The incongruity of the situation was illus-
trated with cruel accuracy by the fact that he
could ill afford the stoppage of his work demanded by the present trend of events. He
earned what might be regarded as a good income by his pen, but his expenses were not
light, and he had deemed himself fortunate the

previous year when he was able to invest a hundred pounds!

As a matter of fact, the interest on his "securities" paid for his gloves and ties; another lucky year might see him provided for life with boots and socks! He pictured himself—if he were idiot enough, when all this turmoil was ended, to pose as a suitor for Evelyn Forbes's hand—explaining his financial position to the millionaire, and wilting under the scornful amusement in those earnest, deep-seeing eyes. Phew! He grew hot at the mere notion of such folly.

Little wonder, therefore, that the driver of the taxi should gaze quizzically after Theydon's alert figure as it vanished in the stairway of Innesmore Mansions.

"Got the hump, an' pretty bad," soliloquized the man. "Gimme a bob over the fare, an' all, so can't be stony. But Lord love a duck, you never can tell!"

Theydon was about to unlock the door of his flat when it opened in his face, and his sister nearly collided with him. She screamed slightly, a certain quality of alarm in her exclamation merging instantly into joyful recognition.

"So you have come home!" she cried. "My goodness! What a fright you've given me!"

"Why?" he said, with a reassuring and brotherly hug.

"I've had horrid dreams. I couldn't rest all last night for thinking of you."

"Is George absent?" George was her husband, a consulting engineer, whose professional duties often took him to distant parts of the country.

"Yes."

"Then you and Miss Beale have been living on tea and scraps. Really, Mollie, I credited you with more sense. Tell me what you ate last night, and I'll diagnose your dreams."

"We dined at a first-class restaurant in the West End," said Mrs. Paxton indignantly. "It would be much more to the point if you explained how you have been living the past few days. I have not been so worried about anything since George was trapped in that horrid mine."

Mollie was on the verge of tears. Her brother resolved instantly to minimize matters, or she would fret more than ever on his account.

"Now, look here, old girl," he said, meeting her critical glance steadily. "Miss Beale has been putting absurd notions into that stylish little head of yours. By the way, is that the latest thing in hats? It suits you admirably."

Mrs. Paxton smiled, though her eyes were glistening suspiciously.

"You can't humbug me, Frank, so please don't try," she protested. "Why are you mixed up in this dreadful business? Why are you constantly meeting detectives? Why did you rush off to Eastbourne yesterday? When did you become acquainted with this Mr. Forbes? Have you seen his daughter?"

Theydon was at least sufficiently well versed in the peculiarities of the feminine temperament to know that he would be safe in answering the last question first.

"Yes," he said. "I have seen a good deal of Miss Forbes recently. Have you ever met her?"

"She was at the horse show last year with Lady de Winton's party. She's an awfully pretty girl, and will be worth millions, I suppose. Some one said that young de Winton was simply crazy about her, but he looks such a sloppy youth that I could hardly imagine those two getting married. Of course, there's the title, yet a title is not everything."

Young de Winton! Theydon had not even been aware hitherto of the existence of a marriageable scion of that noble house.

"That particular young spark has not been in evidence during the past few days at any rate," he commented, and his voice was not so nonchalant as he imagined, because Mrs. Paxton looked up quickly.

"Perhaps it was only idle gossip," she said. "Is Miss Forbes a nice girl to talk to? She struck me as being very animated."

271

"Animated"—while in the company of that undoubted oaf, de Winton! Theydon choked back something tinged with gall as he replied quietly:

"She could not well help being highly intelligent. Her father and mother are charming people. I was introduced to Mr. Forbes owing to a mazagine commission to write an article about his interest in aviation. Now you see how promptly even the most gorgeous bubble bursts when it impinges against a solid little fact. As it happens, Mr. Forbes and I will have so much in common during the next day or two that I am now going to stay with him. I came here to pack a portmanteau. If you'll be a good little girl and listen while I'm at the telephone you will hear all about it."

The words were no sooner uttered than he wanted to recall them. It would be no easy matter to discuss Furneaux's suggestion with any one in Fortescue Square without letting his sister into the secret that the visit was necessitated by considerations of his own personal safety.

Mrs. Paxton's eyes were sparkling with a new interest.

"I had no idea you were on terms of such intimacy with the family," she cried. "Don't tell me, Frank, that your flights have taken you to the elevated region in which millionaires' daughters figure as possible brides!"

"Now you are making me out a Mormon,"
and Theydon grinned fiercely.

"You know what I mean. This Miss
Forbes—by the way, what is her Christian
name?"

"Let me see. I think I have heard it. Doris,
is it, or Phyllis? No, I remember now—Evelyn."

"O, then, if you are so vague on that point
I suppose I must reconcile myself to owning
a bachelor brother again."

He shook his head at her.

"Ah, you women!" he said. "Yet I used
to regard you as quite a sensible person,
Mollie! Now, how in the name of goodness
could I possibly entertain any notion of marrying the only daughter of a man in Forbes's
position?"

"It all depends," was the illogical but crush-
ing retort. "There are plenty of millionaires'
daughters whom I would not regard as good
enough for my brother. And, let me tell you,
the family is making progress. A little bird
whispered the other day that George's name
will appear in the next list of honors. He is
to receive a knighthood."

It was not new to Theydon to learn that
his brother-in-law stood in high favor with the
Government, because Paxton had been ap-
pointed on two Royal Commissions with reference to mining regulations, but he affected

a surprised incredulity as offering a way of escape from an inquisition which he dreaded.

"Dear me!" he smirked.

Therein he erred. His sister gave him a puzzled glance.

"You are not yourself today, Frank," she said dubiously. "You are acting. For whose benefit? Not mine, surely!"

"If your prospective ladyship will pardon me I will now go to the telephone," he countered.

Anything, even a mad jumble of incoherence in his talk with the Forbes household, was better than the troubled scrutiny of those clear brown eyes. Leaving the door open so that his sister could hear his side of the conversation, he rang up No. 11 Fortescue Square.

The butler answered.

"That you, Tomlinson?" said Theydon. "Will you ask Mr. Forbes if I am to turn up in time for afternoon tea? If it is more convenient that I should arrive later I have lots of things to attend to, and can fill in a few hours easily."

"I really don't know what to say, sir," came the astounding answer. "Mrs. Forbes has been shot—"

"Great heavens!"

"Yes, sir. She was merely looking out through the drawing-room window, when some one fired at her from a passing motor car."

"Do you mean that she is dead?"

"No, sir—not quite so bad as that. The bullet struck her left shoulder. A few inches lower and it would have pierced her heart. The doctors are with her now. I—"

Some interruption took place on the line and the butler's voice ceased. Theydon, careless now as to what construction his sister might place on his words, was about to storm at the exchange for cutting the communication. He meant to say that on no consideration would he inflict the presence of a stranger at such a terrible moment, when a coldly metallic, almost harsh question reached him.

"That you, Theydon?"

"Yes," he said. Forbes was speaking.

"I was crossing the hall, and guessed it might be you. Come as soon as you are at liberty. You will be welcome. If we are to be besieged I want some one who will not be afraid to shoot. These policemen are too scrupulous. They saw some cursed Mongol leaning out through the window of the closed car, and could have either shot him or put a bullet so close that his aim would have been disturbed. As it was, my wife only escaped death by the mercy of Providence. She bent slightly at the very instant the would-be assassin fired, and the bullet simply lacerated her shoulder. After this, I'll defend myself and my womenfolk, but I need at least one other man whom I can trust. Will you come?"

"I'll be with you within twenty minutes."

He heard the clang of the receiver being replaced on its rest at the other end of the wire. Somehow, the sound conveyed a new determination on Forbes's part. He had his back to the wall. No matter what view the law took of his action subsequently, he would protect his dear ones at all hazards.

After that, Theydon hesitated no longer.

"Bates," he cried, "throw into a bag such clothes as I shall need for a few days' stay in Mr. Forbes's house. When I am gone, pack your own boxes and take a week's holiday. Go anywhere you like, out of London, but go at once. Send me your address, care of Mr. Forbes, and I'll let you know when I want you again."

"If it's a matter of holdin' out against them—"

Bates intended making a declaration of war, but his employer broke in emphatically.

"I want you to obey my orders fully and unquestionably," he said. Bates promptly became the well-trained valet once more.

"Yes, sir," he said. "Your portmanteau will be ready in ten minutes. Half an hour later me an' Mrs. Bates will leave for my cousin's place in Hampshire."

Theydon returned to the sitting room. His

sister's face was white with fear, but he threw restraint to the winds.

"Mollie," he said, placing his hands on her shoulders, "you are very dear to me, but there is one woman in the world who, if fate proves kind, may yet be dearer. She is in danger. If some one said that of you to your husband, what would he do?"

She kissed him with tremulous lips. "He would act just as you are going to act," she said. "But, dear, can't you trust me? I cannot help, perhaps, but I can pray for you."

"Well, then, Sis, I won't fence with you any longer. There's a sort of feud between Mr. Forbes and a faction in China. He helped the reformers financially, and some supporters of the dethroned dynasty are trying to compel him by force to give them a list of the prominent men who control the revolution. If he yields, it means that nearly a hundred leading men in China—men whose only thought is the welfare and progress of their country—will be ruthlessly murdered. If he continues to refuse, his own life and the lives of his wife and daughter are at stake. These fiends killed Mrs. Lester within a few feet of this very room. They killed her husband six months ago. They tried to kidnap Evelyn Forbes yesterday, and succeeded, for a while, in carrying off her mother, their plan being to torture one or both, even unto death. Heaven help me, I

love Evelyn Forbes, and I would count my life
well spent if I died in defending her. Should
anything happen to me and she is spared, tell
her that, will you—and my spirit will thank
you.''

"We must not think of death, but of life,''
was the brave answer. "Can I do anything?
Could George assist if he were here?''

"No, Mollie. Perhaps I am exaggerating
matters, though the history of this week would
make strange reading if published broadcast.
Indeed I shall now urge on Mr. Forbes the ad-
visability of sending the facts to the press.
London would be stirred to its depths, and
every one of its citizens would be quick to
observe and report the presence of Chinamen
or Japanese in the West End. Some innocent
Orientals would suffer, but the police might
at least be enabled to capture the pestiferous
gang which has committed this latest outrage.
Just think of some cold-blooded scoundrel
shooting at a sweet-mannered and gentle lady
like Mrs. Forbes!''

"Surely the authorities can protect her.''

"That is the wild absurdity of the position.
Of course, you didn't hear what Mr. Forbes
said. The armed detectives on duty in his
house actually saw the Chinaman who fired the
shot which wounded her, leaning out through
the window of a closed car. But they cannot
blaze away at any passer-by merely because

he is, or resembles, an Asiatic. What they dare not do, however, he and I will endeavor cheerfully. Bates!"

"Yes, sir," came the cry from a bedroom.

"If you are packing two bags, put that pistol and a box of cartridges in the smaller one."

"Yes, sir."

Mrs. Paxton at this crisis proved herself a woman of spirit.

"I think you're right, Frank," she said quietly. "I refuse to believe that any British court of justice would blame any man for defending the lives of his wife and daughter, nor you for helping him. If the peacefully disposed Chinese residents in London wish to avoid risk let them keep away from No. 11 Fortescue Square. May I come with you?"

"You, Mollie?"

He looked at her with troubled eyes. For the moment such was the fire in his brain he did not understand.

She laughed gallantly.

"I don't mean as one of the garrison," she said. "May I not make the acquaintance of these people? Sometimes, the mere knowledge that others are aware of one's troubles and sympathize with one is comforting. Miss Beale is not expecting me till tea time. I told her I might lunch with you. Indeed, I promised to call at her hotel for her letters, and that is halfway on your road."

"You're a brick, Mollie," said her brother. "I do believe Evelyn Forbes will be glad to see you. The most amazing thing about this affair is that none of the many friends Mr. and Mrs. Forbes and their daughter must possess in London has the slightest inkling of the truth. I suppose the servants are instructed to tell ordinary callers that the various members of the family are out, or some of them indisposed, or something of the sort. . . . But come along! I hear Bates banging my belongings into the passage. I'm in a fever to be there and taking part in the row."

Soon they were seated in a taxi and speeding to Smith's Hotel, Jermyn Street.

"Have you invited Miss Beale to reside with you while she is in London, Sis?" said Theydon, allowing his thoughts to dwell for a moment on the less tragic side of events.

"Yes. What else could I do? Poor thing, she was terrified at the notion of sleeping under the same roof as a Chinaman."

"I don't blame her. But there's a certain element of risk for you, Mollie—"

"Oh, bother! Don't tell me that a few Chinamen can threaten all London."

Yet even the valiant-hearted Mrs. Paxton yielded to the haunting terror of the bandits when the taxi drew in behind a gray car already standing at the curb outside Smith's

Hotel, and her brother grasped her wrist in sudden warning.

"Sit still," he said. "Now we may get on the track of some of the gang. That is the car which followed me on Monday night."

His sister, of course, did not understand. She had heard nothing of the pursuit and its curious sequel.

"Do you mean it is one of the cars which these men use?" she whispered breathlessly.

"Yes. I'll explain later. But what impudence! The scoundrels have not even changed the number plate."

Unquestionably, the number of the gray landaulet now within a few feet of them was XY 1314. Theydon stooped, opened a dressing case lying at his feet, and took out the automatic pistol placed there by Bates. He put it in the right-hand pocket of his coat.

"Now, I'll reconnoiter," he said, and opened the door. The taxi driver was already gazing curiously in at his fares, wondering why one or both did not alight.

"Be ready to start the instant I want you," said Theydon to the man, and he strolled past the gray car, with every sense alert, every muscle braced. If Wong Li Fu were seated inside he would cover him with the pistol and hold him there until the police came, or shoot him dead if he offered any resistance.

Fortunately, therefore, all things considered,

the interior of the car was absolutely empty, save for a copy of the *Times* on the back seat. Even the presence of the newspaper was significant. In that issue should have appeared Forbes's reply to "Y. M." which Furneaux had suppressed as unnecessary.

There was a chauffeur at the wheel—no Chinaman, but a tightly-buttoned and black-legginged young Englishman—in fact, the real thing in chauffeurs.

"Whose car is this?" demanded Theydon.

"It belongs to the Chinese Embassy, sir," said the man, answering civilly enough, but not unnaturally showing some surprise at the curt question.

"Are you waiting here for some official of the Embassy?" went on Theydon.

"Not exactly, sir, some friends of His Excellency." The man glanced toward the door of the hotel. "Here they are now," he added.

Theydon turned. Two Chinamen, sedate, pig-tailed persons, were descending the steps. With them was Furneaux! One of the Orientals gave Theydon a rather sharp glance, having noticed, apparently, that he was conversing with the chauffeur, but Furneaux, after a stonily indifferent stare, said to the second Chinaman, in plain English:

"Do you mind dropping me at Scotland Yard?"

"With pleasure," was the composed reply.

The three entered, and the gray car made off, leaving Theydon to gaze blankly after it. His sister, though badly scared at first, quickly recovered her self-possession. She even made a joke of the incident.

"As an anti-climax, Frank, that is the best thing of its kind you have ever brought off," she tittered.

CHAPTER XV

THOUGH a prey to that most burthensome of cares—the uneasy consciousness of an impalpable yet ever-threatening evil—Theydon was not blind to the humorous element in the present situation. Mrs. Paxton, of course, did not know who the little man accompanying the Chinamen was.

She had seen her brother stalk the motor car and its presumed occupants in the most approved melodramatic fashion, and could not help noticing his complete discomfiture. Naturally she imagined he had encountered a pair of perfectly harmless citizens of the Middle Kingdom, and, being one of those happy beings more readily swayed to laughter than to tears, rallied him upon an apparent blunder.

"Never before have I discovered a neurotic streak in you, Frank," she said, after she had obtained a couple of letters for Miss Beale, and they were *en route* again. " Come now, confess. If Evelyn Forbes—or, let me see, is it Phyllis or Doris? No, Evelyn. If Evelyn Forbes, then, did not happen to be a remarkably pretty girl, would you really attach such terrific importance to the mad goings-on of a set of Chinese fanatics? I doubt it."

The cab was threading its way through the traffic of St. James Street and Piccadilly on a busy afternoon in the season, and Theydon had much to tell her before they arrived at Fortescue Square, but he sat by her side in silence for a little while.

"Frank," said his sister, at last, "it is not like you to seek refuge in silence. I'm sorry if my chaff annoyed you. Don't forget that you know everything about this mysterious business, and I know very little."

Her sympathetic voice roused him from the stupor which had benumbed his senses.

"I allowed imagination to run away with me, Sis," he said gently. "It was thoughtless on my part. Please forgive me. I suppose those two Chinamen are unofficially connected with the Embassy. At any rate, the man with them, the little man in a blue serge suit and straw hat, is Furneaux of Scotland Yard, a pocket marvel among detectives, the sort of criminal-hunter you read about in Gaboriau, but can scarcely accept as existing in real life."

From that instant he bent his wits to the task of acquainting Mrs. Paxton with the history of the preceding three days. He was aware of the irrepressible trembling which shook her slender frame when he spoke of the

ivory skull found in Edith Lester's underbodice, and the replica of the same grewsome
token sent to Forbes, so suppressed all mention of his own experiences on returning to
Innesmore Mansions overnight.

Furneaux had asked him for the bit of
ivory that morning, and, incidentally, had produced the others from his pocket. The detective gave no reason for his eagerness to
possess these trophies, but seemed to invest
them with great importance. While keeping
up a constant flow of talk with his sister, Theydon tried to puzzle out the detective's motive
for carrying such sinister messengers of death
around London.

Try as he might, he could arrive at no
plausible explanation, but he did not make the
error of attributing Furneaux's action to mere
impulse. Those men of the Yard had a solid
foundation for every step they took. Even the
visit to Smith's Hotel, and subsequent departure in the gray car, meant a definite stride
onward in the fight against Wong Li Fu. Of
that he was assured.

At 11 Fortescue Square there were no outward signs of recent disturbance beyond the
presence of a sharp-eyed policeman at each corner of the row of houses of which Mr. Forbes's
residence formed one of the center pair.
Theydon expected to see a shattered window in
the drawing-room on the first floor, where,

286

presumably, Mrs. Forbes was standing when the shot was fired, but each pane in three large windows was intact, and the windows were closed.

Then he reflected—as, indeed, proved to be the case—that on such a fine day the window would probably be open. Two windows on the second floor and one in the cloakroom near the front door were raised a few inches, but drawn curtains screened from observation any watchful eye which might be stationed behind them. As a matter of fact, armed detectives were hidden there, and they had been given specific orders to shoot without warning any one of Chinese appearance whose behavior was suspicious, while three men were in readiness in the hall to rush out into the square and make an arrest under similar circumstances.

In that fashionable quarter, at that hour, automobiles of every type were passing constantly. At the very next door a well-appointed carriage and pair was in readiness to take an elderly lady for a drive in the park. As yet, none of the other residents in the square had the remotest notion that No. 11 was in a state of siege. The position of affairs, if it were not so desperate, was almost amusing!

Mrs. Paxton and Theydon were admitted without any delay, and Forbes himself hurried downstairs to greet them. He was pale, but quite composed. All the nervous uncertainty of the previous day had vanished. He was armed and willing for the fray. If, as was by no means unlikely, Wong Li Fu staked everything on a gambler's throw and led his cohort in a daylight raid on the house, the Manchu leader would meet with a very warm reception.

Forbes was surprised to find that a lady had come with Theydon, but expressed his pleasure at the visit, which, he said, was just the thing his wife and Evelyn needed.

"Yes," he went on cheerfully, noting the astonishment caused by his words, "Mrs. Forbes is not seriously injured. The bullet lacerated the top of her left shoulder, and the wound is painful but superficial. She positively refuses to remain in bed, so our doctor humored her, provided she promises not to pass the time looking through the drawing-room window!"

Mrs. Paxton, to whose senses the presence of armed detectives and constables in uniform was even more eloquent than her brother's words, glanced about the spacious entrance hall with wide-eyed amazement. Once she and her brother were recognized as friends of the family, the men on duty gave them no heed.

Outside were the familiar sounds of London traffic; within were preparations for conflict. The police carried revolvers openly in leather cases strapped to their belts. On a table near the library door were several automatic pistols ready to be snatched up in an emergency. An alert detective, revolver in hand, was peering through the curtains of the cloakroom; this sentry, in particular, would alarm the garrison if, as Winter had definitely warned his assistants, an attempt were ever made to enter the house by main force.

"I think I must be dreaming," she said, trying bravely to lessen the gravity of the statement by smiling at its inherent absurdity. "Am I in London, or have I been whisked by magic to one of those outposts of civilization where men and women of European race are often compelled to band together for protection against savages? One reads of such things comfortably while dawdling over breakfast, and one wonders idly why people go to such places. But that something of the sort could happen in London—why, it is simply fantastic!"

"It is unpleasantly real, for all that, Mrs. Paxton," said Forbes, leading the way up the stairs. "What else can we do? If the authorities surrounded the house with a cordon of soldiers London would be in an uproar. We want to avoid that, at all costs. I have been in communication with the Home Office, and am advised that, if we decide to put up with the inconvenience, it is better, and actually less risky, to hold out here than seek safety by flight. I understand that Scotland

289

Yard is not losing an unnecessary minute, but there are obvious difficulties in the way of decisive action. It is considered worse than useless to effect isolated arrests, as these tend only to put the other members of the gang on their guard. The chief inspector tells me that he had some hope of being able to make a big haul tonight. The principal drawback is the language bar. Chinese interpreters are few and far between in London, and those who do exist—in the East End, for instance—have long since lost any useful acquaintance with events in their own country. This is a political matter, you understand, and must be fought out on political lines. Strange as it may sound in your ears, the cause of Chinese freedom is at issue in this very house. If Wong Li Fu could secure a list of names now locked in a bureau in my library the Constitutional party in China would perish forthwith for want of leaders. But he won't get it. Thanks to your brother, Mrs. Paxton, his deadliest attack failed yesterday. For to-day's accident we have ourselves to blame. We did not even suspect that his malignity would take the form of shooting the first person who chanced to look out of a window.''

He had halted at the top of the broad staircase while making that stirring declaration of war.

"Pardon my outspokenness," he said, sinking his voice to a lower tone. "I don't want to frighten my wife on my own account. She believes now that the police are hunting these scoundrels in every hole and corner of London. In a sense, that is true, but we never know the moment some extraordinary action may be taken, so we remain constantly on the *qui vive.*"

He heard the telephone ring beneath, and turned quickly.

"I may be wanted," he said. "I'll join you presently. There is my wife's boudoir," and he pointed to a door. "Take Mrs. Paxton in, Theydon. Mrs. Forbes and Evelyn will be glad of your company."

Theydon knocked, and heard Evelyn's voice bidding him enter. Mrs. Forbes was lying on a couch, and her daughter had evidently been seated near her, reading a newspaper.

"I've brought my sister to see you," he explained. "I've been relating such heroic things about you that she simply refused to go home without ocular proof of your existence."

Mrs. Forbes would have risen, but was restrained by the girl's emphatic cry:

"Mother, why won't you behave like an obedient invalid?"

Thus coerced, "Mother" did behave.

"They insist on treating me as a casualty,"

she cried cheerfully. "What is your sister's name, Mr. Theydon?"

"Mollie," he said thoughtlessly, for he had just touched Evelyn Forbes's hand, and the mere contact gave him an electrical shock.

The women laughed, and Mrs. Paxton blushed.

"Mollie Paxton, at any rate," she said, realizing at once that her brother had completely lost all self-possession at sight of his divinity. "Now, as you are going to stay here, Frank, you shall give me the full measure of the few minutes I can spare, so go and talk over your adventures with Mr. Forbes while I gossip with the prisoners."

Theydon saw that his tactful sister had struck the right note. She might be trusted to make herself eminently agreeable. Her bright, smiling manner had already created a good impression, and a lively chat with one who had not passed through the vicissitudes which beset the Forbes family would be an excellent tonic.

"Before I efface myself, may I be allowed to congratulate Mrs. Forbes on her escape?" he said, halting at the door.

"Yes, you may," replied the older lady. "And, just to show that I am convalescent, kindly tell Tomlinson that I am coming down to luncheon, and that Mrs. Paxton will join us."

292

Forbes was leaving the telephone when Theydon regained the hall and explained that he had been dismissed from the feminine conclave upstairs. The millionaire closed the door and motioned his companion to a chair.

"How long will it be before London wakes up to the knowledge of what is going on in its midst?" he said. "Is there anything in the newspapers? I have had no time to read. I passed a rather sleepless night, so did not rise until a late hour. Then Helen was fired at. I need hardly tell you that my time has been fully occupied since."

Theydon gave a résumé of the paragraph which had appeared in at least one of the morning journals, and admitted that some inkling of the truth was bound to gain publicity during the next few hours.

"I cannot understand why it is the reporters are not here by the score already," he went on. "Some passer-by must have seen or heard the shooting. A pistol cannot be fired in a quiet square like this without attracting general attention."

"That is the extraordinary part of it," said Forbes, smiling grimly. "People heard the noise, of course, but came to the conclusion that a cylinder in the car had back-fired. That was the view taken by two policemen on duty within a few yards of the house. A detective stationed in the cloakroom actually saw the man raising the weapon. He, of course, was under no delusion as to what had happened, and ran out instantly, but the car was then traveling at a fast pace, and was out of sight before the nearest constable could even endeavor to stop it. Anyhow, what was the man to do? We cannot expect that he would whip out a revolver, if he carries one, and blaze away indiscriminately at car and occupants if the chauffeur refused to pull up. Really, Theydon, Wong Li Fu has perplexed the authorities more than any desperado known to this generation. He is aware that his hostage has escaped from Croydon, so he calmly drives past my house, knowing full well that it is efficiently guarded, and fires a pot shot at the first person seen through one of the windows. The man whom I have spoken to over the telephone shares that opinion. He is one of the legal advisers of the Home Office. Just to show the baffling nature of the problem, he says that it will be absolutely impossible, on the evidence available at present, to frame a charge against any Chinaman other than Wong Li Fu. Yet we know that he has at least four or five, and probably three times as many, accomplices."

"Have the police yet obtained any real clew as to the whereabouts of the gang's headquarters? They must have some sort of meeting place. They must eat and sleep somewhere."

"That big detective, Winter, came here this morning. He seemed to be very confident, though I think I gave him the worst shock he has received for many a year when I informed him that within an hour after he had left the house Mrs. Forbes had been shot at, and narrowly escaped a fatal wound. It was he who asked me to invite you to come here. I'm exceedingly sorry that our acquaintance, begun so happily, should involve you in personal risk—"

"As for that," broke in Theydon, "I would not change places with any man in England at this moment."

He feared instantly that he might have said too much, and added with a laugh:

"Don't forget, Mr. Forbes, that I write books, some of them—the most popular ones, I am afraid—being of a sensational type. When this tornado has died down, and Wong Li Fu is carefully hanged, and you and your family are recuperating in Sutherlandshire, I shall resume work with a new inspiration. Never again shall I say to myself, 'Oh, that is too far-fetched,' or fear that I am straining my readers' credulity beyond bounds. If a small gang of Chinamen and Japanese can hold up London, bamboozle the best men in Scotland Yard, and keep a man of your position a prisoner in his own house, I need have no fear of adopting any situation my fertile

brain can evolve, because four days ago I
would have scoffed at the things which have
actually happened as quite impossible and
therefore unbelievable."

"Japanese, you say? Why do you mention
Japanese?"

"The American, Mr. Handyside, tells me
the skulls are of Japanese workmanship. He
argues also that the wrestling tricks of which
Winter and I, and Mrs. Forbes in lesser degree, have had some experience, are Japanese.
More than that, a Jap was arrested outside
my place early this morning."

"Mr. Winter said something about it, but
he spoke only of Chinamen."

"I have Furneaux's authority for the statement that the prisoner is a Jap, and belongs
to a society calling itself the 'Sons of Nippon.'"

"But confound it, I have no quarrel with
Japan. If anything, I am one of her best
friends."

"I must get Handyside to propound one of
his favorite theories. He says that a powerful
and growing party among our allies in the
Far East means to keep China in a condition
of anarchy until Japan is prepared, financially
and in armament, to take a commanding share
in the ultimate settlement. But, at best, the
few Japanese adventurers in league with
Wong Li Fu hardly count. Once he is laid by

the heels this feud will evaporate into thin air.''

"If it doesn't, I must ask the Government to provide safe quarters for my family in the Tower," muttered Forbes, rising and pacing the room in the same thoughtful, care-laden way as he had paced it when Theydon first told him of Edith Lester's end.

" You said Wong Li Fu knew that Mrs. Forbes had been rescued from her bonds last night," went on Theydon. "I suppose Winter told you that. Was he only assuming the fact, or have there been developments at Croydon?"

"A motor car drove up to the gate openly at ten o'clock this morning. A police sergeant, jumping to the conclusion that one of his own chiefs or a representative of Scotland Yard was paying the place a visit, incautiously showed himself in the doorway, whereupon the car raced away. It was an unfortunate and, perhaps, costly blunder, but the man is hardly to be blamed. The very audacity of the gang is their best safeguard."

A luncheon gong clanged in the hall. Both men started, and then laughed.

"You see," cried Forbes. "These rascals have got us on the jump. I don't know how long my servants will stand the racket. They are most loyal, and Tomlinson vows that not a syllable has been breathed outside by any of our domestics. But the women's nerves are on edge. A scullery maid dropped a decanter a little while since, and the crash drew blood-curdling shrieks from the kitchen. Come, let us eat, drink, and be merry, for tomorrow we die. The quotation is not a felicitous one. Indeed, it is distinctly ominous, but it seems to meet the conditions.''

He threw open the door, and saw the three ladies descending the stairs.

''Helena,'' he cried sternly, ''the doctor said you were not to stir out of your room.''

''My dear, the doctor is a mere man, and fancies that a woman is not fitted for warfare. He is quite mistaken. When aroused we can be terrible.''

Mrs. Forbes, whose face was paler and eyes seemingly bigger and more luminous than usual, was leaning on Evelyn's arm. She was dressed in a blue tulle costume which lent a fragile air to an already slender form, but she smiled so unaffectedly that even the policeman grinned.

''You certainly look ferocious,'' said her husband, yielding instantly, as she well knew would happen.

''I believe you are all jealous,'' she vowed. ''I am the only one who has really been in the forefront of the battle. No. I forgot you, Mr. Theydon. Didn't that horrid man knock you down?''

"Yes," said Theydon, moistening his lips with his tongue. There was such a peculiar rasp in his voice that it evoked a general laugh.

Obviously the guests meant to avoid serious topics during the meal. Evelyn Forbes chimed in with a reminiscence of her schooldays in Brussels, and soon the talk was general, ranging from the year's Academy to the Ladies' Gold Championship.

Mrs. Paxton, an excellent mimic, was amusing them with imitations of the voice and manner of a certain well-known lady golfer, when she was interrupted by three sharp, irregular cracks which seemed to come from the dining-room windows. Simultaneously a picture frame on the opposite wall was split and a Worcester vase on a sideboard was smashed to atoms.

Theydon, owing to his position at the table, was the first to notice three small, starred holes in the plate glass of the windows.

"Don't stand up!" he said, instantly. "Some one is shooting at the house. Crouch on the floor, for Heaven's sake!"

That urgent appeal was emphasized by a fourth bullet, which, taking a lower flight, barely missed Forbes, upset a Venetian glass flower vase on the table, and buried itself in the lower half of the sideboard.

Forbes, heedless of the possible consequences to himself, sprang to his wife's assistance, and, interposing his body as a shield between her and the windows, led her to an angle of the wall where she would be safe. The younger women, after a momentary hesitation, dropped to the floor and crawled to the same refuge. Theydon ran out. The front door was open.

The police had heard the shooting, the sound of which had been deadened to those in the dining room by the breaking glass and china. But within a few minutes a useless pursuit was abandoned. The fusillade had come from a car which halted close to the garden railings on the far side of the square. Though the trees were nearly in full leaf, and dense shrubberies seemed to shut off every house from any such method of attack, investigation proved that it was possible to estimate accurately the position of the dining-room windows in No. 11.

When Theydon returned he found Forbes and the ladies gathered in the hall.

"Another narrow escape on both sides," he said coolly. "Two policemen were just too late to interfere. Of course, they did not anticipate a move in that quarter."

"Have the—er—enemy made off in a car?" said Mrs. Forbes.

"Yes. A constable in a taxi is trying to follow them."

"Well, then, let us finish our luncheon. I had hardly touched my cutlet."

"By Jove, Helena, that doctor of ours was decidedly in error," cried her husband. "You're right. If we're besieged we must carry ourselves according to the code. Mrs. Paxton, I hope it won't disturb you if a shell bursts before coffee is served!"

Theydon glanced through a window before resuming his seat.

"That volley has done things!" he announced. "London is stirring at last. There's a crowd in front of the house, and a short, fat man is explaining the procedure. Prepare now to receive the press in battalions."

CHAPTER XVI

WHEREIN UNEXPECTED ALLIES APPEAR

ALTHOUGH, as shall be seen, the final and complete defeat and extinction of the London section of the Young Manchus were directly due to forces set in motion by Furneaux, it was Winter's painstaking way of covering the ground that unearthed the fraternity's meeting place, and thus brought matters to a head speedily. For the rest, events followed their own course, and great would have been the fame of the prophet who predicted that course accurately.

In later days, when more ample knowledge was available, it was a debatable point whether or not the inmates of No. 11 Fortescue Square were saved from an almost maniacal vengeance by the fact that a crisis was precipitated. Winter maintained stoutly that the police must triumph in the long run, whereas Furneaux held, with even greater tenacity, that although the gang would undoubtedly be broken up, that much-desired end might have been attained after, and not before, a dire tragedy occurred in the Forbes household.

The pros and cons of the argument were

equally numerous and weighty. They cannot be marshaled here. Each man and woman who reads this record will probably form an emphatic opinion tending toward the one side or the other. All that a veracious chronicler can accomplish is to set forth a plain tale of events in their proper sequence, and leave the ultimate verdict to individual judgment.

Winter was a hard-headed, broad-minded official, whose long and wide experience enabled him to estimate at their true value the far-reaching powers of the State as opposed to the machinations of a few determined outlaws. On the other hand, the amazing facility with which Furneaux could enter into the twists and turns of the criminal mind entitles his matured views to much respect.

At any rate, this is what happened.

Winter was sitting in his office, smoking a fat cigar, and wading through reports brought in by subordinates concerning every opium den and Chinese boarding house in the East End, when Furneaux entered.

"Any luck?" inquired the chief, laying aside one document which seemed to merit fuller inquiry; it described a club much frequented by Chinese residents in London, men of a higher class than the sailors and firemen brought to the port by ships trading with the Far East, and an outstanding feature of the Young Manchus' operations was the intelligent grasp of

the ways and means of modern civilized life
these filibusters exhibited.

"So-so," squeaked Furneaux.

He flung himself into a big armchair, curled
up in it like an animated Buddha, and extracted one of the three ivory skulls from a
waistcoat pocket.

"If you could only speak, you image of
evil!" he muttered. "You're not so dead that
you cannot work mischief. Why the deuce,
then, can't you mouth your incantations?
Then we would listen and learn."

Winter, still sorting his papers, cocked
the cigar inquisitively on one side of his
mouth.

"Oh, I have ascertained a lot about the
inner politics of China," mumbled Furneaux,
irritably, gazing fixedly at the skull after one
quick glance of his colleague. "Every little
helps, of course. I have met some Chinamen
this morning who would cheerfully plunge
Wong Li Fu into a cauldron of boiling oil, and
stir him round with a long stick when he was
in it. One man, quite an important personage
in the jute line, has lost a brother and a
brother-in-law, the one in Canton, the other
in Pekin, and he lays both deaths at the door
of the redoubtable Wong. Another, the fellow who chanced to take up his quarters at
Smith's Hotel, is a delegate sent here spe-
cially to hunt out Wong, and destroy him. I

asked him how he meant to set about it, but his scheme is vague. He's an opportunist of the first water. 'Me catchee and killee Wong Li Fu one time,' was his best effort. I'm going to confront Len Shi with these two in Bow Street. They may worm something out of him. But will they own up if they do? Dashed if I know. The Oriental mind is on a par with their blessed language. It has three thousand ways of expressing one idea, and not one of 'em is our way."

"Has Theydon gone to Fortescue Square?"

"I suppose so. He turned up in Jermyn Street—outside Smith's Hotel, if you please, with a lady in a taxi."

"A lady? Miss Beale?"

"No, his sister, judging from the family likeness. His eyes grew goggled like yours when he saw the gray car."

"Didn't you explain matters?"

"Not I. Gave him the cut direct. My Chinamen are shy birds, and I daren't flutter them by letting them think there are too many foreign devils mixed up in the business. My London Chinaman was the brainy person who got the Embassy busy when Mrs. Lester's death was announced. He saw Wong Li Fu's hand in that from the first moment. Oddly enough, though he and a man from the Embassy followed Theydon from Waterloo to Forbes's place on Tuesday night, and again to Innesmore Mansions, he didn't recognize him today. Or perhaps he did. I don't know. Talk about the impassive Red Indian! A thoroughbred Chink would give a Pawnee chief one glass eye and a coat of paint, and then beat him hollow at the haughty indifference game.''

"My!'' said Winter admiringly, "you've got your tongue loose today. Well, here's an item which should prove useful. Whitechapel thinks we may find a Young Manchu or two among that collection,'' and he threw an official memorandum across the table.

Furneaux repocketed the skull, and was gazing moodily at the report, when a uniformed constable announced that a boy messenger wished to see a "detective" with regard to the typed letter delivered at Mr. Forbes's house on Wednesday evening.

"Show him up,'' said the chief, and a smart-looking boy, wearing the familiar uniform of his corps, was brought in. He glanced around inquiringly.

"Oh, you're the gentleman who came to our Piccadilly office,'' he said to Winter.

"Yes.''

"Well, sir, I haven't very much to tell you, but it was I who took the letter to Fortescue Square. I saw the sender, a foreign-looking gentleman, he was, with funny eyes, and I think I spotted him again this afternoon. He was coming out of a house in Charlotte Street."

"Are you sure?" demanded Winter, quickly.

"He was awful like the man who engaged me, sir, and dressed the same way."

"Did you notice the number of the house?"

"Yes, sir. No. 412."

"Quite certain about that?"

"Yes, sir."

"Good boy. If your information is of any service I'll take care you are not forgotten."

The boy saluted and went out.

"We must look up No. 412," said Winter, quietly; but there was a ring of genuine satisfaction in his voice, because the clew promised well, and it was a complete justification of the straightforward method he adopted in every inquiry, whereas Furneaux invariably preferred an abstruse theory to a definite piece of evidence.

The Jersey man's face had wrinkled as a preliminary to some sarcastic comment on what he termed the "handcuff" way of reasoning, when the telephone bell rang. Winter answered, and at once his self-possessed air fled. Indeed, it was a very angry man who listened, because a subordinate was telephoning from Fortescue Square a full account of the shooting outrage.

The Chief gave a few curt instructions as to

securing the adequate cooperation of the local
police, who should take measures to render
any repetition of such daring tactics absolutely
impossible.

"No one was injured, you say?" he added.

"No, sir."

"Were the ladies very much frightened?"

"They've gone back to finish luncheon, sir."

"Good. Evidently they're all of the right
breed. You can tell them I said so, if you
like. Assure Mr. Forbes that every care will
be taken to protect his house in future. See
that strong patrols occupy every point from
which a gun can be aimed at any window, even
the attics, in No. 11. Phone me again when
you have discussed matters with the district
superintendent."

The receiver clanged back into its hook.
Winter had not foreseen this latest move.
"Sheer impudence," he termed it.

"More bullets?" inquired Furneaux lacon-
ically.

"Yes. A long-range attack from across the
square. Four shots lodged in dining room."

"No one hurt, and no one arrested?"

"Not a soul."

"James," said the little man solemnly,
"Wong Li Fu is making us a laughing-stock.
Are you aware that the newspapers will get
on our track now? Can't you see the head-
lines?—'Another Sidney Street.' 'Chinese

Pirates Busy in London.' 'Scotland Yard Outwitted.' By this time tomorrow the Commissioner will be suggesting that you and I ought to think about retiring on pensions."

Winter jumped up, overturning a chair in his haste.

"Come!" he said. "If that Chinaman in Bow Street won't speak, I'll torture him. What of the other fellow who was caught near Innesmore Mansions?"

"He's a Jap. He knows nothing. He was hired for the job—to put any interfering bobby to sleep."

The chief inspector angrily bundled some papers into a drawer, and threw away his cigar, which he had allowed to go out. Furneaux produced an ivory skull again, and scowled at it, whereupon his superior, snorting with annoyance, strode to the window, and affected an interest he was far from feeling in the panorama of the Thames.

And thus they passed a harmonious quarter of an hour, which came to an end with the appearance of an attendant to announce the arrival of "two Chinese gentlemen to see Mr. Furneaux."

They went down in the elevator without exchanging a word. At the entrance stood the gray car, in which the Chinamen were already seated. Furneaux introduced the chief inspector, and they were whisked to Bow Street.

There in a cell they found Len Shi, a somewhat sullen-looking man whose European chauffeur's livery seemed curiously raffish and unsuitable when contrasted with the more picturesque if sober-hued garments worn by his fellow-countrymen.

At first he maintained the sulky know-nothing rôle which he had adopted successfully with the official interpreter. Furneaux, watching the faces of prisoner and questioners, guessed that small progress was being made, so, waiting until Len Shi was evidently quite satisfied with himself, he suddenly thrust an ivory skull before the man's eyes. The result was unexpected but puzzling. The man was badly scared, beyond doubt, but he now became obstinately silent.

Winter, than whom no living actor could play up better to Furneaux's tactics in a touch-and-go encounter of this sort, assumed a highly tragic air.

"Handcuff that man, and bring him out!" he said to the constable in charge of the cells.

Len Shi blanched. He estimated the legal methods of Great Britain by those which obtained in his own land, and probably thought he was being led forth to immediate execution.

The whole five crowded into the car, and the driver, the same English chauffeur to whom Theydon had spoken, was told to make for 412 Charlotte Street, and pass the house slowly,

310

but not pull up. Len Shi, though quaking with alarm, bore himself with a certain dignified stoicism until he found out where the car was apparently stopping. Then he said something in a panic-stricken voice and the jute merchant, who spoke English fluently, turned to Furneaux.

"Tell the chauffeur to return," he said. "Len Shi will now confess."

Once started, Len Shi talked volubly. The others merely put in a question now and then, and the detectives curbed their impatience as best they might until Len Shi was safely lodged in Bow Street again.

Then Winter led his Chinese helpers into an inner office and closed the door.

"Well?" he said, addressing the jute merchant. The other Chinaman had very little English and could not maintain a conversation.

But, to the chief inspector's surprise and wrath, the English-speaking Chinaman had only a request to make.

"Give me and my friend those three ivory skulls," he said.

"Why?" he said.

"Without them we can accomplish nothing."

"Be good enough to explain yourself. Above all, tell me what Len Shi has been jabbering about. He had plenty to say."

"He told us of the fate of our friends in China. Those things do not concern you. What

311

you want is to have Wong Li Fu and the others
—there are nearly twenty in all—delivered
into your hands. Very well. Give us those
ivory skulls, and bring your men to that house
in Charlotte Street, at one o'clock this night,
and you will take them without a blow being
struck."

"That is our business, not yours," said Winter, gruffly decisive. "I cannot expose you two
gentlemen to any personal risk in this affair.
Kindly—"

"You do not understand," broke in the jute
merchant, addressing the burly representative
of the Criminal Investigation Department as if
he were a fractious child who must be informed as to the why and wherefore of a dis-
agreeable duty. "What will you do? Surround the house with policemen, break in the
doors, and fight? You may, or may not succeed. Some, plenty, of your men will certainly
be killed. That is not good. We do not wish
it. Give me those skulls. I and my friend
will go there. You come at one o'clock, tap
so on the door, and we will admit you. Then
you take Wong Li Fu and all the others.
There will be no fight."

The Chinaman's manner was singularly im-
pressive as he tapped three times on a high
desk to emphasize, as it were, his instructions.
The sound, too, was curious. He did not use
his knuckles, but bunched the fingers of his

right hand together, and rapped on the wood with the long nails which are a mark of distinction in his race.

"We make things easy and certain for you," he added, more by way of painstaking argument than because any further explanation was really necessary. "You do not wish to fail, no? You want to be sure that Wong Li Fu's evil deeds shall be stopped? Good. We do that—I and my friend. We can pass the door-keepers. Can you? No. At one o'clock we open the door and the Young Manchus will be wholly in your power, to do with them what you will. I promise that, and my word is always taken in the city."

Winter turned troubled eyes on Furneaux.

"What do you say?" he muttered irresolutely.

"I think the plan is a good one, and should be adopted," was the instant reply.

Nevertheless, Winter was perplexed. He hemmed and hawed a good deal. Seldom did he hesitate in this fashion. As a rule, he was quick to decide and quicker to act.

"I might entertain your scheme if I were told more about it," he said dubiously, gazing with troubled eyes at the Chinaman's blandly inscrutable face. "Please believe me when I say that I trust your good faith, but I am not sure that even you understand fully the nature of the adventure you have in mind. Wong Li

Fu has already committed one murder in London. He has attempted others, and is absolutely careless of consequences. How can I have any guarantee that you and this other gentleman may not be his next victims? He is a person who displays a somewhat forced humor. We might enter the Charlotte Street house at one o'clock and find your corpses there, with labels and ivory skulls neatly attached.''

"That will not be so," was the grave answer.

"If I agree, what time do you propose going there?"

"About midnight."

"And do you expect the police to leave the whole neighborhood severely alone for another hour?"

"Not unless you wish it. If you so desire you can occupy both ends of the street, and arrest every Chinaman coming away from No. 412, but let those pass who go towards it."

"Will others go there—friends of yours, I mean?"

" Oh, yes. We will overpower the Young Manchus by taking them unaware. We will act quietly, but there will be no mistake. It is you who will err if you do not accept our help."

Then Winter yielded, though not with a good grace. The implied suggestion that the London police could not handle a set of Mongolian ruffians was utterly distasteful, yet he admitted, though unwillingly, that he did not want to sacrifice some of his best men in rushing the place.

"All right," he said. "Hand over the skulls, Furneaux! It is quite agreed," he went on, addressing the Chinaman again, "that I have full liberty of action in so far as preliminary arrangements are concerned? I see your point that Wong Li Fu must not be forewarned, and shall take care that my men are hidden. I have your positive assurance, too, that you are not exposing your own life in any way?"

"To the best of my belief I shall be as safe in Charlotte Street as I am here," said the jute merchant, smiling for the first time during the interview.

"One! Two! Three!" said Furneaux, counting the skulls into the Chinaman's outstretched hand.

For some reason, the action, no less than the words, jarred on Winter.

"I do wish you wouldn't be so d—d theatrical!" he growled.

Furneaux said nothing. He accompanied the chief inspector when the latter escorted the two Chinamen to their car, and whistled softly between his teeth while Winter and he were walking to Scotland Yard. The big man glowered at him once or twice, but passed no comment. When they reached the Embankment, Winter took Furneaux to his room, but left him instantly. He was absent a long time. When he came in again he was cheerfully placid.

Walking toward their favorite restaurant in Soho, they met a newsboy running with an edition of an evening newspaper damp from the press. The boy was shouting, " 'Orrible crime in the West End; Chinese outrage!" Furneaux bought a paper. It contained a lively account of the attack on Mr. Forbes's house and described the mansion as an armed fortress. Scores of police were parading the neighborhood and examining every passing motor car lest it held Chinese bandits. The arrest of Len Shi at St. Albans, and of a Japanese outside Innesmore Mansions, was recalled, and an Eastbourne correspondent had sent a fairly accurate version of the kidnaping of Mrs. Forbes.

" The pack is in full cry now, James," grinned Furneaux. "Tomorrow—"

"O, bother tomorrow! Let's eat, and talk about something else."

"What? Both? Well, now, if that isn't a bit of luck," cried a pleasant voice close behind them, and Mr. George T. Handyside held out his two hands.

"I was feeling kind of lonesome in the hotel, and just strolled out to look at the shops," he rattled on. "Say, can you boys

eat a line? Is there any place in London
where they know what a planked steak is?''

"Planked steak!'' snorted Furneaux.
"When you've tasted a porterhouse steak
grilled by a master hand you'll never mention any other variety again. Come right
along, Mr. Handyside. Tell us fairy tales
about God's own country. We're in the right
mood to believe anything!''

"But what's this story of another shooting
up in Fortescue Square? Is it true?''

Then Furneaux dug him in the ribs.

"This isn't the Wild and Woolly West,'' he
said. "This is London, sir, poor, old, played-
out London, whose beefy citizens do nothing
but eat, talk cricket or golf, and sleep. If
you credit the newspapers, you'll never get us
in the right perspective.''

Another newspaper boy raced past, bawling
loudly.

"All a flam, is it?'' said the American quizzically.

"No,'' said Winter, "it's the truth, and less
than the truth. Let's hunt that steak, and
we'll season the dish for you.''

Winter never erred when he chose a man
as a friend. He liked Handyside, and was
half inclined to drop a hint in his ear as to
the night's program, for the American had
seen Wong Li Fu more than once, and might
be useful for identification purposes.

CHAPTER XVII

THE SETTLEMENT

Now, Len Shi had communicated one vital fact to his compatriots which they had carefully concealed from the detectives. The opening campaign against Forbes had practically ended that day. Thenceforth, for a week, the Young Manchus meant to separate, revert to Chinese costume, live in Chinese boarding-houses in the East End, and thus utterly mislead and bamboozle the police, who, in their hunt for the miscreants, would be searching for Chinamen in European dress and living in European style.

Winter was in two minds whether or not to inform the inmates of No. 11 as to the contemplated raid on the Charlotte Street rendezvous. Ultimately, he decided to say nothing definite that evening. It was better that the threatened people and their guards should not relax their vigilance. "The best-laid schemes o' mice and men gang aft a-gley," and if, perchance, the jute merchant's plan, whatever it might be, miscarried, and some of the desperadoes escaped, they would be stirred to instant reprisals.

But there was no semblance of doubt or hesitation about the measures taken by the police. That night, from eleven o'clock onward, not even a prowling cat entered Charlotte Street without being seen by sharp eyes. Nearly opposite No. 412 was a large warehouse, with a back entrance a long way in the rear, and approached from another street.

At midnight three Chinamen appeared, turned into Charlotte Street from the south and shuffled on noiseless feet straight to No. 414. They knocked, and after some delay were admitted. A minute later three others came from the north, knocked on the door of No. 410 and disappeared, the delay, seemingly caused by a parley with some one within, being longer in this instance.

Afterward squads of Chinamen, exactly 25, all told, came from north and south in practically equal numbers and entered those two houses, but never a man entered, or passed, or came out of No. 412. These more numerous arrivals met with no hesitation on the part of the two doorkeepers. They entered without let or hindrance.

After that there was what is known in theatrical circles as a "stage wait." Charlotte Street, save for its loafers and an occasional belated resident of some dwelling other than those under observation, lapsed into its normal and utterly dismal gloom.

From 12:30 onwards, Winter, stationed on the south side, looked at his watch many times. A little man, mingling with the disreputable rascals on the north side, was similarly fidgety.

A tall, slim man, wearing a dark overcoat, who lurked in a doorway near Winter's post, blew the tip of the cigar he was smoking into a red glow so that he might look at his watch. Another tall man, rather more powerfully built, awaited developments with apparent unconcern. Mr. Handyside, in fact, was in the august company of the Commissioner of Police, and the latter, though eminently agreeable, nevertheless observed an Olympian attitude. Thus might Jove watch a gathering in the Pompic Way!

At 12:45 there was a stir. Out of 410 and 414 came 25 Chinamen. They gathered on the pavement, and did not attempt to walk away, though a sudden and concentrated advance was made by the two sets of loafers, while the doors of the warehouse opposite belched forth a startling array of constables in uniform.

Winter and Furneaux respectively headed the contingents from north and south. An inspector was in charge of the central body, and even a Chinaman who had not been a day in London must have realized that the intent of these swift-moving detachments was to cut off his escape if he meant flight. But not a Chinaman budged, save one, who seemed to recog-

nize the chief inspector, because he stepped
forward and said in suave tones:

"These men are my friends. The others
are inside. They are quite safe. Kindly wait
till one o'clock."

"I must understand what you mean, Mr. Li
Chang," said Winter sternly; for some reason, he distrusted the smooth-spoken jute merchant. "Why have you visited these two
houses, and not 412? And what do we gain
by waiting here any longer? We must have
been seen, and our purpose guessed."

"No," came the somewhat surprising answer. "No one in No. 412 is aware of your
presence. We have taken care of that. As
for the other houses, they provide the simplest
means of access to the center one. Doorways
have been made in the cellar walls and special
staircases built. Consequently, if you broke
open the door of 412 you would find the way
barred by two other locked doors, while the
occupants, if aroused, could escape from
either or both of the next houses. We Chinese have a long acquaintance with the needs
of a secret society. You may take it from
me that the obvious way into or out of an
opium den, for instance, is never the way
used by the habitués."

By this time the commissioner, Handyside,
Furneaux and the inspector had come up, and
the five formed a little group in the center

of a semicircle of detectives and police. There was absolutely no sign of life in any of the houses; save for the raiders and the stolid Orientals, the street itself was deserted. Many eyes, no doubt, were peering through darkened windows, but the denizens of Charlotte Street as a rule attend strictly to their own personal affairs when the police are in evidence.

"What do you advise, sir?" said Winter, addressing the commissioner. "Mr. Li Chang wants us to make no move until one o'clock. It is only a matter of six or seven minutes."

"And what then? Are we to enter these other houses, and not No. 412?"

"Yes," said the Chinaman.

"Have you left the doors open?"

"No. They must be forced. But there are only small locks. The bolts are drawn."

"The places are apparently in complete darkness. My men must use their lamps, and may be attacked."

"No," said Li Chang simply. "There will be no fighting. Those Manchu dogs are helpless. We have seen to that."

"But how? Do you mean that they are stupefied?"

"Bound," said the Chinaman. "Tied hand and foot."

"Again then, may I ask, why wait?"

"It will be in order," was the calm reply.

"I entered into an arrangement with you. I want to abide by it."

Winter breathed heavily. The ways of the Oriental were not his ways, but a bargain was a bargain, so what more could be said?

Suddenly, about two minutes to one o'clock, a curious crackling noise was heard, a column of sparks burst high above the steep roof of No. 412, and the upper windows of the opposite houses reflected a red glare.

"Good heavens! the place is on fire!" cried Winter.

Simultaneously came a shout from both ends of the street. Men were running from the detachment guarding the rear of the premises to say that a fierce fire was raging on the first floor back of No. 412.

"Smash in those three doors!" cried Winter to his helpers. "Drag out every Chinaman you meet! Handcuff them in threes and fours! Arrest these fellows standing outside, but keep the two lots separate!"

"Why are we, your friends, to be arrested?" demanded Li Chang's dignified voice.

"I'll soon tell you why, you slim demon!" shouted the chief inspector, roused to anger by the consciousness that he had been duped. "What fiendish trick have you played on those wretches penned up inside there? But I'll soon know."

He turned to the local officer.

"Better march this crowd of Chinamen straight to your station," he said. "I'll follow soon, and lay a charge."

He felt a claw-like hand on his arm, and wild with vexation though he was, forced himself to listen.

"We are ready to go where you wish," said Li Chang calmly. "But spare your own men. They must not enter No. 412. They will be blown to pieces. Stop them! I shall not warn you twice!"

Somehow, Winter was impelled to obey. The center door was already yielding, but he rushed forward and told the party which meant to enter at that point to abandon it, and reinforce their comrades. A number of detectives and police were already inside the dark hallways of Nos. 410 and 414 when the very walls trembled under the shock of a violent explosion in No. 412, which was quickly followed by three others.

A tongue of flame darted instantly to a height of many feet above the topmost storey, showing that the series of explosions had not only destroyed the whole rear section of the house, and thus given the fire fresh fuel and plenty of space but there could be no reasonable doubt that the bombs, if bombs they were, had themselves been filled with some highly inflammable substance. Thenceforth, the police

could do nothing beyond keeping at a distance
the crowds which soon gathered, and thus
clear a space for the operations of the fire
brigade.

No. 412 was thoroughly gutted. Not a shred
of the building remained except the crumbling
walls at front and back. Its neighbors were
in little better case, and the firemen devoted
their efforts mainly toward keeping the disaster within bounds.

One thing was certain. No human being
had escaped from out of that doomed habita-
tion. The fire, too, had gained hold with a
phenomenal rapidity which argued the use of
petrol, or some kindred agent of irresistible
potency when ignited.

Winter and Furneaux, accompanied by the
commissioner and Mr. Handyside, walked to
the local police station. The American was
the only one who spoke.

"Queer ducks, the Chinese!" he said, seemingly musing aloud rather than inviting comment. "They like to settle their own dif-
ferences. I guess we'd feel pretty much like
that if we lived in China."

No one took up the point thus raised. Winter bent a searching, almost sorrowful glance
at Furneaux, but the little man's eyes were
fixed on the ground, as though he were deep in
thought.

In the charge room of the police station the

twenty-five Chinamen awaited them. Twenty-five pairs of oblique eyes gleamed at the four when they entered, but not a word was spoken.

Winter, of course, singled out Li Chang for a parley.

"Now," he said, "tell me just what happened after you and these others went into the two houses in Charlotte Street."

The Chinaman faced him imperturbably. His manner was as unemotional and his words as slow and methodical as if he were selling jute in his East End warehouse.

"We asked to be admitted, and after giving the password and showing the sign there was no difficulty," he said. "We were in parties of three. As you probably saw, I headed one, which entered No. 410. My friend, Won Lung Foo, led the other. The ivory skulls made matters simple. We explained to the door-keepers that we had just arrived from China, and brought messages of great urgency. Once inside, we gagged and bound the door-keepers. Then we entered No. 412, where we knew that Wong Li Fu would be smoking opium with the remaining fourteen."

"Were there seventeen in the gang, all told?" broke in Furneaux.

"Seventeen Manchus. The rest are—paid men—of no account."

"Queer," muttered Furneaux, almost to

himself. "The story begins and ends with the number 17!"

Again did Winter strive to pierce his colleague with a look from those bulging eyes, but the little man was far too occupied with a singular numerical coincidence to pay any heed to him.

"Well, go on!" he said impatiently, glaring at the Chinaman.

"We went to the big room at the back," continued Li Chang quietly, uttering each word separately, and evidently weighing it in his mind to test its accuracy before use, "and found Wong Li Fu. Him we bound quickly, and very securely. The others we tied in twos and threes. Of course, we brought the two doorkeepers to the same room, so that you should experience no difficulty, but take them all together."

Here Mr. Won Lung Foo broke in. Evidently he could follow English better than speak it.

"Yes," he said. "We wantee you catchee Chineemans all togeller—muchee wantee!"

Then he smiled blandly, and his tongue rolled over his lips as though some fruit or sweetmeat had left a pleasant taste there.

"Then, if your surprise was so successful, what caused the fire?" said Winter, affecting a magnificent disregard of the plain facts.

Li Chang, for once, permitted his immobile

features to show some semblance of anxious uncertainty.

"That," he said, "is a mystery which can, perhaps, never be solved. But it saves your Government much trouble."

In those few words he expressed quite clearly the line he adhered to throughout a long cross-examination. Neither Winter nor the commissioner could shake him. The fire was an accident—the outcome of an extraordinary chance. He knew nothing whatsoever of its origin.

After a protracted debate in private between the two heads of the Criminal Investigation Department, the names and addresses of the prisoners were recorded and they were set at liberty.

Before Li Chang went away Furneaux demanded the return of the three ivory skulls, which were promptly handed over.

"One word in your ear," murmured the detective, *sotto voce*. "Did Wong Li Fu recognize you?"

"Oh, yes," said the Chinaman.

"And you spoke to him?"

"Oh, yes."

The eyes of the two clashed. For once, Furneaux peered deep into the mind of an Oriental, and what he saw there kept him quiet, but he knew, just as surely as if he had been present, exactly what Li Chang said to Wong

Li Fu. He delivered a message from two graves in far-off China.

.   .   .   .   .

And that is all—or nearly all.

The "Charlotte Street Fire" caused only a slight sensation. It became known that No. 412 was a resort of Chinese opium fiends, and the loss of the den and its frequenters was not treated as a National calamity. The shooting at No. 11 Fortescue Square was regarded much more seriously, and the newspapers were full of it all next day.

Thenceforth, however, interest flagged. Mr. Forbes and his family and servants left London for Scotland, and the Amateur Golf Championship came along, so the escapades of a few Chinese fanatics in London were quickly forgotten.

They were forgotten, that is, by most people; but one man, Frank Theydon, went back to his flat in Innesmore Mansions to plunge into work and strive vainly to obliterate those pages of his memory charged with bitter-sweet day-dreams.

Strive as he would, and did, to bury the past under the duties and cares of the present, the radiant vision of Evelyn Forbes remained uneffaceable and entrancing.

But he was built of tough fiber, and resolutely refused an invitation to visit the Sutherlandshire glen in which Forbes and his daughter were sedulously nursing to health and strength the dear wife and mother whose nervous system had suffered far more than she permitted to become known under the stress and strain of the kidnaping experience.

Even when Evelyn herself wrote, seconding her father's most friendly note, Theydon pleaded the exigencies of his profession and filled a letter with an amusing account of Bates's chagrin because he had failed to "bag a Chinaman on his own account," having actually purchased a pistol and fixed it in position before he and his wife quitted the flat.

Three months passed. On August 9, a broiling morning, Theydon was dejectedly reading of preparations for the "Twelfth," when a telegram reached him. It read:

"Handyside has arrived here in his car. Come for the gathering of the clan. We take no refusal. Forbes."

Theydon traveled north that night. He reached the glen in time for dinner next evening and passed a few delightfully miserable days in Evelyn's company.

At last, feeling that he was losing grip and might act foolishly, he announced to Forbes, one night when a glorious moon was shining, and he knew that Evelyn was awaiting him in the garden, that he must leave for London next day.

"Why?" inquired his host. "Has something

unforeseen happened? I thought you meant remaining here till the end of the month at the earliest."

"I'm sorry," said Theydon, chewing a cigar viciously as a means toward maintaining his self-control. "I'm sorry, but I must go."

There was a slight pause. Forbes looked at his young friend with those earnest, deep-seeing eyes of his.

"Is it a personal matter?" he went on.

"Yes."

Again there was a pause. Theydon was well aware that he risked a grave misunderstanding, but that could not be avoided. It might be even better so. And then his blood ran cold, because Forbes was saying:

"Are you leaving us because of anything Evelyn has said or done?"

"No, no!" came the frenzied answer. "Heaven help me, why do you ask that?"

"Heaven helps those who help themselves," said the older man. "That is a trite saying, but it meets the case. I think I diagnose your trouble, my boy. You are in love with Evelyn, and dare not tell her so, because I happen to be a rich man. Really I didn't think you had so poor an opinion of me as to believe that money or rank would count against my daughter's happiness."

He said other things—kindly, wise, appreciative—but Frank Theydon never knew what they were. He managed to stammer out some words of gratitude and then went to find Evelyn.

She had crossed a sloping lawn and was standing by the side of a little stream that gurgled and bubbled in joyous career to the nearby loch. She had thrown a white shawl over her head and shoulders, and looked adorably sylphlike as she turned on hearing his footsteps; the moonlight shone on her face and was reflected in her eyes.

"Oh, you're here at last!" she cried gaily. "The next time I ask any cavalier to escort me he will come more quickly, I imagine."

He stood in front of her, and stretched out both hands.

"Evelyn," he said, "here is one cavalier, at any rate, who offers himself as an escort for life."

The merriment died out of her eyes, and the quip on her tongue failed her. Greatly daring, her lover took her in his arms. Through the open windows of the drawing room floated the tender refrain of a ballad. Mrs. Forbes was singing, and sweet words blended with sweet music in the still air.

Then their lips met, and the dark glen became an earthly Paradise.

THE END